SUNBOLT

BOOKS BY INTISAR KHANANI

The Sunbolt Chronicles
Sunbolt
Memories of Ash
Debts of Fire

The Dauntless Path
Thorn
The Theft of Sunlight
A Darkness at the Door

THE SUNBOLT CHRONICLES BOOK ONE

SUNBOLT

INTISAR KHANANI

Snowy
Wings
PUBLISHING

Sunbolt
Copyright © 2023 by Intisar Khanani
Cover Art © 2023 by Alice Maria Power
Cover Design © 2023 VM Designs
Chapter Header Art © Kerstin Espinosa Rosero

Snowy Wings Publishing
www.snowywingspublishing.com

Library of Congress Cataloging-in-Publication Data
Names: Khanani, Intisar, author.
Title: Sunbolt / Intisar Khanani.
Series: The Sunbolt Chronicles
Description: Turner, OR: Snowy Wings Publishing, 2023. | Summary: A street thief with a dangerous secret helps a noble family flee execution, only to be captured by the dark mage who killed her father.
Identifiers: Library of Congress Control Number 2023913598 | ISBN 978-1-958051-25-2 (Hardcover) | 978-1-958051-32-0 (Large Print) | 978-1-958051-26-9 (pbk.) | 978-1-958051-24-5 (e-book)
Subjects: LCSH Magic--Fiction. | Government, Resistance to--Fiction. | Bildungsroman. | Paranormal fiction. |s Fantasy fiction. | Young adult fiction. | BISAC YOUNG ADULT FICTION / Fantasy / General | YOUNG ADULT FICTION / Fantasy / Epic
Classification: LCC PZ7.K52654 Su 2023 | DDC [Fic]--dc23

A QUICK GUIDE TO NAMES

The Eleven Kingdoms are primarily based on a variety of real-world historical cultures. I have done my utmost to present these cultures with respect, while still creating a fantastical world. If I have erred in my portrayals (which I'm sure I must have at some point), I humbly ask your forgiveness.

Below is a guide for names whose pronunciation might not be immediately evident from their spelling unless you are already familiar with them. Names are in alphabetical order.

Alia – AH-lee-ah

Hitomi – Hi-toh-mee

Hotaru – Ho-taru

Kol – To be fair, I made this one up, so you can pronounce it any way you like and you won't be wrong. I pronounce it like the word "coal."

Mama Ali – Mama 'A-lee, with the 'A similar to "uh" but formed deeper in the throat, without the expulsion of so much breath.

Rafiki – Ra-FEE-kee

Saira –SIY-ra, with the SIY similar to the word "sigh."

CHAPTER 1
A FUTURE FORETOLD

"*Mgeni!* Stay a moment; I have your future for you."

I grin, turning toward Mama Ali. She sits beneath the cloth shade of her market stall, her husband's catch heaped on the wooden counter before her: mounds of sardines, glinting silver bright in the sun. Today there's also a single little octopus that must have gotten tangled in his nets, its fleshy body turned over to show the white of its tentacles.

With her wide smile and heavy girth, Mama Ali is a well-known fixture of the fish market, her laughter booming across the crowded aisles, and her penchant for sharing people's futures indulged in even by the locals. Her son, ten years old and shrewder than a hundred-year-old owl, perches beside her, watching me.

"You can keep my future, Mama Ali," I reply. "It will probably do you more good than me."

My words draw laughter from the surrounding fishmongers. The market stalls are packed tightly together, every counter offering up the bounty of the sea, scenting the air with salt and

1

fish. Above the stalls flap brightly colored cloth shades, protecting both the women and their goods from the sun's heat.

I hear someone ask what she missed and a woman replies, calling me mgeni again. My smile slips a notch. I may have adopted the traditional, brightly colored long skirt and tunic of the local women, as well as the tightly wound head wrap, but my sand-gold skin and the shape of my eyes will always mark me as *someone else.* Mama Ali uses the term as an endearment, but the echoes I hear now brand me as an outsider.

Mama Ali holds out her hand imperiously, a queen demanding tribute from the riffraff that forms her court. "Come, my friend, keeper of secrets, let us see what we can."

"What will you give me?" I ask, hoping "keeper of secrets" is just a phrase she uses on potential customers. Regardless, I don't have the coin to pay her, so I may as well be clear *I* won't be giving anything.

"Give you? Your future, muddle-brain! And, because you are always admiring my wares, I will give it to you for free."

"Oh, very well." I acquiesce none too gracefully, offering Mama Ali my hand. With her palms clasped around my hand, I wait, trying not to fidget too much. I may be running a little late, but there's no reason to think the meeting will have started on time. Besides, since I wasn't invited in the first place, no one will miss me. "Don't tell me I'm going to meet someone new, dark of skin and—"

"Short," Mama Ali agrees.

I nearly choke. "Short?"

She drops her voice. "Well, if I want to be sure it happens, short is so much more likely than tall, isn't it? At least," she nods her head to suggest the market, as well as the rest of the island, "here."

I laugh. I think this must be why Mama Ali and I get along so well. "Right. Short and dark."

"No." She pulls a frown. "For you, something different."

I glance toward the sky, gauging the angle of the late morning sun. Magic is one thing, but divining the future? Not so much. "I really have to—"

"You are going somewhere," Mama Ali intones, closing her eyes. I glance at her son in disbelief. Ali grins wide, his teeth showing pearly white against his earth-brown skin.

"I was before you stopped me," I agree.

Mama Ali heaves a theatrical sigh, squeezing my hand rather painfully. "Somewhere important," she clarifies. She tilts her head as if listening. And Mama Ali hears a lot — she has her pulse on the happenings of Karolene. Maybe there's something she knows. Has she gotten news about the League? Or the Ghost?

She drops my hand, sitting back with a gasp. "Run!"

"What?" I glance over my shoulder, instinctively looking for signs of danger. The market is busy, filled with people laughing and bargaining over the night's catch. There are dozens of stalls crammed together, aisle upon aisle, but nothing and no one seems out of place. There's no sign of either the sultan's guards or hired mercenaries.

"You are *late*," Mama Ali cries.

"Of course I am; isn't everyone on the island always late? That's the way time works here."

She catches my arm, and I can't tell if she's acting or serious. "No, listen to me, Hitomi. You must run now, and—" she hesitates.

"And?"

"Keep running," she says. She points down the aisle. "*Run.*"

"Run, mgeni!" a woman from two stalls down calls, her voice bright with laughter, and then everyone starts shouting encouragement.

Laughing, I duck away from the market stall, zigzagging through the market. I keep up a steady jog. A sprint will attract too much attention and, without a clear enemy to escape, expend too much energy. And anyway, I can still faintly hear the laughter from the corner of the market I've left behind. Mama Ali must be enjoying her joke.

I hop over the tail of a tiger shark lying half-butchered in the aisle, eliciting a sharp word from the seller, and round the corner. The sounds of the market drop to a bare whisper. Not because I've left the market, but because walking straight toward me are a half dozen mercenaries, all with the feared black bands wrapped around their right forearms. They're not just any mercenaries, but part of Arch Mage Blackflame's guard. The sellers on both sides of the aisle are meticulously checking their wares, looking everywhere but at the armed men in their midst. Most of the buyers have already discreetly slipped away.

I stumble slightly, trying to drop into a casual walk. The leader of the guards looks me straight in the eye. His face is long and sharp, his eyes a little too small, too deeply set. His gaze skims my body before returning to my face. A mean, tight smile stretches his lips.

Damn. Damn damn damn. I drop my chin, glancing quickly around to get my bearings. There's no escape down a side aisle here, the stalls packed tightly together. I've come too far to chance turning and running — because turning tail is an admission of guilt. They would be after me with their daggers drawn before I reached the corner. I'm not about to chance my speed against theirs unless I must. So I keep walking, keeping my gaze down, staying so close to the stalls on my left that I graze my hip against the chipped wood of the counters.

"Look what's here," the leader says, calling the other soldiers' attention to me. My steps falter as they veer toward me, quickly closing the distance between us. "What do you think she is? A mutt or a half-breed?"

A half-breed they might not bother because those who are

half-human and half-something-else often have a strength or ability that could cause more trouble than these men are looking for. Unfortunately for me, the secret I guard is fully human. I glance sideways at the fish seller in the stall beside me, wondering if I can count on her. She is young, no more than a handful of years past my own fifteen, her eyes wide with panic. No help there. I swallow hard, trying to ease the fear thrumming through my veins.

I begin to back away, offering a hesitant smile to the soldiers. A smile? What am I doing? I should run—

But it's already too late. Two of the soldiers have moved ahead of the others, circling past me. I'm surrounded.

"Mutt," says one of the soldiers, taking in my features. I feel myself flush slightly. My parents may have been from different lands, but a good number of islanders have other blood in them, even if it dates back a few generations. How else did the noble women come by their sleek hair? Their problem isn't with my bloodline. It's with the fact that I'm a misfit — a foreigner in local dress — and I make an easy target.

"Half-breed," two others posit, their boots sounding unnaturally loud in the quiet. No one wears boots in Karolene, not unless they're soldiers.

"Definitely a mutt," a soldier behind me says. He's come to a stop a couple paces away, no doubt waiting for his leader to make the first move.

"Well, girl, what are you?" the leader asks.

I refuse to answer in the words they've afforded me. "Human," I say. "Sir."

He laughs, sauntering up to me. "Human! Imagine that. What a mess of features you are." If the market aisle was quiet before, now it has gone silent.

I need to find a way out. My eyes flick first one way then another, tracking the guards, looking for an escape route — and fasten on a middle-aged woman across the aisle. She holds something up — a charm? — then points to the next stall down from the one beside me. How I'll get to it, I have no idea, but I suspect I just need to follow her lead.

The soldier reaches forward and grabs my headwrap, yanking it off. I stumble, banging my hip against the stall, and the girl in the stall yelps with shock. The other guards laugh. I grip the counter tightly with one hand, looking him straight in the eye. I have to lift my chin, because unlike the local men, he's tall. Probably a mainlander recruited for the job.

"I'll have that back, please," I say, trying to keep my voice even.

He ignores me, tossing the wrap to the dirt beside his boots. "Scruffy as a dog," he says, eyeing my short, wavy black hair with disgust. The other soldiers hoot with laughter, and I have no doubt that in a moment they'll take the dog analogy a step further. And what they'll do after that....

Skreeeee!

The soldiers shout, ducking down. A small dark object whizzes past over their heads. I leap onto the counter and jump to the next stall from there before the soldier even realizes he's lost me. The woman there grabs me by the waist and swings me down, using my momentum to shove me out the back exit of her stall. I stumble slightly as I hear her screech, "My fish! You stepped on my fish! You better run, girl, or I'll pull your ears off! You scared of soldiers? I'll give you something to fear!"

She's protecting herself. Grinning fiercely, I sprint between the backs of two other stalls and emerge into the next aisle. The woman's shouts have alerted everyone in the next aisle to my running. They are tense and quiet, watching me as I leap into the center aisle. The sellers bend over their counters to see; the customers turn to stare at me.

"Mercenaries," I call. "Blackflame's!"

6

"*Here,*" a woman selling shrimp gestures to me. I race to her stall, the crowds parting and then closing back up behind me. I slide over the counter, dropping to a crouch. The guards tear around the corner after me, but they have to shove their way past the men and women in the aisle, granting me a few precious moments. Once more, I find myself careening through a back exit, this one nothing more than a bit of cloth tacked up over a gap in the wooden planks.

I sprint down the aisle, leaping over a broken crate, and duck through another back exit into a stall in the next aisle.

"What? Who—" An older woman this time, her face lined. A boy stands on the other side of her counter, a coin in his hand. He gapes at me as well.

"Blackflame's guards," I gasp out.

She yanks open a crate hidden beneath her counter and pushes me in, slamming the top down as soon as I pull my head in. I lie on my side, my cheek pressed against ... smooth rocks? In the fish market? As my breathing slows, I take in the faint, woody scent of green coconuts. Of course. I've left the fish market, crossing the invisible line into the fruit and vegetable sellers' section. Karolene's local markets run together, bleeding into each other. It's only the import and export markets, carefully regulated by the sultan's palace, that each have their own special streets.

Curled on top of the fruit-seller's wares, I listen for pursuit. I still have one weapon left: a secret I have kept and guarded my whole life. My friends think the charms and magical items I own come from a connection to one of the mage families living here. It's not an unlikely scenario: that's how most people get such things.

But the truth is that I'm a Promise, a young magical talent, trained in secret by my parents. At least until they died. While I've continued training on my own, I don't know any defensive spells that would do me much good right now. I'd have to make something up, and that could endanger the people who have sheltered me. So I lie as quietly as possible, ignoring the pain of cramping muscles, and hope the soldiers don't find me.

Twice I hear boots pound past. I hear shouts, but no one responds. No matter how many people saw me, and no matter the color of my skin, they will not betray me now. Not to these men.

Slowly, the market noises resume. I lie in the coconut crate, fuming, thinking of Mama Ali. Of all the self-fulfilling prophecies…. Run and keep running. *Well.* If I hadn't started out running, I wouldn't have needed to keep running.

The lid of the crate creaks open.

"Come, it's safe now," the woman says, offering me a hand. She helps me out, and I sit on the floor of her stall, blinking in the bright light.

"Are you well?"

"I'm fine," I assure her. I may have lost my head wrap, but I only ever wore it to fit in better.

"Your hands are shaking," she says, and taking me by the arm, helps me to her own stool.

I look down, surprised to see that they are trembling. I open and close them a few times, squeezing my hands into fists as if I might forcibly regain control of them.

"Here," the woman calls. I jump, then realize she is only hailing a coffee seller. The man serves us each, pouring the cardamom- and ginger-scented brew into the miniature cups set out on his tray. The woman pays him with a coin and he continues down the aisle. He'll stop by on his way back to pick up the empty cups.

I drink the coffee slowly, savoring the rich flavor. The woman leans against her counter, sipping from her own cup, lost in thought. I wonder what she's thinking of, if perhaps she has lost someone herself. So many have disappeared, taken from their homes, the markets, the street. Most made the mistake of voicing dissent, but not all. Sometimes you just have to attract the wrong kind of attention.

I look out to the aisle. A few of the other sellers, those who aren't busy with customers, nod toward me. I smile my thanks. Each of them had the chance to tell the soldiers where I hid, who had hidden me. But they didn't.

I set my cup down on the counter, and notice the shadows on the street — or rather, the lack of them. It is near noon, the market slowly growing quiet as people head home to eat and then rest through the hottest part of the day. Near noon — I bite back a curse as I remember where I'd been headed in the first place. I'm most definitely late now.

I stand up from the stool. The fruit-seller swivels toward me. "Thank you, mother," I say respectfully. I take her free hand and bend over to kiss it.

"Oh, child," she says. "Be careful here. A darkness has taken hold of our island."

"I know, mother," I say. It seems I will always be the foreigner. "Karolene has been my home for four years now."

She nods, warmth lighting her face. "Then go in peace, and do not forget your own mother, who waits at home for you. Stay safe for her."

I force a smile, nodding. She ushers me out the back of her stall, and I follow the tight path down to the end of the aisle, her words echoing at the back of my thoughts. She doesn't need to know that my mother isn't waiting for me, that my mother disappeared a long time ago, when we first came to Karolene, when the darkness that grips this island had only just begun to spread its roots.

CHAPTER 2
THE SHADOW LEAGUE

I plunge into the winding streets and familiar alleys of Karolene. Here, there is no such thing as a straight road — at least, not for long. Each street makes its way around the corners of the buildings that shape it, shifting first one way, then another. The smaller alleys make full turns at what might at first appear to be dead ends, descending side stairs and passing through buildings that have grown up over the alley itself.

As I turn another corner, I nod to two men chatting in a doorway. The alley beyond them lies deserted. They hesitate, then nod back. I hide my grin. I know they're acting as lookouts today, but they know me only well enough to believe I might have been invited. The alley shifts a little, the men dropping out of sight, and I spot the great wooden double doors I have been seeking. They are gorgeous, carved in a floral pattern, inlaid with bronze and painted a vibrant turquoise. Unfortunately, lounging on the steps before them is the one guard it *would* be my luck to meet.

"Going somewhere?" Kenta asks, cocking an eyebrow. For

once, he doesn't have a bottle of rice wine and a frybread at hand, which could mean he's taking his job too seriously to humor me.

"Tell me they didn't put you out here as a guard dog," I say, dropping down beside him as if that was my intention all along. "Isn't that demeaning?"

He grins, showing teeth that are a little sharper than the average man's. "Better than not being invited at all, Tomi."

I grimace. "I'm planning on discussing that with — him." We both know whom I mean: our friend and the leader of the Shadow League, a man known only as the Ghost.

"You can certainly discuss it," Kenta agrees. "Later."

"That would defeat the purpose."

"You should have come earlier, then."

I shake my head, exasperated. "Believe me, I tried. Has the meeting already started?" At this point, there's only a very small chance that it hasn't, even taking into account how late every-thing runs here.

He shrugs, a graceful rise and fall of his shoulders. He is short but slim, with a shaggy chestnut mane mingled with black, and a set of dark brown eyes that dominate his face. There is no ques-tion that he resembles the sure-footed, black-masked tanuki that is his natural form. "Almost everyone's here."

"Almost. The meeting won't have started yet. Plenty of time to discuss what I need." I hop to my feet. Kenta rises with me. We're of a height, but he's faster than me and he loves a good fight. In large part, that's because he loves making fools of his opponents, tripping them over their own feet and knocking them onto their rumps. I've often enjoyed the spectacle, but I'm not interested in taking part.

"Oh, come on," I grumble. "Do you really think he can't handle me? Because if he can't, this whole," I wave my hand vaguely, "*venture* is doomed. I am nowhere near as difficult to handle as some people."

Kenta smirks. "Regardless of what I think, I've been asked to make sure only invited guests enter through the front door."

He looks at me, the sunlight gleaming in his eyes. His lips twitch.

I feel a grin start to spread across my face. "But not the back door?"

"Side door," Kenta corrects me.

"Who's watching that?"

"The kitchen staff."

"Right." I patter down the stairs. "See you on the way out!"

Kenta's chuckle follows me down the alley to the corner.

The side entrance, a nondescript brown door set in the wall, has been left propped open with a brick. I glance up and down the alley, but other than a boy headed in the other direction with a chicken tucked under his arm, there's no one in sight. I tilt my head sideways, peering inside.

The door opens into a dimly lit hallway — but just a pace or two on another door stands open, light falling through it. From the flicker of shadows and the occasional clatter or thump, I would guess it's the kitchen. I slip inside, keeping in shadow as long as possible. A quick peek into the kitchen tells me lunch is being cooked, the kitchen staff preoccupied with their preparations.

All I have to do is ease past the doorway, and I'll be on my way. Except. Except the door behind me is still open, and that's no small risk. At least not for the people meeting upstairs. With a mental curse, I kneel beside the door, ease it open just a fraction more, and lift the brick out. The door swings shut with a slight *click*. I set the brick down and rise, turning back to the hallway.

"Can I help you?"

A young man stands at the kitchen door, a meat cleaver in hand. He looks slightly perplexed, the cleaver clearly a tool of his trade rather than a threat.

"They just sent me down to make sure the door was closed," I say lightly. "I didn't mean to disturb you."

"No trouble," he assures me, smiling. "We didn't realize Master Rafiki wanted it shut."

"He forgot to say," I explain. "I'd better go back up, though."

"Do they need anything else? More coffee? Papaya?"

"I don't think so. At least not yet."

He nods and returns to the kitchen as I escape into the house. I've known Rafiki almost as long as I've known the Ghost, and despite our differences, I've been inside his house more than a few times. Once I find the main hall, I know precisely where I'm going. I make my way from shadow to shadow, up the stairs and into the small but exquisitely appointed library. I can hear the faint sounds of voices coming from the next room, the words unintelligible. I'll have to get closer.

Like most wealthy houses in Karolene, not only does Rafiki's house sport massive wooden entry doors, but also a long, elaborately carved balcony facing the street on each floor. The library doesn't have a door that opens to the balcony, but it does have a window. I slide over the sill, easing my weight onto the balcony to avoid a telltale creak. Hunkering down, I creep along until I reach the window to the next room. This time, I have no trouble making out the words. The meeting has certainly started.

"Are you sure about this?" a man asks, his voice troubled. "You have verified it?"

"I have a number of informants," the Ghost replies, his voice calm. "They all say the same thing: Blackflame will have the Degath family arrested tonight and...." A silence follows, but I can imagine the Ghost's hand cutting through the air. *Execution.*

"The sultan has signed a warrant," he adds. "For treason."

That's bad. Arch Mage Blackflame already plays the sultan like a puppet. Only a handful of nobles have maintained positions that even remotely stand against him; Lord Degath is by far the most powerful and outspoken of them. And Blackflame intends to kill him. He must feel strong enough in his power to make his move now. With Degath out of the way, the other nobles will most likely surrender to his wishes. After all, if *Degath* isn't safe, no one is.

I stare down at the wooden floor, the dust and bits of sand that have collected in the cracks, listening as the men and women within argue the merits of attempting to sneak the Degaths away before the impending arrest. These last four years, I have watched the life of the city slowly bleed into the sea. Oh, Mama Ali still laughs and sells her self-fulfilling prophecies in the fish market, children still play, and the motions of life continue because they must, but there is a silence where there were once words. It lurks at the edge of my hearing. Now people dart glances to the side when they speak, checking for soldiers or Blackflame's mercenaries, where before no one thought twice about the presence of armed men. People have disappeared: men and women who spoke out against Blackflame when the laws began to change, then people who spoke out against the disappearances of their brothers and sisters. Until, finally, people stopped speaking. Such silence at the heart of Karolene has cost them a part of their spirit. Their laughter hides their loss, their smiles hide their grief, their eyes hide a pain that will not be eased.

Of course, they still fight, but the battles are hidden now. After all, complete strangers saved me hardly an hour ago. But these are quiet battles, small shows of resistance; no one dares attract too much attention. For a proud people, one that has prized its independence for four hundred years, such fear is a terrible thing.

"Why have we formed the Shadow League, if not for this?" The Ghost's voice cuts across a droning argument over the risks of taking action.

"The Degaths are not our allies," a man says.

"Of course they aren't," a woman snaps in response. "They are nobility and we are *secret*. It would have been political suicide for Lord Degath to support us. But that doesn't mean he should not have our support when he needs it."

The Ghost takes up the thread of her argument. "Lord Degath presents the natural complement for our work. Without his voice urging change and speaking out against Blackflame, our own work would be much more difficult. The people need a voice, and as careful as he has been in what he says, he is still the closest thing we have to it."

The room surges with the sound of disagreement. I lean my head against the wall, listening to the echoes of fear within. But I needn't worry unnecessarily. This is the Shadow League, and the Ghost, young as he is, has a natural charisma. He also has a brilliant mind for appealing to both types of people in the room with him: speaking at times of logic and strategy, and at other times of duty and purpose. I feel a faint smile touch my face as I follow the ebb and flow of the conversation. By the time the group agrees to vote, there is no question that the Ghost has carried the argument.

I watch as, one by one, the men and women depart from the door below me. If I lean out over the balcony, I know I'll be able to see Kenta on the steps, but I stay where I am as the tops of heads come into view and bob away along the alley. Only one voice remains in the room with the Ghost: Rafiki. They speak too quietly for me to make out their words, but I've heard what I need. Now it's time to join the conversation.

I climb back through the library window and have just reached the hall door when Kenta comes up the steps.

He grins mischievously. "Have your conversation?"

I shake my head, spreading my hands before me in a gesture of innocent helplessness. "They'd already started."

"I suppose it was interesting," Kenta says as the meeting

room door swings open. Rafiki stumbles to a stop when he sees me. Where Kenta is slim, Rafiki is solid, built thick with a bit of a belly. His hair is shaved short, a whisper of fuzz on his scalp. He stands only two fingers taller than me, but he makes up for it with a booming voice and arrogant demeanor.

"You," he says, deep brown eyes narrowing into a glare.

I ignore him, continuing my conversation with Kenta. "Very interesting," I agree. "You missed out. You remember old goat-face of the 'what did they ever do for us' arguments? The Ghost even convinced him to vote for a rescue attempt."

"You were *listening?*" Rafiki's face is a study in fury.

I smile pleasantly at him. "I wasn't invited, so of course I didn't come in. But if you were going to talk as loud as all that, I couldn't very well ignore you."

A voice I know almost as well as my own speaks from behind Rafiki's shoulder. "And where exactly were you, Hitomi?"

Rafiki steps to the side, his anger settling into a smirk, certain that I'll get what I deserve. The Ghost leans against the doorway, arms crossed beneath his cloak, his expression lost beneath the midnight hood. It had been by my advice that he paid a mage passing through the city to charm the hood, filling it with shadows that hide all but the faintest gleam of his eyes. When we first met, he never hid his face, but that was before the Shadow League, before people began to disappear. Swathed in a cloak that has no place in Karolene, he looks like the pale-faced north-erners: exotic and foreign — except that the Ghost's skin is the same as Rafiki's, as Mama Ali's. He, unlike Kenta and I, belongs here.

I clear my throat, realizing the Ghost is still waiting for my answer. "I was admiring the view from the balcony. You really need to sweep out there, Rafiki. Lots of dust. Quite shocking."

"Why, you thieving little—" Rafiki starts toward me, but the Ghost catches his arm, bringing him to a halt. Rafiki turns to him. "How else did she get in here? She's no more than a common thief. *Why* you keep her around I can't imagine."

I bristle. "I didn't need to know a thing about thieving to get in here," I say before the Ghost can answer. "You leave Kenta on your doorstep and think you're safe? Your side door was *open*. I walked right in, and no one even noticed."

Rafiki quivers with fury. "That's a lie! But what can anyone expect from—"

Kenta steps up beside me, his words cutting through Rafiki's like a knife. "I'd watch my tongue if I were you." He smiles, a slow sharp smile that promises all kinds of trouble.

"And that will be more than enough," the Ghost says. "Kenta, you and Rafiki wait downstairs. Hitomi, come inside and we'll discuss why — and how — you came to be here." He pauses. "No mischief, Kenta."

Kenta bumps his shoulder against mine. "As you say, Ghost," he says, grinning. He heads down the stairs. Rafiki sneers at me, still certain that I'm about to receive a tongue-lashing. I repress the urge to kick him as he passes. That would hardly impress the Ghost.

The Ghost opens wide the door of the meeting room, gesturing for me to enter. I pace to the other side of the room. I don't feel like sitting right now. The room is lit by three ornate metal lanterns hung above a large central table. They fill the space with a warm glow, softening the hard edges of the table and the lines of the chairs, and mingling with the shadows in the corners. The table is covered with platters of fresh fruit and tiny, ceramic cups of half-drunk coffee. Unlike the coffee-seller's plain blue cups at the market, these cups depict delicate flowers and swirling patterns in a variety of hues.

The Ghost closes the door and walks toward the table. He leans against the back of a chair, watching me. "You just can't let Rafiki be, can you?" he asks.

17

I throw my hands up in exasperation. "I don't know how you stand him. The man is an arrogant—"

"Tomi," the Ghost says, half-pleading.

I try not to laugh. "I know, I know. You must get tired of playing mother to all our little tantrums."

He clears his throat, but I still hear the amusement in his voice when he speaks. "That's not quite how I think of it. But I wish you would try a little harder with Rafiki. He brings as much to the League as any one of the rest of us."

I glance down at the meeting table. As if I had anything of the sort to offer up myself — a table to meet around, fruit and coffee to serve, an iron-clad reputation of loyalty to hide behind. "I'm sure he does," I tell the Ghost. "I just don't know how you stand him."

The Ghost swings his chair around and sits, crossing his arm over its back. I can't quite make out the expression in his eyes beneath the inky shadows of the hood, but I've no doubt he isn't frustrated with me anymore. That's good at least. "How did you get in, Tomi?"

"I walked in, like I told you. Through the side door. Rafiki might have great coffee, but he doesn't know the first thing about keeping a place safe."

"It was closed. Someone else checked it on their way in."

I shrug. "Well then, someone else opened it. Probably the kitchen staff, since they didn't know Rafiki wanted it closed."

"How do you know that?"

"Because I mentioned it to them, and they were surprised."

The Ghost considers this. "All right."

"That's all?" I ask, half-joking. "You're not going to invite Rafiki in for a conversation about how and why I came to be here?"

"Clearly," the Ghost says, leaning forward and pushing a platter of fruit toward me, "you came for the pineapple."

I can't help the laugh that bursts from my lips. Shaking my head, I drop into a chair and reach for the platter. Pineapple is the one food I never pass up. "Absolutely. Justice served with a side of pineapple. That's what I'm here for."

"Is it really justice you're looking for?" the Ghost asks. "Is that what you want, Tomi?" His voice is velvet and darkness. I wish suddenly that he wasn't the Ghost, that he was someone else with a name and a face, someone I could lean on and laugh with without having to measure my words.

I spear a piece of pineapple and pop it in my mouth. When I'm done chewing, I say, "What I really want is to know why you didn't invite me to this meeting."

"I already knew you'd come."

"That's no answer," I snap, glaring at the darkness beneath his hood. "Do you not trust me? Is that what it is?"

He shakes his head. "I trust you, Hitomi. I knew I could trust you to come here uninvited. I know that when I need your help for the League, you won't let me down." He hesitates, then goes on, "I know you'll fight Blackflame with your dying breath. But I don't want that yet."

My words come out rough. "If you wanted me to come here, why didn't you just ask me?"

"Because this way I don't have to argue about it with anyone."

I want to believe him. I really do. But he's so good at giving people what they need. He knows what I need to hear: that I'm useful, that he needs me, that he can trust me to be myself and come through for him even when he doesn't ask it. I'd like to believe I'm that person, but part of me wonders if that person exists at all. I wonder what he tells Rafiki, what he tells every other member of the Shadow League.

Unaccountably, I feel myself on the verge of tears. I stare at the table, blinking slowly to keep them back. "Right," I say, my voice tight.

"Hitomi—"

"It's fine. It doesn't matter. Let's talk about the Degaths."

I hear him sigh, the faint creak of his chair as he sits back. "Hitomi."

I wait, but when he doesn't continue, I raise my eyes to look at him, start to ask, *What?*

He's pulled his hood back.

I close my mouth, try not to swallow so I don't look like a fool. It's been so long since I've actually seen him that I'd forgotten his face. No, not forgotten it, just let it fade in my memory: skin the deep brown of rich earth, dark eyes with just a hint of laughter in them, his nose and mouth perfectly sculpted. His hair forms slightly looser curls than many islanders', short ringlets that frame his face.

He regards me somberly, looking both young and old at the same time, as if his eighteen years were an eternity. I wonder what his real name is. Once upon a time I thought I knew it, thought the name he gave me when we first met was really his. But even then he was learning to hide himself, to remake himself a hundred different ways.

"All right, Tomi? I trust you."

I nod, still staring.

He grins, his teeth flashing white between parted lips. "I can't be that ugly."

I clear my throat. "What? Isn't that why you wear that hood?"

"One of many reasons," he agrees.

"So," I say, trying to get back on steady ground, "the Degaths?"

"You heard the vote?"

"Yes."

"And you'll help."

It isn't a question, but I answer anyway. "Of course."

"This is dangerous."

"Dangerous?" I nearly laugh. "I almost got picked up by Blackflame's men on the way here just for looking like I do. This can't be any more dangerous than that."

The Ghost sits straight up. "You what?"

I hold up my hands. "Doesn't matter. I hid in a crate of coconuts, and here I am, none the worse for a little exercise." He hardly looks comforted, but I forge on. "Today aside, I know what we might lose. And I won't let it happen." Not again, not if I can help it.

"I'm not sure I should let you do this."

"Why? Because of the stupid guards this morning? They're irrelevant. I ran from them today. I'll be running from them next week." Which is not wholly accurate. I think I've only been chased by soldiers twice before, and both times they'd had good cause. Rafiki was right when he called me a thief, though I only steal when I run out of the odd jobs that keep me fed.

The Ghost mutters something under his breath, glancing away from me. My brow furrows as I lean forward, trying to catch his words. Did he say something about a promise? That's impossible. How can he know anything about my Promise? I've never let him see my magic workings, have kept everything secret — even my parents' names. He can't possibly have guessed....

"What?" I ask, my voice sharper than I intend.

He shakes his head. "Promise me you'll take no unnecessary risks."

"Fine," I say, a little too quickly. It's not a bad oath, anyhow. Who would want to risk more than necessary? I have no intention of dying to help the Degaths. But I understand that if Blackflame destroys all of his political opposition, Karolene will not escape his grasp without a long and bloody battle. And the

Degaths are a family; I don't want to see that destroyed. I look down at my hands, wondering what drives me more: love for my adopted land or loneliness.

The Ghost nods, standing up. "I'll get Rafiki and Kenta. We'll need to plan."

"Thanks," I say. As he reaches the door, I add, "I mean that."

"I know," he says, pulling his hood back up to shadow his face. "But it's I who should thank you."

CHAPTER 3

AN HONEST THIEF

S uggesting that Rafiki is pleased by my inclusion would be like claiming none of the Eleven Kingdoms ever fought a war. Kenta sits beside me while we discuss different options, doing his best to bait Rafiki with sly comments about open doors and thieves. I try to ignore them both, since I have no intention of making the Ghost regret including me.

Our first course of action is simply to alert the Degaths. If they have a contingency plan, then we need not worry. After we spend an hour discussing what we'll do if they don't, the Ghost departs. It's still the full heat of the day — the markets have closed and everyone has gone home to rest. It's the best time to visit the Degath residence without drawing notice.

I know the Ghost will drop his disguise and take the rooftops part of the way, only donning his cloak again once he's actually inside the residence walls. Part of me wishes I could run the rooftops with him, but he doesn't need me tagging along.

Rafiki provided us with lunch — an unexpected treat the likes of which I haven't had in a long time. After I polish off my meal and take care of the remaining pineapple, I head out as well.

It's a long walk and the heat has turned muggy, the sea breeze sluggish. In this weather, home isn't much better than the streets. I share a two-room apartment with seven other women who range in age from my own fifteen years to at least twice that. At four women per room, we have more space than many places I've stayed, though the lack of windows makes even pleasant nights stifling.

Most of the women are already home and resting on their mats. A few murmur greetings as I pass, lifting their hands briefly. I make my way to where I keep my sleeping mat rolled atop the small wooden crate that holds my few belongings. Despite the fact that the box has neither lock nor properly fitting lid, I have no worries about anything going missing. No one ever touches anyone else's property here. It's a strict rule, and breaking it means you'd better find a new place to sleep. So far it's worked well, though I think we all have our own secret emergency stashes hidden somewhere in the city, or with someone else. Kenta has mine, such as it is: a palm-sized book my father used to jot notes in, a hair comb adorned with pearls that my mother left behind when she disappeared, and a few precious coins.

I lay out my sleeping mat and lie down, listening to the soft rustles and occasional snores that permeate the room. It seems like I've barely nodded off before the women begin to rise. I remain on my mat, feigning sleep, and they let me be. I don't want to answer any questions right now. If they notice I breathe too fast for slumber, they don't let on. I sometimes feel like they think of me as some sort of exotic mistake. Maybe it's because I try so hard to fit in, or maybe it's because my features make it clear I never will.

Once the room has emptied, I sit up and rifle through my crate. At the bottom, I've folded my thieving clothes: a set of boy's pants and a faded blue tunic. I change quickly, using a cloth to bind my chest so my figure doesn't accidentally give me away.

A traditional embroidered cap completes the outfit. I'm not sure what we'll end up doing tonight, but I'd rather not look like myself. There's not much chance of hiding my fair skin and strange eyes, but at least this way, if people come searching, they'll be looking for a boy.

I check my pockets to make sure I have everything I need and strap a small knife to my leg. Then I head for the door.

"Where you off to, girl? Goin' ta pick something you shouldn't?"

I pause, turning toward the two women in the outer room. They lounge on their mats, one of them clicking through her prayer beads. They watch me with sharp, hungry eyes.

"Bring it home and we won't say a word," the second woman says.

"I'll bring you some soldiers," I promise, making for the door. "I bet they'll want to hear about that chicken you 'found' last week." They'd been so pleased with their catch, they'd forgotten to save me a piece. I came home to laughter and a platter scattered with bones. Whether I manage to earn a surplus of food or am forced into thieving a morsel, I won't be sharing with those two. I head downstairs to the sound of insults and threats being thrown after me. I don't worry, though. They have as much to lose as I do.

I reach Rafiki's house before the Ghost. Kenta winks at me as I enter the meeting room, as carefree as ever.

"Do you ever worry about anything?" I ask him, dropping into a chair. I eye the table sadly. It has been cleared and no further refreshments have been set out.

"My next bottle of wine," Kenta says with mock seriousness. "When I'll meet my heart's companion."

I snort. "Aren't they the same thing?"

Kenta just laughs, glints of gold flickering in the brown of his eyes.

25

When the Ghost arrives a few minutes later, I can tell at once from the focused intensity of his movements, the purpose with which he sits, that the Degaths have no plan at all.

"We are going to have to be careful," he says as Rafiki shuts the door. "And fast."

"Why didn't you just bring them with you?" I quip.

"They plan on living, not just surviving," he says, unamused. "Lord Degath is making a few discreet arrangements for money transfers. His wife is ensuring that their most valuable belongings will not be found."

"And their children?" They have three, though the eldest two are probably older than me.

"They know nothing," the Ghost says. "And they'll continue knowing nothing until we meet them tonight."

MY JOB IS to rent a carriage and drive it to our agreed meeting place at the edge of the waterfront, near an esplanade frequented by the nobles. The walkway and gardens were built to offer the best views of the sunset, unmarred by the docks located farther south and the fishing dhows that pull up on the open beaches further north. It's the perfect place for the Degaths to walk out, and to get into an unmarked carriage without eliciting interest.

While I get the carriage, Rafiki will arrange a safe place for the family to spend the night. Between the two of them, the Ghost and Kenta will keep a watch on both entrances to the Degaths' residence. If either sees the approach of soldiers, they'll evacuate the Degaths as quickly as possible. Hopefully, though, the family will merely leave for an after-dinner outing as planned. Once their carriage departs their house, the Ghost will join Rafiki and me at the waterfront. Kenta will trail the Degath's carriage in his tanuki form, assuring no one and nothing else follows.

Once they take their walk and transfer to our carriage, we'll transport them to a place for the night. Come morning, the Degaths will depart on one of the fishing dhows — the last thing Blackflame will expect. The sultan's soldiers are sure to freeze all activity at the docks serving the shipping merchants and passenger boats once they realize their prey has escaped. But the dhows are only used by local fishermen. Many are merely pulled up on the beaches once they return from their night fishing. Not only is a noble family unlikely to arrange passage on a dhow, but monitoring the dhows is near impossible.

"The best plans are the simplest," the Ghost says.

I try not to consider all that might go wrong. We've accounted for various contingencies, but the most ominous possibility is that Blackflame won't wait for full night to arrest the Degaths. Part of me wishes that the Ghost *had* simply collected the family when he saw them earlier, planning for their future be damned. But the Ghost seems certain that we'll have enough time to implement our strategy.

My task, at least, should be easy. The Ghost has provided me with a small change purse filled with enough coin to rent a carriage for the night, as well as the name of a merchant who I can claim sent me. There are two establishments that rent carriages, both attached to inns. I feel a twinge of unease when I learn that both carriages have already been rented from the first. But what's the likelihood that all the available carriages will have been taken?

It turns out the second inn does indeed have one available.

"How do I know you'll bring it back?" Master Khalid, the proprietor, demands, eyeing me with suspicion and disdain.

"This is an island," I say, trying to reason with him. "Where could I possibly take your carriage that the sultan's soldiers couldn't find it?"

"Forget the carriage. You could book passage and take the

horses with you, make yourself a pretty penny. You want a carriage for your master, tell him to send me a man who looks like he serves a merchant. Not a boy in rags."

"But—"

"Now get out, or I'll call the sultan's soldiers on you myself."

I stalk outside, furious with myself, wishing I'd argued with the Ghost. Rafiki should have come for the carriage — although I have to admit that the Ghost was right: he does stand a higher chance of being recognized. Still, better that than not managing to get a carriage at all. Or we could have hired an errand boy to pick it up for us. I know a few young men who would do an odd job like this, no questions asked. I let out my breath with a sigh, knowing that wasn't a valid option either. If they ended up being questioned, they'd have no concern turning us over. No, I was the best choice for this job. And now I've failed.

I stand for a long moment, surveying the street. It's roughly cobbled, once a major thoroughfare but now falling into disrepair. The street lies quiet, only a few people passing by on their way home to dinner. I watch them absently: a tall, elderly gentleman with a kind face and a slight limp; two children skipping along, hand in hand; a young man hurrying by, his gaze distant.

I shake myself. I'm only prolonging the inevitable. I'd better get moving. The more time we have to change our plans, the better. If only I'd been better suited to the job the Ghost gave me — I nearly trip over my own feet. Better suited? I'm a *thief*. If the man won't rent me a carriage, I'll just have to 'borrow' one for the night.

Kenta would howl with laughter if he knew how long it took me to figure that out.

With renewed purpose, I start down the street, never looking back. If Master Khalid is watching me, I want him to feel confident that I've given up. At the next corner, I turn and walk on. I circle around by the smaller alleys to the back road that services his stable. It's narrow and edged with refuse, dirtier than the paths between the backs of the stalls at the fish market. But then the fishmongers take pride in their market, working together to keep it clean. It's clear neither Master Khalid nor his neighbors take ownership for the alley that serves the back of their buildings.

The inn stands just two buildings down from where the alley comes to an abrupt end at a wall. There's only one way out. I'll just have to hope no one is coming in when I need to get out.

There aren't too many good niches to observe the inn from. I settle for scaling a boundary wall across the alley and hiding among the branches of a small, sickly mango tree. I pat the tree trunk in apology before picking the only edible mango in sight: a pock-marked, yellow fruit hardly larger than my palm. Despite its appearance, it smells delectable. I use my knife to carve off slices to eat, licking the juice that dribbles down my fingers as I ostensibly observe the inn.

The length of the stables doubles as the boundary wall of the alley. A derelict metal gate, hinges hanging loose, has been left propped against the wall, leaving the entrance to the yard wide open. I tilt my head, but from my vantage point I can't spot where the carriage waits. I'd guess it's inside the yard, probably parked alongside the small stable.

I watch the kitchen door and windows as I finish my mango, gauging the movement within. They haven't yet lit a lamp, so I can't tell from here if anyone's looking out. It must be close to dinnertime, which means the kitchens will be busy. It's not a good time to try to sneak past them. The plan, then, is to sneak as little as possible.

Climbing down from my perch, I cross the alley and peek around the corner of the stables. The doors must face the inn yard; not unexpected but certainly not what I would have liked.

A glance skyward tells me that I don't have time to waste on wishful thinking.

Gathering my confidence, I stroll into the yard, following the wall of the stable and turning at the corner. The carriage waits in the yard just before the stable, directly opposite the kitchen. It appears to be nothing more than a box with a door mounted atop a set of wheels. Who would want to rent *that*? I'm beginning to think Master Khalid is quite the penny-pinching, close-minded lizard-brain.

Breathing a prayer, I saunter up to the stable doors and let myself in, leaving the door cracked open behind me. I pause in the semi-darkness, listening for sounds of alarm, but none come. If anyone noticed me, they must have thought I belonged.

On my left, a horse whuffles. I blink a few times, letting my eyes grow accustomed to the dark. The interior smells overwhelmingly of manure and damp. The humidity has gotten into the walls, and apparently Master Khalid hasn't taken it upon himself to care. I let my breath out slowly, unclenching my hands. Not my concern. I just need to select a couple of horses, harness them, and get out.

The Ghost has no idea how fortunate he is that I've worked odd jobs for four years now. For a short time, dressed in boys' clothes, I'd gotten work at a rich man's house helping in the stables. That lasted until they realized I was a girl, but it was long enough for me to learn everything I needed to know about harnessing a horse to a carriage. And even a little about how to recognize carriage horses.

There are three horses left in the stables, though there are stalls for six. Upon inspection, one of them seems much finer than the other two. He stands a couple hands taller at the shoulder, his coat gleaming in the shadows. Probably a riding horse, I decide. I bring out the other two, leaving one tied to a ring just within the door. They stand of a height, and their builds are similar. I have no doubt they're the horses I need. Now comes the hard part.

"Work with me on this, okay?" I whisper to the chestnut gelding. He swivels an ear toward me. "Quick and quiet, that's what I need."

There's no telling what he thinks of me.

I push the door open gently and lead the horse out to the carriage, acting as if I'm only doing my job. The whole time I'm harnessing him, I expect to hear shouts erupt from behind my back. But there's nothing. As I walk back to the stable, I discreetly glance over my shoulder. There's movement inside the kitchen, but that's all I can tell. Either they're so used to the horses being taken out that they haven't even bothered to look, or they're smart enough to know they've got time to catch me if they're quiet about it. I sincerely hope they're not that smart.

The second gelding, a bay, appears as disinterested in me as he is in pulling the carriage. Once I get him outside, he stands there, unwilling to move an inch, while I yank at the straps and try to get him to move over just a little.

"Come on, mud-brain," I say, almost done with the buckle. "Just shift a little."

He huffs and holds his ground.

"Hey! Hey, you!"

I don't look up. Instead, I smack the gelding's side with my palm and, when he steps sideways, jerk the strap with all my strength. The gelding twists his head around to snap his teeth at me, but he's buckled in now.

"You — with the horses! What are you doing?"

I look up with a smile. A man steps out of the kitchen door, crossing the dirt yard with long strides. Two more men spill out of the door behind him, followed by three young girls. The whole kitchen crew, it would seem.

31

"Just getting them harnessed," I call, throwing the reins up to the driver's bench.

The man hesitates, taken aback. "I don't know you."

"I'm Hamidi," which is not at all what he meant. I clamber up to the driver's bench. "Master Khalid knows I'm taking the carriage out."

He stands in the middle of the yard, frowning slightly. The rest of the workers stand about at his back. "He normally has—"

"You!" Master Khalid roars from the window above the kitchen. "Stop that boy! Stop him! Thief!"

I shout to the horses, snapping the reins. The chestnut gelding leaps forward, dragging the bay after him. I keep a tight hold on the reins, letting the gelding do the work to turn the carriage while the bay dithers. The man from the kitchen sprints toward the carriage. He's moving a lot faster than the horses.

The carriage lurches forward as I shout again, the bay clearly uninterested in breaking into a trot let alone a gallop. If only I had a whip, a stick, anything to prod him with! The man leaps for the driver's bench, his hands closing on the edge as he tries to pull himself up.

"Sorry," I say, and stamp on his fingers with all my might.

He drops down with a shout as the carriage swings out, making the turn onto the road with barely a handspan to spare. Snapping the reins again, I shout at the horses and spot a whip lying by my feet. I've never been so grateful to see one before. I stoop to grab it, nearly losing my balance as the carriage rattles and jerks over the ruts. Behind me, I can hear the shouts of the kitchen staff giving chase, but the alley is too narrow to allow them to run up alongside the carriage. What I need is to get far enough ahead of them that they won't be able to catch up once the carriage leaves the back road.

I brace myself in the seat and crack the whip — or try to. I've never used one before. Cursing, I swing it again, and manage to flick the lazy bay's hindquarters with the tip. He jumps forward, breaking into a gallop and the carriage sways one way and then the other as the horses panic, too confused to match their strides.

We burst from the back road. I haul on the reins, realizing belatedly that we have to turn or we'll run into the opposite building. The horses' hooves skid on the cobbles, and the back of the carriage bounces off the corner of the wall. I grab the driver's bench, nearly losing the reins as the carriage skips sideways across the stones.

And then the bay's hoof catches in a hole where a cobble should have been.

He screams, twisting and falling, and the carriage swings around again, slamming against the building opposite as the chestnut staggers to keep his balance. I drop the reins altogether, hanging onto the bench as the carriage tilts crazily, a wheel smashed. We shudder on another pace before grinding to a halt.

I clamber down on shaky legs and circle the horses. If there's anything I can do to help — but my hopes stutter to a stop with a sickening lurch: the bay's leg is broken. He pants, his eyes wide and ringed with white, as he tries again and again to stand. The reins are tangled, and the angle of the shaft won't let him get his balance well enough to stand. Beside him, the chestnut has just managed to keep his feet. He tosses his head, stamping and snorting, the muscles of his neck straining.

"Stop him!"

The shout pierces the quiet that has wrapped around me. I bolt, darting through the gathering crowd. One man tries to grab my arm as I pass him, but I twist and kick and he releases me with a cry. But now more people are taking up the chase, and I don't blame them. It's one thing to make off with a frybread, and a whole other to destroy a carriage and break a horse's leg.

Fear lends me speed for the second time today. I race down another alley, turn and sprint through the open door of a building. I run up the stairs, ignoring the surprised faces of two women chatting before a door, and burst onto the rooftop. Below, I can hear shouts and cries, as well as the thud of feet on the stairs. Someone saw me enter.

I take two deep breaths, surveying the surrounding rooftops, and then I begin to run. It's one jump up to the short wall at the edge of the roof and then — *leap*. I come down on the next building, staggering forward, already searching for the next rooftop. Run, run, *leap*.

I've done this before, but never in a part of town I don't know, and never actually running from someone. The third rooftop lines an alley. I take the alley with a flying leap, grateful the next building is somewhat shorter, and come down with enough force to jar my bones in their sockets.

I pause to look back. I've left my pursuers behind. All except one, a young man who comes to a stop at the edge I just leapt from, gauging the distance. He's not going to jump.

A quick glance to the alley below tells me that the people on the ground haven't managed to catch up with me yet.

"Listen," I say, meeting the man's eyes. His gaze narrows. He opens his mouth but I cut him off before he can speak. "I'm sorry about what happened, okay? This is for the horse. Get a mage-healer to set its leg properly."

"You're sorry?" he says, taken aback.

"Catch." I toss the money pouch the Ghost gave me across the space between us. The man just manages to catch it. He looks down at it, heavy in his palm, then back up at me.

"It's for the horse," I repeat.

Then I turn and run. I put two more roofs between myself and the chase, then swing down to a balcony, using the wooden lattice as a makeshift ladder. I drop the last few feet to the ground, brush off my clothes, and begin walking.

CHAPTER 4
SAFE HOUSE

I glance skyward. Between the buildings, the strip of bright blue is already darkening. I'm out of time. Swallowing a curse, I head toward the waterfront. Without a carriage, we won't be able to transport the Degaths — it's too long a walk to the house Rafiki has in mind, and the family will be too obviously out of place wandering the streets. I'll have to come up with something else.

I keep a watch out for vacant buildings along the way, pausing at the intersections of alleys, studying the more decrepit structures for signs of occupancy. There are a few. Karolene may be a thriving trade city, but the occasional building does fall into disrepair; businesses close and leave behind empty shells; families board up their houses, intending to return one day, only they never do. Plans have a way of unraveling.

I barely step into the first building before I slip out again, moving on before the squatters I spot can register my intrusion. The second and third have too many broken windows and doors to hide our presence or be in any way defensible. When I happen on the fourth, only a few streets from where Rafiki and the Ghost

35

will already be waiting for me, I know that this one will have to work.

The doors and shutters at ground level are still intact. It only takes me a moment with my trusty lock-pick set to get through the back door. Inside, I light a candle stub I keep for just such occasions and inspect the rest of the building. Past the large back room, a long hall lined by two rooms on either side leads to the front entry. The rooms have precious little to offer: moldering mattresses, blackened lumps that may have once been cushions, a scattering of refuse. But one of them does have a workable door.

Back in the hallway, I find a stairwell built between the front room and these smaller rooms, but the treads have long since fallen to pieces, leaving a splintered framework incapable of supporting weight. My eyes search the stairwell. How did it fall in when the doors and shutters are still intact? I find my answer in the blackened ends of timbers: a fire that must have started on an upper floor. Given how thick the dust — and ash — lies here, there should be no one upstairs.

I cast around one last time, knowing that this is hardly the place to put a lord's family. But we have no way to get them to Rafiki's safe place tonight. It will have to do.

Before I leave, I pull a pouch from my pocket, weighing it in my hand, then extract the string of stone prayer beads within. Better to set them up now, when no one can guess at what I'm doing. I suppose I could tell the Ghost or Kenta about my Promise, if I had to. I can't imagine them betraying me. But there's no reason whatsoever for Rafiki to know. He may be part of the League, but I'm not convinced that he wouldn't report me to the High Council for hiding my Promise and remaining "untrained" — formally, at least.

I shudder. Untrained Promises aren't merely fined or sent to school. At my age, there would be only two options. I could choose to have my magic stripped from me, which would likely take my mind with it. Or I could agree to become a source slave, living in a mage's household and being forced to funnel my magic into the mage's own spells.

No, the wards go up now, before anyone else arrives.

With a quick tug I release the knot holding the loop of beads together. One by one, I line the inside of the building with the beads, leaving them below each window and along the walls, and at both exits. I return to the center of the building and kneel on the floor, cupping the last bead in my hand. I focus on the bead until I can feel it in my mind, feel the old ties that bind it to the circle I have set out, like the filaments of a single-stranded web. Reaching out through it, I slowly wake each stone, renewing old bonds and closing the circle I've created around the building. The bead in my hand grows warm as I send my thoughts out through it, sensing each of its siblings, assuring I haven't accidentally mixed their order and left a gap. But the wards fall into place around me perfectly.

I've cast this spell dozens of times, using it as a protection when I've slept in abandoned buildings or on rooftops. I wonder what my mother would have thought, if she could see me. I've never heard of a mage using prayer beads, but they're stone, the traditional material for setting wards. Keeping them on a string retains their order so that I don't have to recast the spell when I need it. I only need to reawaken it, and, when I am done, be careful to gather the stones in the same order that I lay them out.

My beads also reduce the chance that anyone will notice my magic-working, for an old spell draws less attention than a bright, spangly new one.

Wiping a thin sheen of sweat from my brow, I pocket the final bead and head out. I find Rafiki and the Ghost both waiting in a shadowed alley a block inland from the esplanade.

"Where's the carriage?" Rafiki asks, his voice ringing out loud in the empty alleyway. The Ghost touches his elbow, quieting him, but he too looks at me, waiting. For once I'm glad that his hood shadows his face.

"I couldn't get one. The proprietor didn't trust me."

Rafiki swears. At least he doesn't ask about the coin purse.

"It's all right," I say, keeping my eyes on the darkness where the Ghost's face would be. "I've found a place for them — a vacant building, safe enough until we can get a carriage. There should be one free by morning."

I can't see the Ghost's hands beneath his cloak, but I would guess they're clenched around the hilt of his short sword and his dagger. He must be the most clean-mouthed man I've ever met: When he gets upset, he just goes quiet.

"Where's the building?" he asks.

I describe its location and setup. Just as I finish, Kenta darts into our alleyway. In his tanuki form, he hardly comes to my knee, his honey-colored fur so thick he looks more plump than dangerous. His legs and belly are covered in darker fur that travels up his neck and wraps around each side of his face to his eyes, suggesting a mask that doesn't bridge his nose. His ears, twin triangles atop his rounded face, are furred as well.

He pauses, brown eyes reflecting the twilight, then tilts his head in a question.

"She couldn't get a carriage," Rafiki explains. "Apparently—"

"We're walking," the Ghost says, cutting him off. "Rafiki, Kenta, with me. Hitomi, you stay here."

I bristle at his tone. I don't mind missing the conversation with the Degaths, but I'm the only one who'll be able to feel the wards I've set. "Fine, but I'm coming with you to the building."

The Ghost hesitates. "No," he says, and walks around the corner. Kenta follows, sending me a quick glance, ears perked. I try not to glare at him. Rafiki is already gone.

I turn and kick the wall, which only hurts my foot. How

could I have known that fish-brained proprietor wouldn't rent to me? Is it my fault I don't look like a rich servant?

I put my foot down gingerly, curling my toes to see if I've broken anything, and run over my exchange with the Ghost again. I find myself grinning wickedly. He hadn't barred me from going altogether, just going *with them*.

I follow after the others, setting a brisk pace until I catch sight of them again. Rafiki and the Ghost wait just before the intersection with the road that lines the esplanade. I take up a position at the corner of a nearby building, peering around the wall as Kenta trots back into view, followed by a lone man. Lord Degath. The Ghost must have told him to look for Kenta — or rather, the raccoon dog that is Kenta.

In the fading light, I can just discern the shape of the Ghost's flowing black cloak as he steps forward to meet Lord Degath. I can't make out the conversation from here — they speak with lowered voices — but Degath is clearly worried about the missing carriage. I have a feeling that the Ghost hasn't mentioned that their destination isn't really a house.

"Baba?" A young woman calls as she crosses the street toward the meeting taking place, her voice clear and carrying. "Where is the carriage they said they'd send?"

I stare. Is she mad? Does she have any idea what she's doing? Even if she doesn't care about Blackflame finding her, she's a rich girl entering a back alley. More than a few people would kill her for no greater reward than the dress she's wearing. Not here, I hope, but it still doesn't make sense to take such a stupid risk.

Her father, to his credit, attempts to quiet her, but I can hear her next question: "We *are* going to a safe house, though, aren't we?"

Her voice is imperious, commanding, as if the phrasing of her words as a question is irrelevant. We *will* take her where she wishes. I frown. Her demeanor, her high-pitched insistence, and her use of the words "safe house" — as if we have a network of homes in which to hide fugitives — rubs me the wrong way. I've met plenty of annoying people working with the Ghost, but this is different. Why should it matter to her whether we take her straight to a boat or hide her on the island, so long as she is protected? And where did she get the idea that we even *have* safe houses?

Her father says something in response, and while I can't quite hear his words, I do catch her name: Saira. Even if I hadn't heard him, I would have caught it a moment later when her older brother, Tarek, hurries across the street, calling after her, "Saira. Saira! You're supposed to stay with us."

Lord Degath snaps at them both, ordering them into the alley and telling them in no uncertain terms to remain silent.

I close my eyes for a moment. It never occurred to me that the Degaths would be anything other than grateful. I can just imagine Saira's disgust at the building I've selected. I bite the inside of my cheek to keep from chuckling.

The Ghost finishes his conversation with Degath without further interruption and drifts back into the shadows. Rafiki waits nearby. Degath crosses the street to collect the rest of his family, returning almost before he's left with his youngest daughter, a girl of about ten, and Lady Degath. I can't make out much about either of them in the fading light, other than that they both seem to understand the concept of not attracting attention, hardly speaking at all.

Saira begins to complain again as Lord Degath motions for his family to follow after their rescuers. Just one night, I remind myself, easing back from the corner. One night and we'll be rid of them.

Holding that thought in my mind, I head for the vacant building.

A BLOCK FROM MY DESTINATION, I hear the click of nails on cobblestones.

"Hey, tanuki-boy," I say. "Did you think you could leave me behind?"

Kenta cocks his head as he draws even with me, brown eyes laughing.

"Just don't let on I'm here until they're all inside," I say. The Ghost won't send me away once we're holed up; it's not worth the risk of anyone seeing me leave. Kenta agrees with a soft barking laugh.

At the door, though, he snaps his teeth at me before darting in. I hesitate, glancing from the dark alley to the even darker interior, and realize that Kenta is doing a quick search to make sure no one else has entered. I could tell him it's unnecessary; no one has disturbed the wards I've set. But of course I can't....

There's also the possibility that Kenta might sense the wards, but only if he's actively looking for magic. He likely wouldn't be able to connect the wards to me regardless. There's nothing to worry about, I tell myself at least five times while I wait.

Kenta pops back out of the building, taking up a station beside the door. I nod to him and he dips his head in return. Safe, then, in every way that matters. I slip into the building. Without a candle, it's much slower going. I cross the room by memory, feel my way to the central hallway and follow it to the collapsed stairs. Kicking a few splintered boards away, I squat in a corner at the back. With the shadows as dark as they are, and Kenta there to assure the Ghost there's no need to search the building again, it's unlikely anyone will realize I'm here.

I tilt my head, unable to discern anything until I hear the faint shuffle of footsteps at the door, followed by voices.

"*This*? This is no safe house!" It's Saira, and she sounds furious. Not worried or confused or curious. Irate. I close my eyes. I don't like the sound of her at all.

"It is a house, and it's safe," Rafiki replies shortly. She must have been making quite a nuisance of herself on the way over. "What more do you want?"

"Saira." A woman's voice, hard and sharp as honed steel: Lady Degath. "That is more than enough. These men are saving our lives. At least maintain the pretense of being a lady and accept their help with gratitude."

A short silence. I hear the door creak closed.

"It's so dark," a small voice says — the younger daughter.

"I'll light a candle," the Ghost offers with familiar kindness. "But only for a few minutes. Once we're settled in, we'll have to blow it out. We must be careful not to attract attention."

"Didn't you say this place was safe?" the son asks.

"Yes. It is also supposed to be vacant," the Ghost says, his words measured, as if he were addressing a simpleton.

Light flickers, chasing away the absolute darkness of the hall: the Ghost has lit his candle.

"Follow me," he says. I hear his shoes in the hall, the others behind him. The stairs are past the four small rooms, so there's no reason to think he'll lead the Degaths this far. But if he does, there's a good chance he'll spot me right away.

"Is that a lycan?" the little girl's voice pipes up. I grin as someone hushes her.

Saira snorts with derision. "It's just a dog, Alia. And a fat one at that. Lycans look like wolves."

I almost choke trying to keep from laughing. It's going to be a while before I let Kenta live down that particular snub.

The Degaths settle into their room quietly, Lady Degath making a single cutting remark that assures near silence from her children. The Ghost glides out after a moment or two, pausing in the hallway. I can just make out his form, backlit by the candlelight. I expect Rafiki is keeping watch at the back door. Kenta glances up at the Ghost, head cocked as he waits in the hallway. Together, they start down the hall to the door.

"We need to lock the door," the Ghost says, his voice barely audible.

"If Hitomi were here, she could have done it," Rafiki observes. I blink in surprise. I never would have thought Rafiki would stand up for me. "Too bad she ran. Didn't even get the carriage. You just can't trust a *mgeni.*"

Strike that.

"That's enough, Rafiki," the Ghost says, sounding peeved. Then, "We'll need to bar it from inside."

I rise, stretching out my legs before making my way down the hall. I pass the Degaths' room, keeping away from the light, but I can't resist a look inside.

Lady Degath sits against the wall. On the ground beside her lies a blanket for her two daughters. The youngest, Alia, has already lain down. Saira lifts up a small mirror to inspect her hair. *Her hair?* Vain as well as foolish. I suppose it makes sense.

I continue on to the back room. "All right, boys," I say sweetly. Rafiki and the Ghost both whirl around, daggers jumping to their hands. Kenta's teeth gleam in a laughing smile. "Since you missed me so much, I guess I'll just have to come help out again."

"You're not supposed to be here," the Ghost says, his voice hard.

"Who's going to lock the door for you then?"

"We'll manage."

"Right. Rafiki, you leaving to find that carriage?" I really hope he doesn't go to Master Khalid's inn first. Not that the story of what I've done won't get out soon enough anyway. I'd just rather the Ghost not know tonight.

Rafiki backs out of the door. "I'll be back soon," he assures the Ghost, and hurries off. I can hear Kenta's nails click against the floorboards as he slips away deeper into the building, leaving us to fight alone.

"Hitomi."

"Save it. Two sets of ears are better than one."

He sighs. "There's Kenta."

"Fine. Three sets are better than two," I amend, stepping past him. I interpret his sigh as a sign that he's giving in. I swing the door shut, plunging the room into near darkness. This far away, the candlelight from the Degaths' room is no help at all. Still, it only takes a moment to lift the pins and turn the lock. "This is my fault. I'm not going to leave you to deal with it alone."

"It isn't a question of fault," the Ghost replies.

I shrug, even though he can't see me in the dark. Maybe he believes that, maybe he doesn't. "I can help here," I say. "Let me stay."

Granted, it might be difficult to send me away through a locked door, but making the request offers him some semblance of control.

What he says next takes me by surprise. "I don't like the feel of this."

I rock back on my heels, peering blindly toward his voice. This may be my first time sneaking out fugitives, but the Ghost has helped a handful of other families escape before tonight. He would know if something felt off. "Is it the older girl?"

Silence. Okay then.

"What do you think she'll do?" I ask.

"I can't tell."

I wish I could see what he looks like. I hadn't realized until now how much I'd learned to read his moods from how he holds himself, even without being able to see his face.

"We'll keep a watch on her," I promise. "Do you want me to stay in the room with them?"

"No. Don't let them know you're here." I hear the rustle of his cloak as he shifts. "It's best we get them out of Karolene as fast as we can."

"Faster than we planned?"

He doesn't answer immediately. "We'll see. The dhows are all out fishing tonight, so there's nothing we can do until dawn. I'll send Kenta to the beaches to see if we can move the Degaths out as soon as the fishermen have unloaded their catch." He doesn't name the dhow owner, his words sounding slightly awkward. Because of Saira.

"Hole up wherever you were before," the Ghost continues. "Stay there until we leave, then follow us out. There's no reason for the Degaths to know you're here."

"Where will you be?"

"Here," he says, by which I gather he means the back room, keeping a watch on the door. Kenta must have taken the front door.

"Let me know if..." If what? Even I'm not sure what might happen. "If I can do anything," I finish awkwardly.

"I will," the Ghost says.

I stand up and start toward the hallway, using the faint fall of candlelight as my guide. The Ghost comes along behind me, no doubt to tell the Degaths to blow out the candle.

"Hitomi?" the Ghost murmurs as we near the door.

"Hmm?"

"Be careful."

I turn my head to look at him over my shoulder. I can't make out a thing in the darkness. A hand touches my shoulder, and then the Ghost steps past me to the Degaths' room.

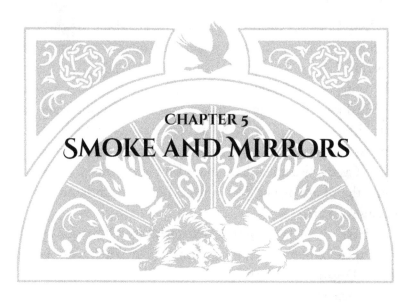

CHAPTER 5
SMOKE AND MIRRORS

I wake with a jolt as the first magical ward flares to life. Leaping to my feet, I turn blindly toward it — it's the bead placed by the front door. I take the hallway at a sprint, skidding into the back room where the Ghost waits.

"What is it?" he whispers from somewhere on my left.

What it is, is impossible. I shake my head in disbelief as the wards along the windows flare up one by one, tracking the presence of the soldiers surrounding us. The only ward that hasn't been triggered yet is the one by the Degaths' window. That isn't a coincidence: they're leaving space there for anyone who decides to jump out.

"We're surrounded," I whisper.

Kenta growls. I hadn't heard him following me down the hall.

The Ghost shifts, straining to listen. "Are you sure?"

"Yes."

"It doesn't make sense," he says, almost to himself. "How could they have found us?"

The realization hits me like a slap in the face   ᶻ
older girl. She has a mirror."

"Mirror?"

"A locator spell."

A moment follows that should have been fill
sound of a curse, but instead holds the Ghost's silence. Then he
moves past me. "Hide."

I don't answer. Instead, I follow him to the Degaths' room.
His footsteps pause as he lights the candle again, leaving it
burning on the floor. The Degaths barely have time to register his
arrival before he crosses the room and hauls Saira to her feet.

"The mirror," he snarls as she yelps and tries to pull away. He
shakes her. "Now!"

The others scramble to their feet, Degath pushing past his
wife to reach for his daughter. And then Saira laughs.

"Oh, the mirror. Why didn't you say so?" She pulls it from
her skirt pocket and holds it out to the Ghost. He releases her and
takes it, stepping back. From the door, I can just see the milky
white surface looking back at him.

Degath stares at it, then turns to his daughter. "What is that?"

The Ghost drops the mirror and grinds it to pieces beneath
his heel. "A locator spell. We are surrounded."

"A — what?" Degath stumbles.

The girl straightens her back, smoothing out her clothes.
She's taller than me, proud in her seventeen years. "It's okay,
Baba. He promised our safety in return for the Ghost. A safe
house would have been nice, but it's the Ghost he really wants."

"Who told you that?" Degath asks, his voice hoarse.

"Master Blackflame himself," she says proudly.

Degath raises a hand to his face, shielding his eyes as if he
cannot bear the sight of his daughter.

The Ghost turns toward the door, then pauses. "Degath?"

47

..did not know—"

"Give your wife and your other daughter blades — you have weapons?" The man nods. "If they go down fighting, they might have an easier end."

"We're not in danger," Saira insists, her voice growing shrill. "Baba—"

"There must be a way," Degath begins, ignoring her.

The Ghost shakes his head. "We are surrounded."

With the stairwell collapsed, there's no other escape. I drop into a crouch. "Kenta," I murmur to the shape beside me. Kenta tilts his head toward me, his body coiled as tight as a spring. "The stairs have fallen in, but the floorboards are sound. We can boost the Ghost up...."

Kenta meets my gaze.

"If he won't go willingly, we'll have to make him. Help me?"

He dips his head.

The Ghost sweeps out of the room.

"This way," I murmur, and he turns, following me. The faint sound of boots scrapes at the edge of my hearing. The soldiers are in position. Any moment now they'll begin their attack.

"We need to get you out alive. We can boost you up the stairs." I grab the brooch that secures his cloak and pull it open.

"I'm not leaving." The Ghost backs up, away from my hands.

His cloak slides half off his shoulders. I yank the cloak the rest of the way off. "You're the *Ghost*. You can't die here. The League needs you. We'll boost you up the stairwell. Climb to the next floor and hide."

"They'll know I'm gone."

"Not if I'm wearing your cloak." I swing the heavy fabric around my own shoulders.

"No—"

"She betrayed us, don't you understand? Blackflame must know about your informants! He planned this in advance, gave that mirror to Saira *knowing* the League would help Degath. If you die here, the League will fall apart. Your informants might already be dead—"

Something rams against the back door, rattling its hinges. At the same moment, a similar assault begins on the front door. The Ghost's hand drops to the hilt of his sword, as if the only support he needs is Kenta, who has no weapon but his teeth, and me, with nothing but a slim knife strapped to my calf. But he doesn't draw his sword.

"I know," he says softly, surprising me. "Blackflame planned this well. I'll go up, but you're both coming with me."

"It won't work. We're surrounded and they won't stop until they find you. Kenta—" I mean to call for Kenta's help, though what I expect him to do I don't know. I can barely hear myself think over the pounding on the doors.

The Ghost glances up into the stairwell, barely lit by the faint glow from the Degaths' room.

"There's no *time*," I shout.

Kenta steps forward in his human form, his bare chest rippling with muscles, and whacks the Ghost over the head with a length of wood.

I step back, speechless. The Ghost stumbles against the wall, shaking his head to clear it. That wasn't quite the kind of help I'd intended.

"Move," Kenta says, grabbing the Ghost by the shoulders and propelling him beneath the overhang of the floor above.

"Kenta," I say, as he offers his hands, fingers interlaced, for the Ghost to put his boot in. The Ghost glances blearily between the two of us. "Kenta! He's not going to be able to jump now."

Wood shatters — the back door has given in. Kenta whirls toward the hallway.

"Come on." I grab the Ghost by the shoulder and hustle him

under the broken stairs to where I hid before. He definitely isn't doing well: he doesn't even protest. "Kenta!"

The Ghost sits down heavily, his back against the wall, just as Kenta appears at my shoulder. "You too," I hiss. "Someone has to keep him safe now that you've knocked his brains loose. You're a better fighter than me."

"They'll see us," Kenta murmurs as he drops down beside the Ghost.

"They won't," I promise. Kenta transforms to his tanuki form in the space of a breath. I try to gather my thoughts. No time, I think, as feet pound down the hall, coming to a stop before the Degaths' door. *No time.* I kneel before them, center myself for what I have to do.

"Hitomi."

I glance up, ready to curse the Ghost, and find him handing me the hilt of his short sword. His hand wavers slightly as he holds it out. His sword. *If they go down fighting, they might have an easier end.* I snatch the sword from him and pull my mind back to my spell. Fortunately, I'm surrounded by what I need most: darkness. Reaching out, I gather the shadows around me and lay them over my friends like a velvet cloak of night and smoke, pulling and tugging at the shadows until I can barely see the two men even though I kneel before them. It's a clumsy spell, made too fast and with wrinkles and snags that might unravel at any moment, but it's the best I can do. Distantly, I hear screaming.

"Don't move," I pant, my body drenched with sweat.

But an arm reaches out of the shadow and pulls off the boy's cap I wear. I'd forgotten it.

"*Don't move.*" I pull up the cloak's hood to complete my disguise. As far as I can tell, the spell has fallen back into place around my friends. "Good-bye," I whisper. Then I run — or try to. The magic-working has unbalanced me, and I stagger as I start forward, barely managing to keep my feet.

A faint light still spills through the Degaths' doorway. I can hear shouts and cries, can see the flicker of shadows through the doorway. But all I can truly make out are dimly lit forms and the brief gleam of light on blades as the soldiers in the hall turn toward me. These aren't your usual soldiers, but an elite squad. They turn with practiced ease, swords in their hands, every move calm, calculated. Completely unworried.

I smile, a wild, feral thing Kenta would have been proud of, and launch myself at the foremost soldier. I have to make this look like a struggle, at least a little. The narrow hall works in my favor: only two can face me at a time. However, the fact that I never learned swordplay, and that I'm still off-balance from my last spell, makes the fight brutally short.

The first soldier meets my sword with his own, blocking my swing and throwing my arm back toward the wall. I duck and twist, just avoiding another blade, and bring my sword back around in time to clumsily block the second soldier's attack — and lose my footing as my sandal skids on the floorboards.

I stagger, throwing myself sideways as a blade slides past my ribs. I'm not quite fast enough to outstep the second blade the soldier uses. It knocks my own sword from my hand. Panic surges through me. I twist away as the sword skitters across the floor, yank my knife free from its sheath. A woman screams — Lady Degath? — but there's no way I can reach her. I throw myself forward, slicing my knife toward the soldier's chest, and another sharp edge flashes in the corner of my vision.

I don't look at it, expecting it to cut into my neck. In that moment, when there is no more running, I know one truth: *I don't want to die.* It is a hopeless knowing, as quick and strong as a single heartbeat. And then the flat of the blade slams into the side of my head.

I fall to my knees, stunned. A boot plows into my back. My face meets the splintered floorboards, and then a man's weight slams down on me, pinning me to the floor. He rips the knife from my grasp, and, with the help of another soldier, binds my hands with ruthless efficiency. They search me quickly, checking my pockets, frisking my arms and legs, checking the empty sheath at my calf. I stare across the floor, trying not to think about what I'll do if they realize I'm a girl, and find myself looking through the Degaths' doorway into the glazed eyes of Lord Degath. A few drops of blood trickle from his lips to form a perfectly round coin of darkness on the floor. I swallow back bile.

"Who'd have thought the Ghost couldn't fight worth shit?" one of the soldiers sneers as they haul me to my feet. They wear the uniform of the sultan's soldiers rather than Blackflame's mercenaries, and yet they don't seem any different.

I look up, catch the measured gaze of the second soldier — not a soldier, I realize, taking in the embroidered rank marks at his collar. A captain.

"He wasn't trying to kill us," he says.

"Then what the hell—"

"He was trying to get killed." The captain steps forward, holding my gaze. "Isn't that right?"

I force a smile through bruised and bloodied lips. At least they haven't figured out I'm neither a boy nor the Ghost. "Some people don't mind blood on their hands. I do."

The man holding me spins me around and backhands me across my face. I fall against a wall. My vision jumps, and all I can think of is how the Ghost must have felt when Kenta hit him with that board.

"*Hold.*" The captain's voice rings out through the hallway. "We bring him in alive as we were ordered. You will not let him taunt you into killing him."

"If only you'd been as stupid as the rest of them." I turn my

52

head to meet his eyes. He offers me the shadow of a smile, one fighting man to another, I suppose. Then he turns and walks into the massacre he ordered.

I follow him with my gaze, forcing myself to keep looking past Degath's sprawled form. Behind him lies his wife, her eyes rolled back, showing only white, her face taut with a pain now departed. Blood stains the front of her dress.

At the back of the room, the two girls cling to each other. I crane my neck to see the third form crouched beside them: their brother, clutching his arm to his side, blood seeping through his fingers.

A part of me is sorry, sorry that the little girl and her brother are still alive, sorry that they will pay the price of their father's choices and their sister's betrayal. Just as I will.

CHAPTER 6
MONSTER

T he soldiers prepared well for their raid. Outside, we're loaded into a prison carriage: a metal box on wheels, with one small, barred window in the rear door. Further on, a wagon waits to take away the dead.

"You can't do this!" Saira cries as she is pushed up into the carriage behind me, her sister clinging to her in silence. "Stop! Master Blackflame promised — you weren't supposed to kill anyone! Wait — where is my brother?"

She gets her answer a moment later when Tarek is shoved into the carriage, the door slammed shut behind him. Leaning my head back against the cold metal wall, I listen to the lock click. If I still had my lockpick set, picking it would have been a moment's work.

Saira continues to rail against the soldiers, half-hysterical, until Tarek says, "Saira, stop. It's no use. *Stop.*"

His voice is low and weak, and I remember belatedly that he had been bleeding. If his wound hasn't been bandaged, we'll need to do something about it fast. I move toward him, sidling down the bench. Now that the carriage rattles along the road, I don't trust myself to keep my balance. Not after the spell and the blow to my head.

I hesitate before I speak. They've all heard the Ghost's voice, and with Saira's betrayal as fresh as the blood on Tarek's arm, I don't want to risk anyone discovering I'm not him. Not until the Ghost has had enough time to escape.

I lower my voice to a whisper, barely loud enough for Tarek to hear me over the clatter of the carriage. "Where are you bleeding?"

"My arm. But they bound it for me."

Saira makes a strangled sound.

"Shut up," Tarek say tightly. "This is your fault. All of it. You *killed* them."

"I didn't!" Saira's voice rises until it screeches in my ears. "No one was supposed to die! The soldiers weren't supposed to attack *us*, just...."

"Just me," I say, then berate myself for speaking aloud. I move back down the bench, training my gaze on the opposite wall.

"Why did you want to kill the Ghost?" Alia asks.

"I didn't want — I just — it was a negotiation! Master Black-flame promised...." Saira shakes her head.

"Promised that he'd keep his political enemy safe if you handed over the Ghost? Oh, how he must have praised your smarts." Tarek's voice is heavy with sarcasm. "You'd save Mama and Baba from what? The sultan's displeasure? While creating some amazing alliance with Blackflame?"

"The sultan wants Mama and Baba dead—"

"The sultan does what *Blackflame* wants!" Tarek is shouting now. "*Blackflame* wanted them dead, and you gave him the perfect opportunity to kill them and catch the leader of the Shadow League at the same time."

"No," Saira whispers. "He promised...."

"And you believed him." Tarek's words drip disdain.

Saira doesn't answer.

As I half-expected, instead of taking us to the city prison, we're admitted through the gates to Blackflame's private residence. Why take us to the sultan's prison when Karolene's Arch Mage is the true power? He meets us in the courtyard, smiling as if he has just been given a gift. And he has, I think grimly.

The soldiers haul me out of the carriage and shove me to my knees. I try not to wince as I hit the cobbles. Blackflame stands a few paces away, watching the spectacle of his prisoners being unloaded with undisguised pleasure.

Wilhelm Blackflame looks nothing like his mage-name would suggest. He's tall and broad-shouldered, with a thick mane of golden hair that curls where it brushes his shoulders. His skin shows pale, marking him a northerner. He is naturally strong, neither big-muscled nor going to fat. With his wide forehead, defined jaw, and cleft chin, his features are a little too strong for beauty. But what his body fails to show and his mage-name only implies is this: the pure magical power lurking behind his eyes.

"Welcome, ghost-boy," he says. He tilts his head to study me. The soldiers have pulled my hood back, exposing my face. Thankfully, with my hair shorn short and my grubby tunic and trousers, I look as much a boy as I do a girl. The additional layer of my cloak conceals anything my tunic doesn't. Apparently, Blackflame's sources aren't as informed as they seem: he doesn't realize that I'm the wrong race.

"Oh, it's my pleasure," I say, keeping my voice as low as I can. I'm not sure how long I'll be able to keep up the pretense of being the Ghost, but I intend to give my friends as much time as I can. "It's good to know you've been losing sleep over me. Or do you make a habit of personally receiving your prisoners in the middle of the night?"

His nostrils flare, and I sense the soldiers shift behind me. I doubt too many people mouth off to him. But then he laughs, and I find I much prefer him angry to amused. "Say what you like now, boy. I'll hear you screaming for mercy before I'm done with you. I'll have every name of every person who so much as smiled in your support out of you."

I swallow hard, trying to look unconcerned. I'm not so stupid as to think I'll last long against a skilled torturer.

"Nothing to say to that? Ah, I thought you had a bit more courage. You might roar like a lion, but you haven't the claws to prove it. More of a puppy, I think."

"Easily said when you're standing free with your mercenaries at your beck and call," I snap. "I've never bought my loyalty." Not that I've ever had anyone loyal to me, come to think of it. Not the way he means.

"A pity. If you had, you might not be here now. I always said you were a fool to trust every man in need of saving."

"Degath *did* need saving." I try to push myself to my feet. The soldiers holding me shove me back down by my shoulders. "*You* turned his daughter against him."

He laughs. "Where is the precious girl? Don't tell me she died with her parents."

"No, Master Blackflame," the captain says. "We've done as you ordered. The children are all alive."

"As you ordered?" Saira's voice wavers with disbelief. I can't imagine how she's held on for so long. I suppose the alternative, the reality of what she's done, is too much for her to accept.

Twisting my head, I can just make out her form as she clambers down from the prison carriage. "But you promised me my parents would be spared!"

"You must have misunderstood, my dear. I said I would spare

Lord Degath's life. And, if I'm not mistaken, there he is behind you."

Saira wheels around to see her brother at the foot of the carriage, helping Alia down with his good arm. Tarek raises his gaze to Blackflame, squaring his shoulders. "If you think I'm more likely to ally myself with you than my father, you are mistaken," he says, his voice shaking with fury. "I would rather slit your throat."

"How charming." Blackflame chuckles, shaking his head as if Tarek were a child showing off a new trick. "Little Lord Degath, you are not half so quick as your father. Let me clarify your situation. You are, by all accounts, dead — or whisked off by the League, perhaps. No one will know where you are; no ally will come to your support. No *Ghost.* I think a few years behind stone walls followed by an execution would do you good."

"You're a monster!" Alia shrieks, holding tight to her brother's hand.

I close my eyes. Blackflame hadn't mentioned her. Why did she have to draw attention to herself?

He smiles. "No, little Degath, I am not. But I will be sure to introduce you to one shortly." He turns to the captain. "Take them below."

WE ARE MARCHED DOWN to the dank underbelly of Blackflame's mansion. The wide room might have felt spacious had it not been for the cages lining one wall and the torture table and instruments set out in the center. Additional implements — chains, spikes, hooks, and various blades — hang from the wall behind the table. By the time we've each been locked into our respective cages, Saira is sobbing hysterically. Tarek maintains a stoic silence, but I'm not sure how much of it is due to shock and blood loss.

My cage is barely high enough for me to stand, and it allows me only three steps in any direction. I am at the end of the row, with a wall on one side and Alia's cage on the other. Beyond her are her sister and then her brother. After him I see two more cages. One I think is empty; the other holds a dark shadow pressed into the farthest corner.

I sit down, leaning against the wall, and try to think through the pounding in my head. I hurt all over: my knees where they hit the cobblestones, my back and ribs where I'd been kicked, and my head where the captain hit me with the flat of his blade. Add to that the drain of my magic working, and I can barely see straight.

Still, if I can pick the lock....

I scoot over to the bars. "Alia," I call, pitching my voice low. "Alia!"

She lifts her head from her hands. Her face is dry, her eyes glazed. She looks worn down by experience, her ten years no longer filled with innocence. In the emptiness of her expression, I catch a memory of my own and my heart stutters. Damn Blackflame to a hundred agonizing deaths.

Alia blinks slowly. "Ghost?" she whispers, her voice numb.

"Yes," I reply, silently promising that I will be her Ghost, that I will get her out of this. If it's the last thing I do, I will save her from watching the rest of her family die. And, as much as I despise her sister, I will save what is left of her family as well.

"Can you untie my hands? I might be able to get the locks open, but not if I'm tied."

"What are you saying to her?" Saira's voice from the next cage is wary. As if she has any reason to suspect me.

I swallow a sharp retort and make myself explain. "If she can untie my hands, I might be able to pick the locks. If either of you have anything I can use. Hairpins, maybe?"

"I've got some," Saira says, tearing at her hair. She gathers a few in her hands and holds them out to Alia. "Take them to the Ghost."

"What did he mean by a monster?" Alia asks.

Saira flinches. "I don't know. But if the Ghost can help us escape, we won't have to find out."

Alia wipes her nose and reaches for the pins. She barely has to shift her position to offer them to me.

"I can't take them until you untie my hands," I remind her. "See if you can loosen the ropes."

I sit with my back pressed up against the bars, my hands shoved as far through as I can manage. Alia picks at the knot, sniffling now and then. "I can't see it," she says finally, pushing my hands away. "And it's too tight."

"You need to keep trying," Saira says from her cage.

"Come on, Alia," their brother calls. "Try again."

She does. I murmur encouragements, praying for the ropes to loosen. It feels like hours later when I finally twist my hands free. I have no idea how late — or early — it really is. I fumble for the hairpins, my fingers too numb to lift them.

"Can you do it?" Alia asks, her voice peaking with worry.

"Yes," I say, wishing the ropes had been a little less tight. My fingers are clumsy, slow. "Let me just get my hands working again." I shake them out, rubbing my fingers until they feel like I've plunged them into a fire, flames licking at my veins. When the burning begins to subside, I pocket the hairpins and scoot over to the door.

The lock is simple enough. I can lift the pins of the lock, but the thin metal clips aren't strong enough to turn the tumbler. I break two of the five I have trying. What I need is something to apply torque, something with more substance.

"Ghost?" Alia asks, her voice plaintive.

"I've almost got it," I mutter. "Do you have anything else I can use? Saira? Tarek? I need something a little stronger than hairpins."

They check their pockets, but like me the soldiers stripped them of their belongings.

"Do you have any more hairpins?" I press. Saira pulls the last pins from her hair, passing them through the bars to Alia. Unbound, her hair falls down her back in a cascade of black. Just the flow of her hair speaks to her noble heritage.

I gather what I have, then set aside four hairpins. It's only a three-pin lock, but it's best to keep a spare in case I break one. If I can solder the remaining metal together, that should be strong enough to finish the job.

I turn my back to the Degaths. Folding my legs beneath me, I cup my hands around the hairpins and lean down so that I'm curled over them. Even here, in the near dark, when I may already be dead, I dare not let my secret out. Instead, I let myself look beaten, and, my cloak obscuring my actions, I pour my magic into the palms of my hands.

I draw on everything I have: on the stone of the walls surrounding me, ancient and unconcerned, born of the earth; on the air, cool and heavy with damp, life-giving yet laden with the scent of death, a memory of pain. When I open my eyes, I see blearily that the pins have sealed together into a single misshapen wrench.

It's done. The wrench is made; the pins are ready. I have only to open the cages and find a way out. Darkness drips onto my fingers. I raise a hand to wipe blood from my nose, my motions slow, unsteady.

Holding the wrench in one hand, I grab hold of a bar and pull myself up. The cage tilts around me. I stagger, my feet clumsy, heavy as stone.

"Ghost?" Alia asks.

I shake my head, trying to clear it, and lose my balance, falling backwards. The last thing I hear is Alia's voice calling to me as my head hits the floor. "Ghost? *Ghost?*"

I WAKE to the sound of boots, the low rumble of male voices in conversation. I squeeze my eyes shut, open them slowly. The dark bars of a cage stare back at me. My memories snap into place. I try to scramble to my feet, but my sense of balance is off. Fighting a wave of dizziness, I crouch on the floor, swallowing down bile. Something metallic has rolled between the stones before me: my torque wrench.

As swiftly as my shaking fingers will let me, I slip it into my pocket alongside the hairpins. When I look up, I make myself focus on the men. Blackflame strides toward the cages, his golden mane falling about his shoulders, his mage's robes flaring as he walks. In their way, the four mercenaries behind him are as ornamental as his robe.

A tall, slim figure keeps pace with him, his short chestnut hair emphasizing the paleness of his face. He wears a rich ensemble of a tailored shirt, brocade vest, fitted pantaloons, and immaculate boots. A northman? As he offers Blackflame a grin, I catch the gleam of lantern light on unnaturally long incisors.

No.

No.

I scramble toward the bars between my cage and Alia's. "Alia — Alia! Listen to me. Whatever you do, don't look at the men." She stares back at me. She looks terrible: pale-faced to the point of sickliness, with dark bruises beneath her eyes. "Don't look at them! Do you hear me? He's a—"

"Child," the creature says, his voice a friendly baritone. "Who is your friend?"

"*Alia!*" I lunge for her, grabbing her sleeve and yanking her toward me before she can finish turning her head. "Don't look!" I can feel the call of his voice even though I'm not his target. I have to fight to keep my gaze on Alia.

She jerks back to look at me. "What's wrong?" she whispers.

"Monster," I whisper back. "A fang. Don't look."

Her eyes widen with horror. Not because he's a fang; I suspect she has met more than a few. The fangs that come to Karolene are often wealthy, moving in elite circles and visiting the court. But they also belong to clans who have signed treaties with the High Council of Mages, treaties that assure they never drink from an unwilling victim.

From her expression, I know that Alia understands as well as I that this fang is not safe like those others. This fang has come for her blood.

"How precious." The stranger chuckles softly. I hear the click of his boots as he comes to stand before my cage. "How long do you think you can protect her, girl?"

Blackflame makes a strangled sound. I keep my eyes focused on Alia. "That's no girl, Kol. That's the Ghost."

The fang, Kol, sniffs the air. "I know a girl when I scent one. I take it your Ghost is meant to be a boy?"

"Open the door," Blackflame orders, his voice dark with fury. *He knows.* If there's one thing his spies have ferreted out for him, it's that the Ghost is unarguably a man. Well, at least I can distract them from Alia. Still, I cling to her until a soldier rips me away. As much as I don't want the fang to harm her, I don't want him to touch me, either.

They haul me from the cage. I manage to salvage some dignity, standing up straight even with my arms pinned tight behind me. I force a smile through cracked lips, tasting the dried blood smeared there from my nosebleed. "What's wrong, Black-flame? Catch the wrong person?"

He hits me across the face, only it isn't just a slap. It contains his rising fury, fueled by his magic, and it rips me from my captor's grip when no amount of my own struggling would have. I slam against the wall, collapsing in a heap on the floor.

Now would be a good time to black out, I think groggily. But I don't.

I watch as a set of men's embroidered slippers approach, flickering apart into two sets and then resolving back into one as I blink my eyes. A hand grabs me by the front of my cloak and hauls me up. I choke as the cloth tightens around my throat.

"Where is the Ghost?" Blackflame hisses, his face barely a hand span from my own.

"Wouldn't tell you even if I knew," I say, and then, marshaling my forces, I spit at him. Considering he's only a little farther away than my own nose, it's impressive how little of my saliva actually hits him. He curses, hurling me across the room. I hit the ground with bone-jarring intensity, rolling twice before coming to a stop sprawled against the torture table.

Blackflame bends over me as I struggle to inhale, to force air into my lungs before I suffocate. "How did he escape?" He glances toward the cages, toward Saira. "Was he even there to begin with?"

"Oh, he was there," I manage. I try to sound amused, but I'm wheezing too hard to sound anything but pained. "Waited until the Degaths were settled, and then headed out. Your soldiers were just too stupid to put things together. They knew I couldn't fight, but did they notice I don't have a scabbard for my sword? Or that my cloak is too long? But then ... you didn't notice, either."

His features twist. He lifts me up so that my toes barely brush the floor. The cloak flaps around them, clearly made for someone at least a head taller than me. Blackflame drops me onto the torture table.

Oh God, no.

"You know," Kol says, "I'm curious just how much fight the girl has in her."

I flinch.

Blackflame pauses. A smile plays over his thin lips. The only sound in the room is the painful gasp of my breathing. "Oh?"

"I might have a use for her. It would be slow," Kol says, crossing the room to us, "and painful. For both of them."

"Both of them?" Blackflame echoes.

"Yes," Kol says absently. "Look at me, girl."

I force my eyes shut, shaking with the effort. A hand touches my face, fingers tapping my eyelids. I feel sickeningly exposed, pressed flat against the table. "Come now, don't you know it will be easier if you look?"

I shove his hand away, clenching my jaw with the effort to keep my eyes closed. He chuckles, the sound coming from just beside my ear. "Open. Your. Eyes."

His hand closes around my neck; his curved nails, pointed and razor sharp, slice into my skin.

"*No*," I gasp, twisting away so that, even though my eyes open, I still escape his gaze.

He rocks back, satisfied. "Perfect. That little debt we've been discussing, Blackflame? This girl will cover it. If you wish, of course."

I force my eyes closed again, even though Kol has turned his attention from me. My breath rattles in my chest. I try to focus on what I've heard: Blackflame has been dealing with a fang, has put himself in debt to the creature. A debt that might be paid for with my life.

"You may have her," Blackflame replies. "So long as she dies."

"She will. But first, breakfast." Kol turns to face the cages. "Alia, dear?"

My eyes pop open. In her cage, Alia gazes back at him, her lips parted, her face going slack. "No," I whisper. I scrabble to sit up, sliding off the table to land in a heap on the floor. I use the table leg to pull myself up again. "*No.*"

"Hold her," the fang says without looking back.

The soldiers grab me, their grip viciously tight. I can hear Saira and Tarek calling out to Alia as well, desperately, hopelessly. Just as a viper may hold a mouse with its gaze, mesmerized into paralysis, so can a fang hold a human. Kol has chosen Alia, and now she waits for him, empty-eyed and all unknowing.

Blackflame opens the door to Alia's cage.

At the fang's gentle beckoning, she goes to him, drifting forward slowly. He tilts her chin up and, with a pleasant smile, bends down and buries his fangs in her neck.

I can hear a woman screaming, and it takes me a long moment to realize it's not me. I still don't have enough breath for such deep, ragged cries. It's Saira. Beneath her voice I can hear Tarek weeping. Only Alia makes no sound, her body slowly going limp in the fang's embrace.

Finally, Kol straightens, his tongue flicking out to lick crimson from his lips. All I can think is how obscene he looks, how sickening he is. Alia's body crumples slowly, almost gently, leaving her heaped on the floor like so much rubbish. A soldier steps forward to return her to her cell.

Kol turns toward me, pivoting so fast that I catch the burning blue of his gaze before I can help myself. His eyes are the unending expanse of summer skies, the innocence of robins' eggs. The color of death.

I jerk back, letting the soldiers' grip on my arms provide the shock of pain I need to break eye contact.

Twisting my head away, my eyes strain in their sockets, as if I

66

might peer through the flesh and bone of my skull to find his fang's gaze once more. I feel his fingers brush my cheek. "You do know that I can take your blood whether you look at me or not, don't you?" he asks. "It just goes easier for you if you cooperate."

I clench my jaw, my eyes sealed shut.

"Oh, this will be fun," he croons. Then, to the soldiers, "Put her away. I won't need her until I leave."

CHAPTER 7
BLUE SILK

I wait until the sounds of our captors' footsteps fade, then begin a count to a hundred to be sure of their absence. The only sound is that of Saira calling to Alia, her voice low but constant. I don't look, can't bear to study the girl's tiny, collapsed form.

My count completed, I pull the torque wrench from my pocket and assess it critically. It's slightly bent, of varying thickness, with a bulge toward one end, but it might be serviceable. The vital thing is to get out and to maintain my strength for the escape. Alia will need all the help she can get just to keep up with us, and there's no telling what we might meet if we do manage to leave the room. I can't afford to weaken myself with another spell.

It takes five tries before I manage to pick the lock. I swing the door open and feel the attention of Tarek and Saira snap to me — as well as that of the other captive. I had forgotten the silent shadow of a creature in the cage beyond Tarek's.

"Can you get us out? Ghost?" Tarek asks, his voice wavering between anxiety and hope.

"I'm not the Ghost," I say gruffly. I walk over to Alia's cage, trying not to look inside to where she lies. Instead, I focus my attention on the lock. It's the same as mine, and the door swings open after only three attempts. Inside, I crouch beside the child, touching her shoulder hesitantly.

"Let me out," Saira orders from her cage.

"Shut up."

"Is she okay? Is she—"

"Alive," I confirm. Alia's breath flutters in her chest, and her cheek is cool to my touch. She's lost too much blood, but she's hanging on. Cursing Kol, I leave the cage and go to Tarek. Saira can wait. At this point, if I don't get to her, I don't think I'll care.

"Is there really a Ghost?" Tarek asks as I work the lock. "Or is it just a cloak you pass around?"

"There's a Ghost," I say shortly.

"Wouldn't he come for you?"

"Not if he's smart," I mutter.

"What?"

"It doesn't matter," I say. "We're leaving now, not waiting for a rescue attempt. Can you carry Alia? With that arm of yours?"

"Yes," he says, his voice turning rough. The moment the door swings open, he pushes past me. He pulls Alia onto his lap, whispering her name as if it has the power to call her back to him. If her dark skin was pale before, now it is sallow as the yellow moon, her eyes ringed with dark circles, her neck bruised.

I take a deep, shaky breath and move on to Saira's cage. At least she has enough sense to ignore me, standing by the bars and watching her brother instead. I'm getting better at working with the hairpins and lumpy wrench, but my eyes keep sliding away to the other prisoner, the one who was here before us. A man, I think. He's sitting up, watching us, dark greasy hair obscuring his face but probably not his vision. I have no idea how old he is, where he's from, if he's even human. But he is a captive, just like us.

I swing open Saira's door, stepping back to let her out. She doesn't even glance at me as she hurries to her sister's side. I turn away and find myself caught by the dark-eyed gaze of the other captive.

"Let me out," he says. His accent is thick, unfamiliar, but his words are still intelligible.

I approach his cage cautiously. "Why are you here?"

"I made an enemy." He crosses the cell, barely able to stay upright, collapsing to his knees as he reaches me. But when he grabs hold of the door, he shakes it, the iron bars rattling in their frame. "Let me out."

I cast an apprehensive glance at the stairs. When I look back at him, I focus on his hands wrapped around the bars: thin and bloodless, the nails ending in razor sharp points. I back away, horrified. "You're a fang."

"I'm not like him," he promises, his words coming quickly. "I won't harm you — or them. I swear it. Just let me out."

I swallow hard.

"Please," he says, reaching out a taloned hand between the bars. "My clan has an agreement with the High Council," he promises. "Not like that other one. I won't harm you."

I hesitate. I'd like to trust him, but all I know about this fang is that he's hungry. I've already seen one horrifying reason to avoid a hungry fang. I shake my head. "I'm sorry."

"No," he says, rattling the door again. "No! Let me out."

"What's going on?" Tarek asks. He cradles Alia in his arms, Saira at his side.

The fang has stilled, watching us. I nod toward him. "He wants out."

"And?" Saira asks.

"Fang."

She blanches. Tarek curses and pushes past me, making for the door. "We've got to get out of here. Leave it."

70

The fang calls after us.

I hesitate. "Maybe I should just...." Let him out? Let him make his own way, separate from us?

Tarek wheels around. "You're supposed to get us to safety, aren't you? That's what you were supposed to do in the beginning, before she," he tilts his head toward Saira, "betrayed us. So: Get us out. Get Alia out."

I drop my eyes to Alia. She's still unconscious; her eyelids twitch once or twice. I nod and start for the stairs. The fang calls after me, but I close my ears to his pleas. I can't be sure he won't attack us. I need to get the Degaths — and myself — out safely. I can't play hero to everyone who needs it.

The door at the top of the stairs is locked. Tarek and Saira flatten themselves against the wall to allow me to pass. Behind us, the fang shouts and rattles his door. We don't speak. It takes me more tries than I'd like to work the lock. My tools are hardly well made, but eventually they get the job done.

I crack the door open and peer down a dimly lit hall. The place appears deserted, the window at the end the only source of light. We scuttle out, our footsteps and breathing loud in our ears. Once we've closed the door on Blackflame's little dungeon, the fang's noise can barely be heard.

We slip into an empty room, shutting the door behind us. From the window we can see gardens segmented by high hedges spreading out before us, which tells me only that Blackflame has brought his own gardening techniques with him. I don't recall the last time I saw hedges like these. Nor can I see any clear path leading to a back gate.

"Does anyone know a way out other than the front door?" I ask. It would be a lot easier if we didn't have to go bumbling through the whole mansion looking for an exit.

"Yes," Saira says. She keeps her eyes on the view, as if she can't

71

bear the sight of Tarek's glare. "There's a side door to the gardens, and a path to the carriage house from there."

"Good." I point outside at a window a few rooms down, situated conveniently beside a large hedge that will shield us from view. "That's how we'll get to the gardens. From there, it's on you." I hope I can trust her not to get us all killed. It's a flimsy faith, but walking out the front door of the compound would be a death march.

"A window?" Saira shakes her head. "We can't. Not with Alia...."

"We'll figure it out. We have to move fast. Blackflame may already know we're gone."

"How?" Tarek asks sharply.

I'm almost ready to shout in exasperation. "He has magic. And he's not stupid. He could have wards set, he could have — I don't know what. I'm not a mage. Now let's move."

"Right," Tarek says, turning for the door. "Move." And that's our great escape plan: climb out a window and run. At least it's simple. The Ghost would approve.

I count windows, and then follow after the Degaths. The hall remains fortuitously deserted. The fall of sunlight through the window suggests early morning. The household is likely focused on breakfast — the servants getting their charges ready for the day, the cooking staff preparing the meal, and the residents getting ready to eat it. That, and as we tiptoe down the hall, there's also the possibility that the servants prefer to avoid this hallway, knowing what takes place below.

I crack open the door to the room I hope the window belongs to, then push it open with relief. It's a cluttered storage room, full of things and empty of people. The others hustle in behind me. The window is one over from the hedge, but I don't want to take another chance on the hallway. I ease open the shutters, then lean out to take stock of the near-palatial house around us. We're at one of its sides; windows rising in rows above us. It can't be helped. If someone looks out and spots us, we'll just have to pray they don't manage to catch up with us.

"Here," I say, turning to Tarek. "Give me Alia, and I'll pass her down to you."

"I can carry her," Saira insists, reaching for her sister.

"Would you just listen to her?" Tarek snaps. "She's doing a lot more to save your life than you deserve."

Saira flinches. She looks wretched, her hair in disarray, her face pinched with worry, her eyes dark with guilt and self-contempt. *Good.* After all, it's her fault her parents are dead, her sister has been drained to within an inch of her life, and we're running for our lives. I hope she feels even worse than she looks.

I suppose I should be kinder. She never meant for any of that to happen — except to the Ghost. Maybe, if I get out of this alive, I'll be able to be more generous. Right now, I can't manage it.

"Get down," I tell her. "It will be easier to hand her over if you're both there to take her from me."

Tarek passes Alia to me as Saira lowers herself from the window. Alia's eyes have opened, but her gaze is glassy, unfocused. She's breathing hard, even though she's barely exerted herself. "She needs a mage-healer," I tell Tarek. "She's lost too much blood."

He nods.

"Listen, if we get separated, there's someone who can help you. There's a tea house called The Golden Cup." I quickly describe how to find it and what to tell the proprietor. I have no doubt Kenta will come running if he gets the message, but hopefully it won't come to that. Hopefully, we'll all get out of this together.

Tarek listens carefully, ignoring Saira's whispered questions from below. I don't suppose she'll ever learn to be quiet. Then he

73

lowers himself from the window. I lean out, Alia light in my embrace, and hand her down to their waiting arms.

"Come on," Tarek whispers.

I hesitate. "Just a moment," I whisper, and move back to the door. I'm not sure what exactly I'm thinking, other than that I hate to leave the fang still caged. But when I reach the door, I hear the faint tread of boots in the hallway: soldiers.

I bolt back to the window, sliding out onto the sill and dropping to the ground with a soft *thud*.

"Hurry," I whisper, reaching up to close the shutters. Tarek and Saira require no further urging, setting a brisk pace through the gardens. Saira takes over the lead as she gets her bearings.

About halfway through, I jerk to a stop, holding up my hand. Tarek nearly plows into me from behind. He has the sense, at least, not to speak, his eyes darting to my face. I can hear the soft crunch of boots on gravel. Many boots.

"They're behind us," I whisper. "And they must know which way we're going, or they'd be shouting and running."

The Degaths stare at me.

"Run," I say. "Fast."

We tear through the garden, Tarek puffing under his burden. Past an ornamental fountain, across a grassy square, and — shouts erupt behind us. A dozen soldiers pour into the open space, almost near enough to catch us.

I spring forward, pushing Tarek ahead of me. We swerve around the corner of a hedge. Ahead of us, the path forks: one turns and leads into another section of the garden, its visibility blocked by shrubbery, the other passes under a stone arch.

"Go." I shove Tarek toward the far path, knowing Saira will stick with him. Then I whirl and make for the arch, pounding through it without a backward glance. Split up, there's a higher likelihood that at least one of us will escape, especially if the soldiers part behind us. They'll be easier to outwit that way.

But I miscalculate. Given the choice between three miserable fugitives and catching the Ghost, the soldiers take off after me. All of them. Together.

Panting curses, I careen around the corner of another hedge and find myself facing a picturesque pond, lotus flowers floating serenely before me. On the far side, conversing with Blackflame beneath an ornate blue and white gazebo, stands the one person who could bring me to a standstill. I stare, bewildered, hearing only the thundering of my blood in my ears.

It can't be. It can't be. But it is. Swathed in a silk kimono of varying shades of blue, she looks like an artist's rendering, a person who truly belongs among lotus flowers and gazebos. Except that she cannot possibly be here.

Gravel crunches behind me. I should not have stopped — I take one step forward, my eyes still glued to the figure in blue, and then a body crashes into me, slamming me to the ground. What follows is a brief and hopeless tussle, me against ten soldiers, all of them armed. It ends about where it began, with my face pressed into the dirt and a great deal of weight on top of me. Even though I'm frantic to get away from them, I can't quite focus on anything other than the need to get to the woman in the kimono. I need to see her face clearly. I need to *know*.

I twist around, searching for the soldier in charge. "Who's that?" I ask. "In the gazebo, the woman?"

"Shut up," he says as I'm pulled to my feet.

"That's not the Ghost," one of the soldiers says. "That's the bloody impostor."

A confusion of voices follows. I squeeze my eyes shut, then quickly open them again and try to find the woman. She's turned away and is descending the steps from the gazebo.

"The girl?" one soldier asks. Another says, "The Ghost isn't so clumsy," and another, "The Ghost isn't so *short*."

My eyes follow the woman. Turn around. *Turn around.*

75

The soldiers fall silent. Blackflame strides toward us with fury written across his face.

"What about the others?" he asks, hardly sparing me a glance.

"We're still searching," one of the soldiers responds.

"Who is that woman?" I demand, straining at the soldiers' grip, trying to see past Blackflame.

He must not hear me properly, or maybe he can't imagine that at this precise moment I couldn't care less about him. Or me. "That was very foolish, girl. Did you really think you could escape me?"

I launch myself to the side without a thought for the mage in front of me. I only make it a step or so, given the number of soldiers hanging off of me, but it's just enough to see the woman's back as she departs, her shining black hair cascading over cobalt and turquoise silk. And I know, I *know* it's her. But I still need to hear it.

"Her," I gasp, wishing I could point. "Who is that woman?"

He shifts uncertainly, glancing over his shoulder and then back at me, momentarily forgetting his ire. "Do you know her?"

"Who is she?"

Blackflame smiles, a lazy turn of his lips that brings me back to myself: restrained by soldiers and at his mercy. "That is my current pet. Hotaru Brokensword. A pretty thing, isn't she? Though a bit obtuse. It's always helpful when they are so exceptionally blind and stupid." He chuckles, watching me.

Even though it's the name I expect, even though I recognized her the moment I saw her, the name slams through me with the force of an earthquake. It's a name I know as well as my own, just as I would know the fall of her hair, the way she walks. Just as anyone would know their own mother.

"Oh," Blackflame says, his voice sweetly malicious. "She's still alive. Had you heard differently?" He leans closer. "She's simply chosen to stay with me."

"*Liar.*" I bare my teeth at him, wishing I had Kol's fangs and could rip his throat out.

"What do you care?" he asks. He pauses to study me, really study me. If he hasn't recognized me yet, I'm certainly not telling him.

"Brokensword has more honor than you," I say to distract him. "She can't know what you really are. She can't know what you've done here."

He laughs. "Ah, but she does. She knows precisely what I do."

I shake my head. He can't be right. My mother would never — but I just saw her a handful of minutes ago, healthy and strong, and unrestrained. No one's forcing her to stay here. If she wanted to find me, she could have. How hard can it be for a mage of her caliber to find her own daughter? But she hadn't bothered.

Blackflame leans toward me. "She has even become an advisor of sorts to me."

The fight goes out of me. I sag in the soldiers' grip, sick with his words, with my mother's desertion. Blackflame chuckles as he watches me. I pretend to ignore him. The anger that burned through me has gone out, quenched by the realization that my mother chose this life over me. Chose Blackflame.

Still smiling, he gestures to the soldiers. "Put her under guard and find the Degaths. I don't care what you have to do, I want them back."

An hour later, I stand with my arms clamped against my side and stare at the cobbles in Blackflame's courtyard, trying not to consider what Kol has in store for me. I've spent what felt like a small eternity under close watch in a cell of a room, unable to coax any information from my guards. Blackflame's guards were almost immediately relieved by Kol's: the fang lord's bid to assure he doesn't lose his claim on me in the unfolding chaos of the Degaths' escape.

Kol is, of course, far more dangerous than his escort, but I suppose he must keep up appearances. What human lord would travel alone? The guards are useful, at least, for handling prisoners.

The guards straighten to attention as Kol and Blackflame cross the courtyard toward us. In the gardens, Blackflame was calm, still relatively certain the Degaths wouldn't evade recapture. Now he vibrates with pent-up fury. I keep my face down so that he doesn't notice my pleasure. They just have to make it to the tea house I told Tarek about, and they'll be all right. With the help of a mage-healer, Alia should recover.

They have a much better chance of surviving than I do.

"If I had not already given you away," Blackflame tells me, "I would look forward to taking you apart, bone by bone, sinew by sinew."

Is it strange to be grateful that I've been traded like a goat, especially when I can hardly expect mercy from Kol? I glance toward my unlikely savior. Kol has added boots and soft leather gloves to his attire of the night before. As further protection from the potentially damaging rays of the sun, he wears a short cloak that brushes his thighs, the hood pulled up to shade his face. But I still catch the faint quirk of his lips revealing his amusement. What does he care if his meal escaped? He still has me. If I had the energy, I would fear him, fear that smile, but as my delight in the Degaths' escape fades, I feel hollowed out, my heartbeat echoing in my lungs.

My mother is here. And well. My mother, who was supposed to be dead, who came here for help and never returned. I swallow the bile in my throat, barely registering Blackflame's threats, his ire washing over me like water over a stone. Four years I've thought her dead, scrabbling to find my next meal and keep a roof over my head, while she has dressed in silk and wandered sunlit gardens. How could she have forgotten me? How could she be *here*?

Blackflame turns on his heel, leading the way from the courtyard. Kol falls into step beside him, the guards prodding me along after them. Instead of approaching the gates, or calling for horses, we make our way through the gardens to an unpretentious square in which a quaint stone arch has been built, a hedge grown up around it. The white wooden gate, latched closed with a hook, gives the impression of some prosaic, feminine hand at work. Which is ridiculous. There is nothing prosaic or gendered about a magic portal.

I lick cracked lips, staring at it. I could be wrong, of course. I haven't seen one up close in years. But why else would we come to a stop before this particular arch? What other purpose could it serve than to allow Kol and his men to arrive and leave unremarked, without a carriage and, now that it occurs to me to look, with no more baggage than a few large packs strapped to the guards' shoulders?

Blackflame unhooks the gate, swinging it open. He casually sets his hand on the stone of the arch, his lips shaping a single word. The view through the gate shivers, rippling as if what fills the gate is more water than air. Kol nods to Blackflame and steps forward, the light bending around him and pushing him through to another place. It is as if the sunlight has suddenly failed him.

The guards follow after Kol, and before I can think whether it would do any good to struggle, I'm shoved into the portal. The sunlight falters within the portal, bright strands spidering out to wrap around me in a vortex of darkness streaked with light, intertwined and spun into a whirlwind of impossibility. I am pulled and twisted, invisible hands squeezing my lungs until I think my heart will stop, and then I am propelled by unseen forces *out* — into the normal world.

I stumble slightly, but the guards around me are equally disoriented, and they allow me to regain my balance on my own. I take a gasping breath and smell the fresh scent of pine. It shocks me in a way that Kol's stronghold, a towering edifice of ugly gray stone rising above us, does not. There are no pines in Karolene, nor on the nearby mainland. I inhale again, but catch no trace of the sea.

Kol pauses on the path leading out of the muddy courtyard where we arrived. He glances back to me. I look away, fighting the urge to turn all the way around and see what the other end of the portal connects to — a doorway? Or another arch? And can it be activated from this side? But then, even if it can, I don't know how to work one, and I don't want to risk the consequences of bungling it. I've heard more than enough stories of left-behind limbs or people accidentally falling off cliffs they never meant to step out on.

"Bring her inside," Kol says. "Have her fed and see that no one touches her."

Fed? How uncommonly generous. It must not be a kindness at all, I think as the guards take me to the kitchens, just a different approach to brutality. But where is the cruelty in feeding a person? It's only as I sit on a bench, a bowl of stew warm in my hands and a heel of bread beside me, that I realize the viciousness of it: if I am strong, I will be able to fight longer and harder before succumbing to the death he has planned for me.

But no fear of the future can stop me from tearing into my food. It's a simple meat and vegetable stew seasoned with herbs I have no names for. Despite the seasoning, it tastes bland as oatmeal cooked in water. Where am I that the people know nothing of spice? Still, all I've eaten in the last day is the food I'd snared from Rafiki's house. While a meal a day is about average for me, after the day and night I've had, I'm ravenous.

A servant refills my bowl twice. None of the cooking staff speak to me, or to the two soldiers who remain with me, eating their own meals while they wait. But the workers talk amongst themselves, and their language is not one I've heard before. Karolene's language has become the lexicon of trade for most of the Eleven Kingdoms, what with the vast majority of shipping routes passing through the island's port. Both Kol and the guards he brought on his visit speak it fluently. But it is not the language of conversation here. Further, I cannot place the looks of the people. They are light-skinned, though not as light as the northmen, their hair ranging from sandy brown to deep chestnut.

I am too tired to grapple with the possibilities. I can worry about it once I've gotten home. There are much greater things to worry about than that for now.

By the end of my meal, I'm slow and heavy with contentment. Regardless of what cruelty Kol may intend in granting me this reprieve, I plan to take full advantage of it. As the soldiers set down their bowls, I rise, ready for them to escort me on.

"Where are we going?" I ask, hoping their meal has loosened their tongues.

"A holding cell," one of them says, his voice gruff.

"And then?"

We leave the kitchen in silence. Finally, he says, "To the tower room, I expect."

A tower. Not the easiest place to escape. I watch him from the corner of my eye, attempting to assess whether his expression is any grimmer than before. "What's there?"

He doesn't answer. It's the other one, a younger man with an ugly gleam to his eye, who says, "You'll see soon enough. We'll be listening for your screams."

"Oh," I say, pretending good humor, "I wouldn't wait around for that if I were you."

"You'll scream," the younger one says. His smile makes my blood run cold. "Won't she, Ger?"

"Only if she fights it," the other soldier says.

We've reached the holding cells, a stretch of rooms with bars as their fourth wall, lining a hall that's bookended by a blank wall at one end and a guard room at the other. I'll be stuck here as long as I'm too weak to take on the contingent of guards assigned to the cells.

"She's a fighter," the younger soldier says in response. "Just think of the screams we'll hear."

The first soldier doesn't answer as he unlocks an empty cell, but his hand on my arm as he guides me in is unexpectedly gentle. That unsettles me more than anything he might have said.

CHAPTER 8
THE TOWER ROOM

There are two types of fugitives, the Ghost once said: those who sleep so they can face the unknown well rested, and those who stay awake for fear of what might come. It turns out I'm a sleeper.

Having spent the better part of the last day and night alternately running and getting bruised and beaten, and well aware that Kol will come for me again, I need to get as much rest as I can. Any attempt to escape would be an exercise in futility. So, without further ado, I wrap myself in my borrowed cloak and lie down at the back of the cell. I move only to ascertain my improvised lockpick set is still safe in my pocket before drifting off to sleep.

I wake a few times, rising to relieve myself or drink more water from the bucket left for me by the door. Unable to tell the time of day and still exhausted, I quickly slip back into slumber.

I wake finally to the sounds of a conversation echoing down the hall from the guardroom. It's an argument about who has to go somewhere—with me, I suspect. While the soldiers bicker, I stretch out my muscles, pain rippling from the myriad bruises

I've collected since Saira's betrayal. Thankfully, as far as I can tell, all my ribs are still intact. The bruises are dark, but none are so deep that they make movement difficult. I can still run.

The quarrel winds down, and two soldiers start down the hall, their shadows long, the lantern light from the guardhouse bright at their backs. I don't recognize either guard from the escort Kol had with him. One of the guards unlocks my door and jerks his chin at me. I don't make them wait; I'd much rather stand on my own two feet and avoid more bruises.

As we walk, I keep careful watch, counting turns, glancing down halls and up stairwells, trying to map out the building so I can find my way to an exit if I manage to escape. But I needn't have bothered.

We leave the castle proper and cross an open yard to the base of a tower built into the castle walls, its ramparts lit by torches. At one time it might have been a watchtower as well as a defensive point; now it's nothing more than a prison with a view—one with dark windows. A cool night wind blows, bringing me once more the scent of pine, as well as woodsmoke.

The sky is full dark, but I'd guess dawn is near, which means Kol has allowed me almost a full day's rest. As much as I needed it, every one of these "kindnesses" unnerves me further.

The fang lord meets us at the foot of the tower. I keep my gaze averted, steadily watching the wall. I'm careful not to let my eyes drop. I'm not looking down; I'm looking *away*. He chuckles as if I've shown some endearing trait and unlocks the door with a key from his belt. Simple lock, I note.

Then he pulls back a bolt.

That will be a problem. There's no lockpick that can slide open a bolt. And I can't assume I'll have the energy to expend any magic on it, not if there's something upstairs I need to escape from first.

We start up the stairwell, Kol in front, then the soldier

holding the lantern, followed by me and the second soldier. I count the steps to keep from thinking about what's waiting above. What can be worse than Kol? Is *anything* worse than a sadistic fang? I concentrate on the stairs. I'll have my answer soon enough.

Two hundred thirteen steps later, we reach the top. Kol unlocks a second door, then slides back another bolt. I swallow hard. Okay, I'll have to use magic on this bolt. Then hide in my cloak, waiting for someone to enter the tower, and slip out behind their back ... After I escape whatever waits within the room. My plan is beginning to sound more and more hopeless.

Kol pauses to survey the interior, then motions the soldier with the lantern forward first. He enters cautiously, his other hand on his sword hilt. Behind me, the second soldier tenses. As if I'm not worried enough already, even these two battle-hardened, fang-serving soldiers are afraid of what's in there.

Kol reaches back to grab my shoulder, then shoves me through the door ahead of him, his grasp too firm for me to twist away.

"Good morning, Val." Kol's voice booms cheerfully through the tower room.

I risk a glance up. The lantern light is just bright enough to illuminate the circular room, the two windows dark holes to either side of us. A prisoner sits against the far wall, his legs crossed, back resting against the stones. He is tall and gaunt, so thin his face is but a skull stretched over with skin, his eyes so faintly colored that I can almost imagine they are not even there. His hair falls to his shoulders in a straggly fringe of white. His tunic and pants hang off his frame, and his hands resting upon his knees are little more than sinew and bone. If he were human, he would be dead.

"You've been looking a bit thin lately. I've brought you a treat." Kol starts forward, dragging me along with him. The prisoner rises and steps toward us, his movements deliberately slow. Caught in Kol's grip, my feet stumble over the stones. From what Kol has said, his prisoner must be another fang like himself. A starved one, weak enough that even if I do look at him, he might not be able to mesmerize me with his gaze. But dangerous enough that the soldiers fear him.

We cross over a dark mess of a design drawn on the ground, and then Kol shoves me forward once again, harder this time. I half-fall, sprawling at the prisoner's feet, my heart slamming against my ribs. No no *no*. I have to stop him before—

A bony hand wraps around the nape of my neck, the fingers cold and strong as iron. I brace my hands against the stone, trying desperately to pull away, and then, abruptly, I go still, sighting my salvation.

"I can pick that," I whisper, barely loud enough to hear myself. The fingers convulse, tightening with bruising intensity. "I can pick that lock," I repeat, my voice low enough that surely, *surely* Kol can't hear.

"Barely more than a morsel," a voice rasps, as dry and brittle as old bones. The hand releases me. I jerk back, scrambling away from both Kol and his prisoner until the wall brings me up short, a mere five paces away.

"A morsel? I bring you a girl fairly bursting with years, and you call her a morsel?" Kol demands, infuriated.

The creature laughs, a sound like dead grasses rustling. "Half-starved and nearly as cold as I am. You've leeched the years from her already."

Kol takes a step toward us, eyes flashing. "I haven't drunk from her yet, but if you've no use for her, I can easily take her."

No. I press myself against the wall. The creature—Val, I remind myself—shrugs bony shoulders, the movement sickeningly clear beneath the thin fabric of his grimy tunic. "I've more use for your soldiers."

"My—" Kol turns, but Val is fast, faster than a creature so gaunt has any right to be. He sweeps forward, sidestepping Kol at the same time that one of the soldiers drifts over the knot on the ground, his eyes wide and glazed beneath the rim of his helmet.

Val's hand closes on the man's shoulder. Kol roars, charging between them to shove them apart. Val laughs as he falls back, sprawling with casual disregard upon the floor. The other man stumbles, thumping against the far wall, his empty gaze still trained on Val.

"Get out, both of you," Kol snarls. The remaining soldier dashes forward to grab his comrade's arms and drag him from the room.

Terror squeezes my chest. However hunger-weakened this fang is, his ability to mesmerize is just as strong as Kol's.

Now he tilts his face up, leveling a darkly amused look on Kol. "Your men run like startled rabbits. Their noses even twitch the same way."

"You drink of what I give you," Kol says, ignoring Val's words. He lashes out with his foot. Val tries to roll away, but the boot catches him hard in the ribs.

Kol hunkers down as Val struggles to sit up. "If you will not have the girl, I'll drain her myself."

"Why bring her at all?" Val wheezes.

Kol's nostrils flare. "I grant you a moment of mercy, and you throw it back in my face?"

He surges to his feet, turning toward me. I drop my gaze back to the stones. The window is too far—he'll catch me before I get to it, and even if I manage to avoid him, it offers me only a fall to my death. There is no escape there. If I can gather enough magic —but I don't know what I can do against Kol, and his prisoner, and two more guards waiting on the stairs.

I press myself against the wall as Kol stalks nearer, my gaze flitting back to Val. He's on his feet, his expression hard, empty.

He'll help me. Surely he must, after I promised the ability to open his chains?

Kol halves the distance between us and keeps on coming. My gaze darts back to Val, then to the window, my back pressed hard against the wall. There's no way out—

"I'll take her," Val says. Relief, however weak, slides through me. He'll keep me alive, at least long enough for me to negotiate something better than the chance Kol would likely afford me.

Kol pauses, turns to regard Val. His voice drips false concern. "Oh, indeed? Are you sure? Perhaps you should know a little more about your meal."

"I think not," Val says, his voice quiet. His eyes have the hard coldness of metal.

I jerk my gaze down, my heart thundering. I can't risk being caught by his gaze, can't risk looking at either of them. I push myself to my feet, even though there's nowhere to run.

"She's a bit of a martyr. You do like the innocents, don't you? They must taste sweeter."

"They all taste the same," Val says flatly.

I flinch, even though I know he must be playing a game now, to keep me out of Kol's clutches. He may still mean every word he says. Maybe I am nothing more than a meal that happens to know how to pick locks.

"Ah, that's a pity," Kol says.

"Not really."

Kol snorts, shifting his balance carefully. He's on guard now, even though he clearly doesn't fear his prisoner. "After all the trouble I went through for her, too," he says with mock sorrow. "Would you believe, she helped a family fleeing a political execution? You know how things are in Karolene. She was working with some local hero called the Ghost, and she pretended to be him in order to ensure his freedom. She even managed to help the family escape after Blackflame caught them. Alas, she didn't get away herself. If such selflessness doesn't taste sweet to you, I can't imagine what does."

"Vengeance," Val says and leaps for Kol.

But Kol is waiting, and the fight is over before it even begins: a flurry of movements I can barely follow—a punch blocked, a kick, a snarl, and then Kol hurls Val away, half-flying over the stones to slam into the wall. He doesn't, however, take into account the chain still attached to Val's leg. It snaps tight around Kol's legs and sends him thumping to the floor.

Val lies against the wall and laughs that same brittle laugh, filled with the rustling sound of dead things, as if the pain in his voice is of no account. The soldier looking in from the doorway stares, eyes wide. I glance back at Val with sudden understanding —he didn't expect to beat Kol. But he did manage to embarrass the fang lord before his own soldiers, and that is a victory of its own.

Kol spits a curse, struggling to his feet and kicking the chain away. "I'll take her myself, then."

"Take her," Val says. "Leave me one of your soldiers instead. They're a bit more of an armful than your martyr will ever be."

"I'll leave you *nothing*."

"So predictable," Val says, leaning against the wall, his lips stretched wide in ghastly amusement. There's something odd about his smile, something that doesn't quite add up, but I can't think what.

Kol's hands curl into fists, his face white with rage.

"You'll have to come get her, though," Val says affably. "There's the chain to watch out for." He rises, crossing the few paces between us in a heartbeat, his hand closing on my shoulder before I can think to run.

I swallow a whimper as he yanks me around to face Kol, my back pressed against his rib cage. I try to twist free, but his grip tightens, his hand catching my wrists and pulling them against my chest. I keep my eyes focused on Kol's chest, not daring to look up any farther. It's a game for them, and I am nothing more than a pawn. I have to believe my offer meant something to the creature holding me captive now—that his aim is to keep me alive long enough to help him without appearing to care about me one way or the other.

"I'll hold her for you," he says, lowering his face to brush mine, his gaze on Kol. And then he goes still, his fingers tightening as I tremble against him.

"Will you?" Kol grins, baring his fangs. "I think you haven't half the willpower you pretend to, Val, my boy. Even as weak as you are, you can scent her now, can't you? Sweet and young and so very tasty. Why not have a little sip?"

Val growls, the sound reverberating through me and turning my blood to ice. Twisting, he shoves me against the wall, his back to Kol.

I scream, kicking at his legs, trying to yank my hands free, but there isn't enough space to move anymore. He's too close, his chest crowding me in, one bony arm shoving up against my throat to pin me to the wall, the smell of him filling my lungs with the scent of decay—and *hunger*.

"Easy," Val mutters, his gray gaze trying to draw me in. I clench my eyes shut, turning my face away, but I can feel his gaze tearing at me, and my face turns back toward him despite myself. I let out a ragged cry, my traitorous eyelids beginning to open. *No.* With a jerk, I smack my head back against the stone, the pain giving me something to focus on other than him and the pull of his gaze. But I can't fight him much longer. I'll have to use my magic, come what may.

Something cool and papery dry brushes my ear, and I hear one whispered word: "Pretend."

Abruptly, his gaze releases me, the change so sudden I would fall were he not still pinning me to the wall. My breath comes in

90

great, trembling lungfuls. I don't know what he wants of me, what I should pretend. He takes my chin in his grasp. I try to pull back, but my head is already pressed hard against the wall, my eyes still clenched shut. There's nowhere to go ... and then he's letting me go.

"Fall," he murmurs.

I do, my legs giving out as he steps back so that I sprawl on the ground, my cloak's hood falling sideways to obscure my face from Kol. I crouch there, trying to hold my breath, breathe as slowly as I can, but I'm shaking and I know Kol will see it. He'll know I'm not dead. He'll know—

"Is that all?" Kol asks. "You stupid girl! You let yourself be caught." He's disappointed—because to all appearances I didn't fight Val's gaze as successfully as I did Kol's. He *wanted* Val to feed from me while I screamed, the pain bright and burning without his gaze to take it from me.

Val snarls a stream of curses at Kol, shoving away from the wall above me to glare at his captor. As if the act of feeding when starved is a victory for Kol over him.

Kol laughs. "She's still got some life left in her. It's rude to leave a meal half-eaten."

"I'll finish her when I want."

"Will you? Do you really think you can hold out? Come now, it's been what, six weeks?" Kol pauses as if thinking. "Why, I believe it's been at least eight."

"Then I had best make her last."

Kol smiles coldly, baring his fangs. "If she isn't done by dusk, I will help you with her."

Val takes a step forward, hands clenched tight. But Kol merely chuckles and turns toward the door. My mind races, searching for a way out.

I push myself up slowly, painfully, until I'm teetering on all fours. It doesn't even take any pretending.

"What about me?" My voice rings out, rasping only slightly. I try not to flinch from the sound of it.

Startled, Kol swings around to stare at me.

I glare at his boots. "Dusk is a long time away. I'll need lunch."

"Lunch?" Kol repeats, as if he can barely believe his ears.

"Your soldiers hardly fed me. You don't want me fainting from hunger, do you?" I ask, a trace of mockery creeping into my voice.

Even without looking at his face, I can hear the answering sneer in his voice. "Indeed, no. We'll see if your meal grants you any further strength."

He swivels back toward Val. "James will bring up her lunch. Perhaps, if you haven't finished her yet, he'll find another use for her."

Val makes no answer. I stay hunched where I am, savoring the gift Kol has unintentionally granted me: the promise of a way out during the daylight hours, when most fangs will have taken shelter. Now all I have to do is make a friend of Kol's enemy here, make sure he doesn't kill me, and ... I hesitate.

What is it about simple plans always backfiring on me? This one begins with the starving creature locked in the same room as me sparing my life.

Kol turns, pacing to the far wall beside the door. A chain lies in loops upon the floor. He lifts the cuff at its end and tosses it across the room toward us, the chain clinking behind it.

The rusted iron cuff comes to a stop a few paces away. My eyes skim over it—it's hard to tell from here, but surely the lock won't be any more complicated than the others I've seen here.

"Chain her," Kol says into the quiet.

"There is no need," Val replies.

"There are windows," Kol says lightly. "If she jumps, you won't get a replacement."

"She won't jump. She's already mine."

I bite my lip hard, hating them both fiercely.

Kol grunts. "Then see that you finish her."

He walks to the door, collects the lantern, and a moment later is gone, the click of the lock overloud in the silence.

In the darkness left behind, Val moves slowly to the wall, easing himself down to sit. The only sound is the faint clink of his chain as he shifts his legs. The windows allow in the first faint rays of dawn, but it is not yet light enough to see him clearly.

The windows.

"You're not a fang," I whisper. There's no way he could be. The sunlight through the windows, day after day for as long as he must have been here, would have slowly burned his skin, leaving him blistered and covered in lesions.

"No." The sound of his voice, like nails scraping stone, makes me shudder.

"Then what are you?"

He doesn't answer. He doesn't have to, because in the ensuing quiet I go through the list of every race I've heard of, every race that feeds off humans and uses its gaze to incapacitate us, and come up with only two possibilities. I've already ruled out one....

"You're a breather."

Silence falls again, but this is a tight, dangerous one. A breather. I swallow hard, my palms damp. They suck their victims dry, like fangs do, only it isn't blood they take. It's breath. It's life. Some say, it's souls.

I have to get out. Now.

Kol and his men will have reached the base of the tower by now. I can pick the lock on the door, and ... then what? If I can force the first bolt open with my magic, I will still have to contend with the second bolt below. If I manage both, it will be a repeat of the flight from Blackflame's house, only at night. With a

93

fang on the loose. Or rather, with a fang *lord* on the loose, along with however many fangs work for him. Even with the food and rest I've had, I'm still not strong enough for much magic working; the bolts will drain what energy I have.

I glance out the window again, pulse racing. Soon the sun will rise. In daylight, I'll be able to navigate my way out, Kol will likely be resting, and my chances of survival improve immensely. Not that fangs can't come out in daylight; they just prefer not to —and I'd prefer not to meet any on my way out. I might be able to outrun a human guard, but fangs are another matter entirely.

All I have to do is keep the breather from attacking me. In point of fact, as far as I can tell, he hasn't even shifted in my direction. Despite his hunger and my initial, desperate promise to open his shackles. My eyes track back toward him. He must be nearly mad with hunger. He's an emaciated husk of a creature.

"How long have you been here?" It's not until the words sound in my ears that I realize I have spoken.

I don't expect him to answer, but just as my attention moves back to the bolts I must contend with, he says, "Perhaps a year."

"You've ... fed?" I know he has, at least once, probably more.

"Yes."

Terror coils in my stomach. But Kol mocked him for being kind, taunted him with my perceived innocence. Which means that this creature, Val, may not be half so evil as Kol himself.

I look away, toward the window, trying to reconcile this with all I've heard of his kind. *Breathers cannot be trusted*, my father told me, years ago, before I lost him to illness and my mother to Blackflame. *Breathers are death and darkness and all things dangerous.*

The first rays of sunlight, bright and clear, break over the window sill, illuminating the far end of the room. It doesn't seem possible that sunlight could share the same space as this starved being. "Why does Kol keep you?"

"It is a longer story than you want to know."

"They give you innocents to feed on," I say slowly, anger warming my chest.

"When they run out of other victims." He smiles, a ghastly stretch of parched lips over yellowed teeth. "You are only the second true innocent to be chained with me."

My skin crawls. How many has he murdered in his time here? His only sustenance would be other lives. He would have to kill more than once to survive a full year. Kol starved him two months this time, but there's no telling what happened before that. "Have you tried to escape?"

"I am bound, as Kol would have bound you, but my chains bear every protective charm and sigil on them our captor could buy. I cannot break them."

My gaze shifts to the cuff lying empty and open upon the stone floor. I force myself to cross the short distance to study the manacle and the chain soldered to it. They are made of iron, a material by its very nature heavy and at odds with magic. They are, as the breather implied, void of protective symbols. "What is your chain made of?" I ask curiously.

"Silver," he says.

From where I crouch, the metal shows dark, but perhaps it's only tarnished. Silver is soft, something that the creature, once fed, might untwist with his bare hands, unless it has been ensorcelled. What he needs is a key—or a thief with a lockpick.

He and I both know it. But how can I think of trying to free a breather? He is a thing of darkness. Should I help him, I have no surety he won't kill me before moving on to Kol.

I purse my lips. *Our captor*, he said. Kol has abused him almost past bearing. As long as the breather spares me, what does it matter if he attacks Kol?

"If I can find a way to free us," I say, raising my gaze to his chest, "will you swear not to harm me?"

"You cannot free me, little one," he says. His voice would be gentle were it not so harshly rasping.

"I might," I say. Why else did he spare my life and keep Kol from killing me if not to help him escape?

"There is a sigil in the stone there. I cannot pass it even if my chains are released."

I blink in sudden understanding. That was why he waited for the soldier he mesmerized to come to him. My eyes scan the stone. A sigil. What are the chances that I'll recognize it? And be able to change it? And how can I trust this breather not to attack when he learns what I am?

I can't. Not only will he despise me for my magic, but he'll drain me in order to gain enough strength to effect his own escape. For whatever reason, he left me my life and I'm not going to sacrifice it back to him. I don't let myself think about it any further.

I can feel the breather's milky-gray gaze on me as I scramble across the room to the door. Sliding my improvised tools from my pocket, I set to work on the lock. It's surprising, really, what simple locks rich people use—but then I guess the possibility of escape never occurred to either Blackflame or Kol.

Behind me, Val makes no sound. By his own admission, he can't reach me. The only dangerous thing about him is his breather's gaze. Between his own weakness, this distance between us, and my turned back, I should be able to fight it.

My hands slow. I stare blindly at the door. He is weak, just like the fang I left behind in Blackflame's dungeon. And, just like the fang, he will die in his prison. As much as I tell myself that it will not be I who have killed them—that the blame lies with Kol, or Blackflame, or someone else entirely—the truth is that this is my choice, now: to leave him behind.

And he is letting me go. He has made no attempt to stop me. He hasn't tried to trick me into turning around so he can catch my gaze and keep his meal from leaving. In truth, he made sure I wasn't even chained. I've been hungry. I know what it feels like when your stomach is so empty it gnaws at itself. I've tied a strap around my waist and cinched it tight because the pressure gives some small relief. Such hunger consumes your awareness, nibbles at the edges of your mind.

I've begged, pleaded, stolen—and been beaten—all for a half-rotted fruit. But I've never, ever been as hungry as the creature behind me.

I rest my forehead against the door and close my eyes, wishing I could make a cocoon in the darkness behind my eyelids, spin a tiny shelter to keep myself safe from my thoughts. But it's no use. I've already damned one fang to his death because I feared him. I cannot leave this creature behind as well.

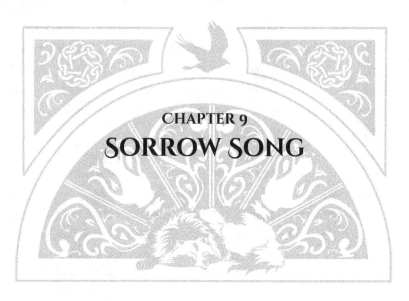

CHAPTER 9
SORROW SONG

I turn to face the breather. Val. "If I can do something about that sigil, or whatever it is, and free you, do you swear not to harm me?"

His brows rise with disbelief. "You are a mage?"

"No, but I've seen a thing or two. If I can do it, we still have to wait for them to bring my meal. They'll unbolt the door and that'll be our chance. Just promise you won't turn on me."

He smiles, a quirking of cracked lips that raises the gooseflesh on my arms. "Is that why you asked for food?"

I shrug. "I figured if you didn't kill me, I'd need to make sure the rest of the way out would be clear." I wave my hand toward the window.

"Is it?"

"If they unbolt both doors, we still have to get through the main gates — or find a back door. But I think it should be possible."

He nods, the wiry tips of his hair brushing his shoulders. "All right."

I take a breath and let it out.

I cross the floor to the symbol and hunker down to study it. It seems to be nothing more than a dark ink permanently staining one of the stones. I trace the intricate pattern it makes with a finger, following the twists and curves that form an unending knot. That doesn't seem right, somehow. My mother taught me sigils; we had barely begun when Baba fell ill and our lives fell apart. Still, no sigil she ever showed me — and she let me flip through her books more than a few times — looked like this. Sigils are symbols, characters, not knots.

I press the tip of my finger against the center of the pattern and open myself up to the magic that pulses through it. *A flash of teeth. Screaming. Blood spattering on the floor. Pain pain pain—*

I snatch my hand away and clutch it to my chest, my heart racing. The breather neither moves nor speaks, but I can feel his pale gray gaze on me. I take a moment to catch my breath, compose my mind. Then I ask, "When you try to cross this, what happens?"

"There is pain."

I figured that. "What kind of pain?"

He shifts, tilting his head slightly. Finally, he says, "My blood stops in my veins, my lungs cannot draw breath, and my eyes see nothing but red."

I look down at the knot on the floor. "Did you see how they made this?"

"A woman," he says. "Not much older than you are."

There it is. I wrap my arms around myself to keep in the horror. Blood magic. Blood taken by force and spilled here to make this spell. "Did they kill her?"

"Of course."

I don't know enough about blood magic to be certain he's right. Is killing necessary to make such a spell? And then I realize Val meant that of course Kol killed the woman. What else would a monster like that do? That's not to say the casting required it.

Unless it did. I stare down at the knot, wishing I knew more about blood magic. It's not exactly the sort of thing either of my parents would have taught me.

I study the knot until its image is imprinted on the backs of my eyelids when I blink. I chew my lip and scratch a bite on my leg and fidget until I glance up and catch the breather's stare. He leans against the wall behind him, watching me. Which doesn't help at all. I stand up and begin pacing, trying to decide what to do.

I could still just leave him — except that I can't. He's granted me time and safety; he clearly doesn't want to kill me. We have the same enemy. And now *I've* given *him* a hope of escape. Twice. Once to save my own life, and then again of my own accord. Which leaves me with the unsavory option of dabbling in dark magic for the first time in my short life.

"Do you have anything that will draw blood?" I ask the breather.

He shakes his head. Saira's hairpins, the sharpest things I have, are still too dull to do the job. I try and fail to work a splinter off the door, though I do manage to rub the tips of my fingers raw. But I need more than a drop or two of blood. With a muttered curse, I walk to the window. I can see a portion of the castle keep, the outer wall rising up to embrace the base of our tower, and then beyond that lies a land of hills, low meadows, and forested slopes.

"Where *are* we?"

"Gadon."

I wheel around to stare at the creature. "But that is — that is...."

"Far and far from Karolene," he agrees.

I lean against the sill weakly. Even recognizing how strange it was to scent pine, even with the foreign herbs in the food, I had not really believed I could be so far. I had not taken into account the sheer distance that could be covered by a single step through Blackflame's portal. Somewhere in the back of my mind, I had been sure I would return to my mother, and quickly. It would be a short hike to the nearest coast, and then I could find work on a ship bound for Karolene. But Gadon is landlocked. It is easily a month's journey to the southern coast through a land I do not know, on roads I have not seen. Even if I were to find a portal, I wouldn't know how to use it.

I might be able to make the journey, I think fiercely, but first I must get out of this tower. I lean over the windowsill, studying the outer surface. It is terribly smooth: no ledge has been built below the window, and only occasional slits show in the curving wall where the stairs descend below us.

I whistle softly, but I can neither see nor hear any birds. It would have been too much to hope for pigeons wintering in the tower stairwell, flying in through the window slits. My mother always told me to focus my whistles toward the birds I wanted, but now I can't see any.

My mother, I think, staring blindly at the ground so far below. She's alive. Here I am, caught in a tower with a breather, surrounded by blood magic, my only hope of escape to somehow overcome the guards and get out before an alarm is sounded. And she is resting in a garden gazebo, swathed in silk, her hair falling free.

My hands shake on the sill. I push myself away, but I can no longer see clearly, my eyesight blurring. I blink hard. Turning, I slide down the wall, one hand massaging my temples so that the breather can't see me. Just in case a tear gets loose. I don't know how long I sit there, struggling with my emotions. They are dark and ugly and I don't have names for them. "Despair" seems too absurd a word; "abandoned" hardly carries enough weight. My mother. My *mother*. How could she have left me? She wasn't held in Blackflame's garden by force, that much was clear. She promised to return to me, and what? She forgot?

"Girl," the breather says, calling me back to the room. The shadows have grown a little shorter since I last looked. I am tempted to close my eyes, to stay where I am, but he speaks again. "*Girl.*"

"Yes."

"What were you looking for through the window?"

"Birds."

"Go and look again. I hear some now."

I stumble to my feet, staring out into the over-bright light. It is near noon. Where did the day go? I close my eyes, drinking in the warmth of the autumn sun. Faintly, I hear what the breather has: the warble of swallows.

I whistle softly, knowing that it is the current of my whistle that will carry to them, rather than the sound itself. But my whistle is leaden on my lips, heavy with sorrow, the loss of my mother. The swallows do not hear, or they cannot bear to answer my call. I try again, and their warbling stills, but they don't come.

I purse my lips to whistle one last time, but I cannot steady my breath enough to give it strength. I slide down to my knees, my hands clinging to the windowsill, gasping for air. My sobs are dry, brittle things, as though they come from a land of famine and drought. I do not know what I cry for, or why, except that I do not know what I am anymore, or why my mother would wear silks, or why my old friends the birds have forsaken me.

Something tickles my hand. I lean my head against the wall, swallowing a sob, and feel it again — something small and slick rubbing against my fingers. I look up. An old crow perches on the sill, tilting his head to watch me, his beak still pressed against my finger.

"Little brother," I whisper. The crow caws in response, hopping away from my hands and inspecting the room with a beady eye. I wonder what he will make of my companion. I lick my lips and whistle faintly. *Little brother.*

He flutters his wings, and I hear his voice. It is the sound of autumn leaves and chill breezes. *Why so sad?*

We are caged.

The crow considers this, then hops down to the floor. I turn to face him. *No wings,* he notes wisely.

Tied by magic.

The crow peers about, then turns to look at the creature. I correct myself: Val.

Dark brother.

Yes, I say.

Heartmate?

No, I say so forcefully the crow hops back, startled.

But then he gives a little caw of amusement and tries again, *Nestbrother.*

Flockbrother.

He considers this. *Caged?*

Caged, I confirm.

Sorrow song, the crow says sadly, and I know he will help.

I point to the blood knot on the floor. *Need key.*

The crow hops over and angles his head to eye the knot. He pecks at it experimentally before hopping back to me. *No key.*

I smile faintly. I didn't expect he would have a way to break the enchantment hidden among his feathers. And it isn't a key I need, not in the sense the crow will understand. *Bring sharp silver shiny?* I try instead. Most importantly, *Sharp?*

Sharp, the crow responds cautiously. He takes wing, flapping out the window. I'll just have to hope he doesn't bring back a rusty nail that will give me lockjaw. Wouldn't that be ironic?

Val's voice pulls me back to the room with a shock. "How hard was it to hide your Promise?" The old fear dries my throat.

He nods toward the window, "Consorting with crows. I hope you are not always that obvious?"

He's laughing at me. "Not normally," I say cautiously, somewhat unnerved by his amusement. By all accounts, he should be wishing me dead. Especially since it was another mage who trapped him here.

"Your parents hid you," he guesses. At my nod, he continues, "And taught you?"

I shrug, remembering my mother's warnings. *Never trust another with your secret.* I can't undo what he has seen, but I can play it down. "It's just whistling."

He says nothing in response, and I don't dare look him in the face to read his expression. I glance away from him, waiting until the crow flaps back up to the windowsill, a nice shiny sewing needle in his beak. He sets it down, then hops along the sill, watching me. *Sharp.*

Life light, I whistle back to him, the traditional praise used by birds.

Fair winds, the crow replies in farewell. It is almost a question, as if he wants to ensure I need nothing else. But I don't want anyone to see me try this magic, not even an elderly crow.

Sheltered nests, I respond.

With a final glance for Val and me, the crow drops off the windowsill, swooping out over the countryside with a joyful caw. I watch after him, not really wanting to turn back to Val. I may as well have admitted some training. There's no way to avoid it now. The longer I take, the closer we get to lunch and the creature James. Safer to trust this breather than to risk waiting.

With heavy footsteps I return to the blood knot and kneel before it. The needle is sharp enough that a good hard jab draws blood from the pad of my thumb. I pinch it to make the blood well up and use the blunt end of the needle as a stylus. Starting at the center of the knot, I trace the pattern until just before it connects again at the center. Instead of closing the pattern, I turn the trail out, smearing the last drops of blood so that the line disintegrates.

Okay. I stare at the knot, waiting. Nothing happens. No pulse of power. No fading of the old spell. I glance uncertainly at the breather. He looks back at me, expression inscrutable. It's like looking at a breathing skull and wondering what it's thinking.

I take a steadying breath and press the bloodied pad of my thumb to the center of the knot. *pain pain PAIN*

"Release," I gasp, which is not the right word at all. I don't know the Olde Tongue. Not well enough, at least. Bending over the blistering, burning point of agony that is my thumb, I draw on the warmth of sunlight and the swallow song once more audible. I draw on the slumbering stone beneath me, and the ancient air born and reborn, and the certain beating of my heart, the pulse of blood in my veins. "*Get out.*"

Blood wells up — not from my thumb this time, but from the knot. The whole symbol pulses, writhes, bulges with dark liquid — the same dark liquid that rises up between the stones to pool on the floor. I scramble back, watching as the knot disappears beneath the growing puddle of black blood.

A hand reaches up out of the center of the pool, a hand composed completely of light, glowing gently. It grips the stones, and slowly, slowly, a figure pulls itself out of the blood. I press myself against the wall behind me. The woman before me, her form half-obscured by her own radiance, pays no attention to Val or me. Kneeling on the ground, she braces one foot, turns her face skyward, and then she launches herself up, arms spreading as if they were wings. For a moment that lasts an eternity, she rises, and then she departs in a blinding flash of light.

I blink. Once. Twice. Three times, the vision of her ascent still glowing before my eyes.

"That was..." I begin, but can't go on. Horror still clings to me, thick and viscous, only slightly mitigated by the awe of the woman rising. "That was...."

"A soul," the breather finishes for me.

I shudder. No magic should take such a toll. No mage should bind another so.

I totter to my feet and take a tentative step forward, leaning over the puddle to look for the blood knot. I can't make it out, but I doubt it matters. "I think you'll be able to cross now."

"I imagine so."

A faint clink. I shake my head to clear my thoughts, pushing away the exhaustion that hovers at the edges of my consciousness. The breather is still chained. I cross the room, stumbling slightly as it tilts. The magic-working has taken more from me than I would have liked.

Kneeling before the breather, I realize that he doesn't sit with his legs perfectly crossed. His cuffed ankle sticks out just a little, keeping the manacle from touching his other leg. Now, he straightens his leg more, bringing it closer to me. I breathe slowly through my mouth, trying not to draw attention to my breath at all. He has given me his word, I remind myself. I'm going to have to trust it.

I turn the cuff, noting in the bright noonday light that the skin beneath it is black and withered. The rest of his leg, while not damaged, exhibits the same sickening skeletal thinness as his face. I wipe my hands on my pants, trying to ignore the dark smears they leave behind, and set to work on the lock. I can almost forgive Saira her sins for having worn hairpins.

Hardly a minute later the cuff clicks open.

With the quickness of a hawk diving for its prey, Val's hand closes on the back of my neck, holding me frozen before him.

"Never been taught?" he whispers. This close, I can see his gray eyes flicker. I flinch, jerking my eyes away to focus on the wall behind him. "For a Promise hidden from the mages, you know a great deal of magic."

I try to keep my voice steady. "I know enough not to kill anyone."

"You have it backwards," Val says, his voice the rustle of dry leaves. "Mages train *to* kill. It is an art form among them." The blood knot certainly stands testimony to that.

"My father didn't kill." I'm not ready to say anything about my mother. I don't know what to say about my mother.

"Your father?"

I try to shift away from him, from his breath that smells of the stale air of moldering crypts, but his hand grips me tightly, his skin burning cold. I might be able to break loose, at least for a moment, but then he might easily give me his death's kiss.

"Your father?" he repeats.

If I lie, I suspect he'll see through it, and that won't go well. But my father died four years ago, and lived about as far from Godan as you can get. What's the likelihood that this creature will know his name?

"Rasheed Coldeye," I admit. His lips curl back from his teeth, and his eyes — his eyes are as bright and hard as silver coins. He's going to kill me.

"We must plan how to get out," I cry, my words tripping over themselves as I wrench my gaze away.

His eyes move over my face, then fall to my hand, still clutching the misshapen torque wrench. Abruptly, he releases me. I half-fall back, dragging myself away from him. He watches me impassively.

"We must plan," I repeat unevenly.

"We have no weapons, little one. Unless you can conjure one."

I shake my head. I doubt I could push a bolt at this point, let alone transform some item into a weapon. But....

"We have one advantage," I tell him, "surprise."

Val tosses the silver chain away from him. The cuff swings out, arcing through the far window, and clatters against the outside wall. Its chain stretches back to the bolt, a dark line in the bright of day. "So we do."

CHAPTER 10
BREATHER

I sit on the far side of the pool of blood, facing the door. Swathed in the Ghost's cloak, with the hood pulled low, I present a strange picture, for breathers don't draw blood, and by any reckoning — blood or breath — I should be dead, not sitting.

So, when the door swings open to admit the creature James with my lunch, I command all of his attention.

"What the hell?" he growls, his voice so deep I can almost feel it through the stones. I hold my breath as he walks toward me, then pauses a bare pace or two away, pivoting toward the sight of the blackened chain stretching to the window. My own chain runs across the floor to me, disappearing beneath my cloak to give the appearance of binding me.

James chuckles. "Vallie, lad, did you forget you were a breather and savage her? You're not much of a fang, you know. Or," he laughs again, "a bird."

Behind him, a guard has entered carrying a meal tray and a lantern. His eyes dart about as he sets the lantern by the door. Hidden in the shadows on the other side waits Val.

James takes two steps forward, his boots squelching in the blood. His hand closes around the front of my cloak and he hauls me up. "Well, let's have a look. You might still be good for something."

I find myself staring into a wolf's face, fangs gleaming. *Lycan.* I've heard of them before, men who can shift to wolf form at will, who can even adopt a demi form as James has, with a tall muscular human body and a canine head. Just as Kenta had, only he never looked half so terrifying as this creature.

I close my hands on James's fist, trying to loosen his grip, gasping as the cloth tightens around my neck. He yanks my hood off with his other hand. His lips draw back into a leering, animal grin. "Oh yes, you're still with us. Perfect."

His words leave me with no doubt as to his intentions. I shout, flailing at him, trying to land a kick, but my legs are hampered by my too-long cloak. *Where is Val?*

James laughs, tossing me to the floor. My breath whooshes out of me, and for a moment I'm stunned by the impact, my ribs and back shuddering from this new abuse. I struggle for air, scrabbling sideways on arms and legs that will hardly answer to me, and then James's weight slams down on me, pinning me to the ground.

He laughs, his hands ripping at my cloak, tearing it open. I try to twist away from him, my body pinned beneath his weight. If I can just land a good punch—

His hands close on my wrists. He holds them together with one of his own, his breath panting loud and moist in my face, canines gleaming. *No.*

A bony white hand loops under James's muzzle, yanking him back and lifting him half off me. James releases me with a yelp of surprise, his arms wheeling through the air as he tries to catch his balance.

"Hello, James," Val says softly, and, leaning in, he — *breathes.*

I don't know whether it is I who screams or James. Perhaps it is both of us. James withers, his broad shoulders collapsing, his thick wolf's pelt silvering and falling out in clumps, his teeth bared in a rictus of pain. I can feel his body shriveling, the weight that pinned me to the ground dissolving.

Val takes one more breath, his mouth hardly a hairsbreadth from the other's muzzle, and James groans, a sickening death rattle that gurgles in his throat and twists his fingers into disfigured claws.

The breather straightens and tosses James's body away. It thumps onto the stones beside me, a dead thing.

Val's eyes meet mine as I cower before him. They are slate gray now; his hair, night shot with silver; his face hardly older than my father's had been, the skin smooth. I stuff my fist into my mouth to keep from screaming again.

He stoops and unbuckles James's sword belt, wraps it around his own waist, then checks the corpse for additional weapons. I scuttle away until my back presses against the wall.

Val holds out a dagger. "Can you fight?"

I shake my head jerkily. He slides the dagger into his new sword belt. "Come," he says, the word a command, and strides from the room, his bare feet silent on the stones. I hesitate a moment, caught by the fall of sunlight on James's aged body. Averting my eyes, I find myself looking at the guard's corpse instead.

I had forgotten about him. He lies on the stones by the door, his arms flung out, the contents of the meal tray he held scattered beneath him. Unlike James, there's no sign that he died in pain. Indeed, I don't remember him screaming, don't recall that he made any sound at all. As I stare, I see his chest lift slightly, then settle again. *He's alive?*

"If you fall behind, you will die," Val says, his voice hard but no longer brittle. I jerk my head up. He stands in the doorway, waiting.

For a long moment, we look at each other.

"Shouldn't you...." I start to say, then stop.

"What?"

For a man who spent a year in a cell, he might have learned a bit more patience, I think, my mind curiously detached.

"Swap your clothes?" I point my toe toward the fallen guard. "As a disguise?"

Val steps back into the room. "Good thought."

I turn away from him, waiting as he strips the man down and dresses himself. When I turn back, I see that he has even donned the helmet with its curling face guard. The illusion is complete: he looks like nothing more than a guard — a slightly older, grizzled one, but a guard nonetheless.

"All right?" he asks. I nod. He leads the way down the winding staircase carrying the lantern. I am grateful it survived the fight unharmed; I wouldn't want to try these steps in the near dark of the stairwell.

At the bottom, Val hangs the lantern from its peg and motions for me to stay back. Then he steps out, sauntering along the wall. I retreat up the stairs until I'm out of sight of the door. I wait, wondering if I trust Val to return. Will he consider our deal complete now that we're free of the tower, or will he come back? Certainly, he has the better disguise for escaping.

Something rustles in the room below. I start, then ease forward, pressing myself against the wall and peering down. A rat raises its long face, its eyes glinting, and then scurries into the shadows, just as someone enters. I freeze.

"I have an idea." Val's voice reverberates in the stairwell as he starts up toward me. "The gates are open, and you are dead."

I swallow. "I'm dead?"

"Someone must carry your body out. You understand?"

He doesn't wait for my response. He bends over and catches me around the legs, then straightens easily, tossing me over his shoulder like a sack of potatoes. I grunt as my stomach folds around his collarbone, my arms flailing.

"Try to be a little more convincing," he suggests, hitching me up higher. "Remember you're dead now." I clench my jaw, head spinning, and let my arms hang down. "Better," he says. "Hold your breath when we pass the guards."

He leaves the tower and makes his way to the castle gates. I close my eyes, my face rubbing against his leather jerkin, and try not to think. His shoulder is broader than I expected, and hardly bony at all. I take a shaky breath, let it out slowly. We'll be through in a few minutes. Then he'll go off to wherever his allies live, and I can start back to Karolene.

"What's that you got?" a voice calls out. I'm surprised I understand. But perhaps the guards come from different lands, and need a trade language to converse in.

Val turns toward the speaker. "That girl as was fed to the prisoner."

"She dead?" The voice comes closer, and with it the sound of other boots.

Val continues toward them. "Aye."

"You sure?" Val pauses as a hand catches my hair and twists my head to the side. It is all I can do not to grimace. The man holds my hair a moment longer, until my breath begins to burn in my lungs, and then he releases me, my face thumping down into Val's back. "Pity. She mighta been some fun."

"The other ones came out looking old," says a second soldier. "How's she still young?"

Val shifts. "Couldn't say. Wasn't about to ask. Maybe she killed herself from fright before he got to her."

The soldiers snicker. "You saw him?"

"Aye."

"What's he look like?"

"Skeleton thing. Bit like a demon." He readjusts his hold on me, reminding the soldiers of his burden. "Where should I put her?"

"Haven't taken one out before, eh?" the first man says. "There's a ditch off the road a bit. Just go on down to the marker and take the path into the forest. You'll see it."

"Or fall in it," another soldier laughs.

"Easy enough to get out if you're alive," the first soldier assures Val as we start forward again. Val only grunts in response, and then we are through, his boots crunching the gravel. He continues down the road with me over his shoulder and doesn't let me go until we've entered the woods.

Before I can speak, he holds a finger to my lips, then hustles me down the path.

We smell the ditch before we reach it. The stench of dead things rotting permeates the air. I stagger to a stop some paces away, gagging, but only bile comes up. I wonder if the woman Kol killed for the blood knot was thrown here. I wonder how many other victims he has sucked dry, and how many of Val's previous meals lie here. My stomach coils into knots.

"Keep going," Val says. "This path will go on past the ditch."

"How do you know?"

"The ditch can't be that old; the marker has stood there fifty years at least." His hand tightens on my arm, jerking me forward. "Walk."

He drags me on, beyond the pit of bodies and over a low rise where the breeze blows sweet and clear. I gasp, inhaling great lungfuls of air as if I might breathe out all the horror of the ditch, all the terrible things I have seen today. But Val gives me no respite, pushing me on.

"I have to stop," I tell him. "We're out now. You go on — wherever you're going. I have to stop."

"Within a few hours someone will realize that James is missing. They'll go to the tower and discover we're both gone. Meanwhile, the soldiers will remember that I have not returned from throwing out your body. By dusk there will be a search mounted, with dogs following our scent — fangs have no trouble hunting at night. Stop here and you die."

"Where do we stop then?" I cry.

"We don't."

With more strength than I realize I have, I dig my feet in and pull back. Val turns toward me. "I am human," I tell him, "not what you are. The magic-working has taken my strength. I cannot go a year without food or drink; I have gone three days with only two meals, and I am weak. Leave me here, and when I can, I will go on."

Val leans toward me. "You have a choice, girl. Force yourself to keep walking, or give your breath to me. I will not leave you behind to speak your story to my enemies."

"You said you would not harm me."

"I say many things," he says, his teeth glinting. "Decide."

"There is no choice," I whisper, taking a step forward. He doesn't answer, but then his hand appears before me holding a small roll of bread.

"Where did you get that?" I gasp, snatching it from him.

"They were bringing your meal," he says. "The rest couldn't be saved, but I thought you might want that."

"Thanks." I bite into it, unsure what to make of him.

"Now walk," he says, his voice as cold as ever. "And don't stop."

At first, I am able to keep up well, for I'd had some rest between releasing the blood knot and James's arrival. But as the miles pass my strength fades. I lose track of where we walk, going numbly where Val guides me, his hand on my elbow. I stumble often, on rocks or roots or rises or dips or nothing at all. Finally, I fall, my knees giving out beneath me.

Val bends down toward me, and I push away, my hands scrabbling at the dirt. "No. I can walk. Don't."

"Hush," he says, as if he were my father comforting me.

"Please," I say, my sight filled with the vision of James dying. I stagger to my feet, but fall with the next step. Only Val's arms reaching around me keep me from sprawling face-first in the path. He lifts me up as if I were a babe. I wait for his face to turn toward me, for his lips to part and steal my life, but he does not look. Instead, he starts walking.

I rest in his arms, my cheek sliding against his chest. He walks steadily, his stride long and certain even in the gathering dark. We move faster than we did when I walked. The only danger is that he will tire of carrying me. It is not a fear I can comprehend. I give in to exhaustion and slip into a dreamless sleep.

CHAPTER II

THE ENEMY OF MY ENEMY

I wake to the distant sound of running water. I turn my head, listening, and the darkness around me resolves into a shallow cave. Val rests on his back. His hands are folded, corpse-like, on his chest. Had I not seen him in the tower, I wouldn't recognize him now. Where before he had been nothing more than bones held together by a scraping of skin, he now seems unremarkably human. The guard whose clothes he took had broader shoulders and hips, but not by much. Even his eyes have lost their paleness, growing dark as the night we have walked through.

"Awake?" he says without looking at me.

"Yes," I respond, my voice scratchy.

"There is a stream below, if you need it."

I sit up, pulling my knees to my chin, my gaze on the ground between us. I hadn't really expected to wake up this morning.

"You," I begin and stop. Perhaps I shouldn't ask.

"Yes?"

I clear my throat. "Why did you help me?" *Why did you carry me when you could have taken my breath as your own?*

117

I can feel his eyes on me, studying me. "I gave you my word."

"You said otherwise when we were walking."

He laughs, a quiet patter of amusement. "I was trying to frighten you. I needed you to walk as long as you could."

Well, it certainly worked. I drop a hand to the dirt, trace a circle in it. "You left that guard alive, too," I finally say.

"I left him a few years," Val admits. "Though I suspect Kol will take them from him anyhow."

"He didn't scream," I say, my mind still on the fight.

"No."

"Not like James."

Val smiles. "Not like James," he agrees. A chill creeps up my spine, runs cold fingers over my arms.

He sits up and draws his dagger. He begins to clean it with a scrap of cloth, his fingers moving in smooth, sure strokes. I watch him work, noting the line of his shoulders, the tightness around his eyes. There is something left he means to say, and it has nothing to do with how James died. I could go down to the stream now, but he would be waiting for me when I returned. So I wait.

It doesn't take him long. He shifts, turning the dagger over to inspect it, and says, "Your father was Rasheed Coldeye, Arch Mage of Falinor."

"Before he died," I agree. I wonder how he knows this, why a breather would care what rank a mage held. But I'm not about to ask.

"And your mother was a mage as well?"

"Yes."

"Then you are trained." The words are hard, his voice cold. He knows I lied to him in the tower, just as I have lied to anyone who has come near me. My whole life has been built on falsehoods, but each was rooted in truth. At least I can give him the truth behind this.

"I was never formally apprenticed. My parents ... didn't want that. So they taught me in secret, every night after their own apprentices left." I lift a hand, then let it fall. "In the eyes of the High Council of Mages, I'm no more than a wild Promise."

He studies me, weighing my words. "Why would your parents hide you?"

"I suppose," I say slowly, looking up, "because they did not want me to learn to kill."

For a long moment, his eyes hold mine.

"Do you not know what a breather's gaze can do?" he asks abruptly.

"It's a bit like a fang's, isn't it?"

"It is nothing like," Val says, his voice soft. "A fang mesmerizes. He holds his victims still; if he is strong, he might beckon them closer, might leave them standing motionless after he turns away."

I know this, have seen it happen far too recently to forget it. "And a breather?" I ask.

"If we wish, we can take your will, your thoughts, and shape them to our own."

I shake my head as if to clear it. Surely I misunderstood. "You — *what?*"

"One of the guards at Kol's fortress realized you were alive."

"One—" I stumble, further confused.

"He knew you were alive," Val repeats. "He saw something — an eyelid twitch, your pulse, I don't know. But I took that thought from him before he could share it. I am not very strong just now, and there is a chance he'll recover the memory soon, but it gave us enough time to get this far without being caught."

I stare at him, wondering how what he claims can be possible. He stole a man's memory — and not a faded one, half-forgotten beneath the weight of newer experiences, but a critical discovery of a moment before.

"No wonder mages hate breathers," I murmur.

Val tilts his head, as if he cannot quite follow me. Perhaps it is the wrong reaction, but his words help me fit together the pieces of an old puzzle, one I'd almost forgotten about: the true reason for the deep hatred between mages and breathers.

The High Council was formed to regulate the use of magic in the aftermath of the Great Burning — a terrifying war in which mages unleashed calamity upon calamity on the Kingdoms as factions fought for supremacy. To the High Council, control is everything. "You could look a mage in the eye and control him, couldn't you? You could take his will from him, use him as you wish. And that would be...."

"Any more terrible than a man without morals or conscience becoming a mage?"

I laugh, the sound startled out of me before I can help it. "Perhaps not. But certainly a terrifying prospect to the average mage, used to being his own master."

"To *anyone*," Val says, enunciating his words carefully, "used to being her own master."

I'd have to be an idiot not to understand his warning. But I don't know how to respond. For some reason, I don't want to be the one to look away from him. He didn't just warn me because he intends to betray my trust. It's that he doesn't want my trust. Too bad for him. If we're traveling together any further, trust is going to be vital.

"I see," I say slowly. And then, "I told you my father's name."

"Girl," he says, exasperated.

"Mine is Hitomi."

Shaking his head, Val returns his attention to his dagger. But he knows as well as I the power inherent in names. And the trust marked by sharing them, especially with a would-be enemy.

I push myself to my feet. "I'm going to see about that stream," I say.

He doesn't respond.

Our cave is set in a sandy bluff that rises above the stream. The opposite side is wooded, the trees tall and lovely. They are mostly bare now, their branches sweeping the sky in elegant curves. Interspersed among their ranks stand solitary pines, showing tall but heavyset, sheathed in their armor of needles. The moon hangs low; dawn brightens the far reaches of the horizon.

I kneel at the stream bank and drink until my head spins. Then I shove my sleeves past my elbows, washing as much of my arms as I can as well as my face and neck. I scrub hard, trying not to think about the dead woman's blood that may still be dried on me. Once I'm satisfied, I push myself to my feet, ignoring the ache in my legs. Now that I've quenched my thirst, I find that I'm hungry as well. Today promises another long trek, not something I'm looking forward to on an empty stomach.

I glance around hopefully, assessing the nearby bushes. Perhaps I can find some late berries along the banks, or a handful of nuts. I start forward, stretching out the kinks in my legs and back as I walk. I'm not quite sure what I'm seeking. I've never picked my own berries or foraged in a forest, but surely it can't be that hard? And if it comes to that, I can whistle a question to the birds.

Fifty paces on, I come to a bush heavy with blue-black berries. I kneel beside it, studying the fruit uncertainly. I know that some varieties are poisonous, but how does one tell them apart? Plucking a particularly plump one, I roll it between my fingers, then pick it apart and smell it. It bleeds a sweet-scented black juice over the tips of my fingers.

Nearby, a dog growls.

I look up, the berry dropping to the ground. Further down-stream on the opposite bank, four dogs crouch, their teeth bared. Behind them, holding tight to their leads, stands a guard. He doesn't move, his eyes scanning the low bushes and sparse tree cover. Four soldiers ride up behind him, and then I see more behind them.

The man's eyes meet mine. "There!" he shouts.

I bolt, the sound of shouts and the thunder of hooves echoing in my ears. If I can just reach Val before they catch me — then what? They'll kill him, too. He might be able to stop three or four, but a dozen?

I swerve away even as I see him crouched at the mouth of the cave, his dark eyes watching me. I splash through the streambed and plunge into the forest, weaving through the trees. A horse pounds past me, and I skid to the side, trying to avoid it. My breath comes in quick hard gasps as I pivot. A boot catches me from behind, slamming hard against my ribs. I sprawl on my hands and knees, each breath sending a rush of pain through my back.

I have to get up. Swallowing back the pain, I stumble to my feet as the horses surround me. They snort and stamp at the ground, reined in tight by their riders. Straightening my back, I turn to face their leader, and find Kol's blue-eyed gaze trained on me.

"You just don't want to die, do you?" he says. Though he appears calm, his words are steeped in fear and fury. I keep my eyes on his shoulder. "How is it Val let you go?"

I shake my head. He drops from the saddle, sauntering over to me with predatory intent. Every instinct I have screams at me to run, but I've already tried that. I won't give him the satisfaction of chasing me the three paces it will take him to bring me down on foot.

My breath rattles in my lungs. Kol comes closer and closer, until he towers over me. I stare straight ahead at his chest. He bends his face down and murmurs in my ear, "Perhaps I should have kept you for myself."

I jerk back. He laughs, his hands closing on my arms, and

then he twists my right arm behind me. My back arches, and it is all I can do to keep from baring my neck to him. I clench my eyes shut.

"Do you think you can fight me?" His long-fingered hand tightens its hold on my right arm and then — tearing pain. My body spasms, a ragged cry spilling from my lips. His eyes pin me, horrific in their blueness.

"Where is he?"

I fight the hypnotic power of his gaze, knowing what he is, what he will do to me. To Val. "Gone," I spit.

His eyes narrow. I can feel my senses slipping, the wider reality of horses and armed men fading into an indistinct blur. There is only the overwhelming truth of his eyes. "Liar," he says lovingly. "How did you two escape?"

Liar, I think back at him, hating this: the deep wide calm of his eyes, the sweetness they promise. I twist in his grip, welcoming the pain that washes through me, giving me some focus other than his eyes.

I give him the simplest truth I have. "I picked the locks."

He throws his head back with a shout of laughter. The horses shy away in alarm. He tosses me down, and as I land his boot drives into my stomach. I curl around it, hearing myself scream. Darkness edges my vision. His boot drives into me again and again, and then he is crouching over me, yanking my head up by my hair.

"Where is he?" Kol roars. I have no breath to answer him with. "*Where is he?*"

"We ... parted," I wheeze. "Last night."

"The dogs were following his scent," Kol says. "He's still here somewhere."

"They must have ... followed mine." I close my eyes, trying to think. He transfers his grip to my throat, lifting me to my knees. His face is perilously close.

"Where is he?" His fingers tighten around my throat.

"I don't know!" I choke out. "We parted. I kept walking.... My scent!" I cry as his grip turns vicious, "It must be stronger than his."

He drops me. I lie on the ground, watching the way the dead leaves stir in the faint breeze. The horses move, breaking the ring that circles me. Kol's hand reaches down and closes on my shoulder, lifting me up as easily as if he plucks a flower. He drops me over his saddlebow, my head knocking against his knee. The saddle bites into my stomach. I turn my face away, vomiting water over the horse's leg.

I don't know how long we ride. I know only the digging of the saddle into my stomach, the shrieking pain of my arm as it swings against the horse's flank. Finally, Kol lifts me, turning my head to face the trail. He has pulled up the hood of his cloak, and donned thick gloves against the burgeoning sunlight. He is well prepared to stay out, which means I can't hope for him to take shelter any time soon.

"You left him how far from here?"

"I ... don't know." I stare at the path blankly. I slept through this part of the journey. I have no landmarks to describe to Kol.

"Do you think if I take a sip or two from you, you might remember?"

"I don't know!"

"Let's try," he suggests, turning my head toward him. He smiles, his fangs bared.

"If the girl says she doesn't know, then she probably doesn't," a voice says from behind us. Kol drops me and wheels his horse around.

I barely manage to break my fall, landing hard on my knees and my good arm. My other arm hangs uselessly from my shoulder.

"Val," Kol says, his voice strangely uncertain.

Mounted on horseback, Val appears completely at ease, one hand holding the reins, the other resting on his thigh. His horse, a sleek gray mare, waits patiently where he stopped her, a good twenty paces back.

His horse? I look around and count only six of the guards that came with Kol. I blink, count again, wondering if the pain has affected my vision. Hadn't there been near a dozen?

The two closest to Val shout and charge him. His horse rears. He yanks the reins, turning the mare in time to bring his sword around. It flickers like a ghost, something there and gone, passing between the soldier's helmet and chain vest. The man flies from his saddle, blood spurting from his throat. Val meets the other soldier head on, kneeing his horse forward. His dagger flashes, deflecting the guard's blow as his sword plunges into the man's midriff. His movements are swift and lethally precise. The second guard slides sideways off his horse with a shriek, landing on his back with a sickening thud.

The remaining guards back their mounts away, glancing wide-eyed toward Kol. I wonder if they recognize the horse Val rides as one of their own, stolen from a fallen comrade. He wears the clothes he took last night, though he has foregone the helmet. His hair hangs down in a thick, dark mane, his eyes flashing in the growing light. They are not quite as dark as I remember. Nor does he look as old as he was.

"Waste of blood," Kol observes.

"Let's finish this," Val says.

"Such a shame." Kol draws his sword. "I would have liked to keep you a little longer."

Val doesn't answer. Instead, he drops his gaze to Kol's mount. The horse pauses and then — relaxes, its eyes dilating slightly, even its expression gentling. There is no indication that magic is at work, no prickling of my senses to alert me, but I have no doubt that Val is using his gaze.

When he looks back up, he smiles coldly. "Come then," he says.

Kol's horse won't move, ignoring the tap of his heels. It gazes toward Val with equine adoration, and remains still as stone despite Kol's kicks and the smack of his blade against its flanks.

"You have a choice," Val says. "You can remain on your horse, who loves me better than you, or you can fight me on foot."

"I don't see you dismounting," Kol snarls.

Val drops down to the ground without a word, relaxing into a fighter's pose, weapons at the ready. Then he tilts his head, a challenge.

I watch him, unnerved. Isn't a horse a warrior's greatest weapon? So why would he abandon his own after beguiling Kol's? Does he care that much for a fair fight? Or perhaps he isn't as good a horseman as Kol is. Whatever his reason, I hope it's a good one.

Kol dismounts, careful not to turn his back on his enemy, his face black with fury. "You'll pay for that little trick, breather."

"I said that I would kill you, fang. I intend to keep that promise. Come."

They move toward each other casually, their swords ready but their motions easy, unhurried. And then they stop. They say nothing, make no move, and yet I cannot shake the sense that they are fighting, that something crucial is being decided in the very stillness of the air.

They meet so quickly that I can't tell who moved first. Their swords clash almost faster than my eyes can follow, the clang of steel ringing in my ears. Behind me I hear a curse that sounds more like wonder than anger, for both breathers and fangs move faster than any human. I'd heard of such things before, but seeing it raises the gooseflesh on my arms.

They fall away from each other, parting as if by unspoken agreement. They circle each other and then slide into stillness once more, their eyes meeting steadily. Kol, with his own hypnotic gaze, seems to have no trouble looking into Val's eyes.

The fighters come together again in a fury of glittering silver. When they part, I see a line of blood across Val's chest. It's a shallow wound, hardly a scrape, but I hear the soft exhalation of the guards and know that it is a sure sign of victory to them.

Kol laughs. "Do you think you can beat me now? After losing to me a year ago and starving since then? While I've grown stronger?"

"Grown lazy," Val says.

Kol lunges forward and again their blades flash, and I see the blur of their movements, the obscene quickness of their cuts and parries. When they part, Kol is breathing hard, but Val bleeds from a second cut, this one to the arm he holds his dagger with. Val should be faster than Kol — should be, because breathers are said to be faster than every other race in the Eleven Kingdoms — but he isn't. Not after a year spent moldering in the tower. And Kol knows it.

I bite my lip. If Val dies, so will I. His fight, whatever its history, is mine as well. I have no distraction to offer Kol, nor any weapon to turn against him, but I have what my parents gave me in the hours that they spent with me and the blood that flows in my veins.

I scoop up a handful of leaves and dirt. It is all I have to work with. Whatever I do will have to be fast and simple: something that moves with the quicksilver speed of their blades, something that Kol will not see or expect. But what I hold are things of slow growth and gentle decay. I let them crumble through my fingers, trying to think of what else I might use.

Kol and Val stand stone still, the sunlight igniting the highest branches of the trees around us. The sunlight. While it is not lethal to fangs, it can be. All things burn at a certain point, and fangs burn a little faster than the rest of us.

I gaze up toward the rays of light, my mind racing. I can't reach that high, but perhaps I don't have to. Sunlight has touched everything around me, from the trees to the leaves and the earth below me. How many times have I tapped the essence of the things around me as I've worked my magic? I have only to draw it out.

I press my hands into the leaf-littered earth and draw on the sunlight stored there, pulling the last golden drops from the withered leaves, stealing the remains of its warmth from the air. I draw on the flicker and flash of the swords, the energy coursing through the living things around me — the horses, the guards — pulling from them the sunlight they have stored in their bodies, transformed and transformed again. I draw it all into myself, until my very core burns.

When I look up, Val and Kol stand apart, but Val has lost his dagger, and Kol has ripped his sleeve. I focus on Kol, fanning the white hot fury within me with my breath, with my outrage. I think of how Kol has treated his prisoners, and how Blackflame gave him Alia; I think of the deaths of Lord and Lady Degath, and the betrayal of my mother, and the creatures I have destroyed in my attempts to do good: the horse with its broken leg, the fang left behind to die in his cage. The blaze builds within me until it is a flaming inferno — and then I release it.

The fire roars out of me with the shriek of lightning wrapped in thunder, searing my throat and eyes and nose, turning all I touch to ash. I do not see where it goes, for in its absence I have gone blind, and over its thunder I can hear no sound.

Through the earth pressed against my cheek, cool and soothing, I feel the thud of horses' hooves, the fading reverberations of animals fleeing. And then only stillness.

CHAPTER 12

MEMORIES OF ASH

I n the darkness, someone holds a cup of water to my lips. I drink greedily, swallowing great gulps until it reaches my stomach, and then I am retching up coals and ash. What is left after a fire? The burnt-out skeleton of what was, a few charred remains. Nothing that can hold water.

Later, there is water again. I open my mouth for it, but there are only small sips. They wash the soot down my throat, pool in the heat-born cracks within me. I learn after that to expect only a little at a time. Water, broth, whatever I am given is poured in tiny trickles between my parched lips.

I cannot say how much time passes, for what is time when there is only darkness? But eventually the darkness eases. I become aware of a faint brightness around me, a twilight I have made myself. I realize I need only open my eyes. Daylight pours in, harsh as the whitest lightning, and I moan with the pain of it.

"Hitomi?" a voice whispers from far away, or perhaps just beside me, but I am already reeling back into the night.

The next time, I only crack my eyes a little. I focus dimly on long brown objects that sway nearby. Trees? I take a breath, trying to slow their movement, and it rattles in my chest.

"Hitomi," the voice murmurs above me. I find myself looking into a set of violet eyes. How strange that they should appear so serious.

I open my mouth to answer, not sure what will emerge as my voice. What comes is a cough so hard and hacking that I taste blood mixed with cinders. It is a good taste, though, for it means that not everything within me has burned to ash.

After that, I spend more and more time with my eyes open. The violet eyes slowly gather more features, resolving into a face I think I know, and after a few days I find the name *Val* floating in my mind.

I discover that we travel through rugged foothills leading up to mountains. At first, Val holds me before him on his horse. As I grow stronger, he rearranges the packs strapped to his second horse, making a nest to hold me. He uses a rope to tie me to my seat that I should not fall, and he takes the lead, my horse's reins looped through his saddle.

I notice that I wear layers of clothes that stink of sweat and dirt. I am wrapped in a mottled gray cloak to protect against the winter cold, the snow that settles on my shoulders, Val's hair. I realize that I have no hair. It is a strange moment when I raise one arm awkwardly to touch my head and find only smooth skin beneath the cloak's hood.

"It will grow back, I expect," Val says when he sees me. I do not know how to answer him.

By the time we reach the mountain paths, I find my voice. It is a smoky, shadowy thing, but it carries meaning past my lips, for which I am grateful. "What happened?" I ask as we sit beside a small fire.

Val turns his violet gaze on me, silent. I think he will not answer, but then he moves to toss a twig on the fire and says, "Do you remember Kol?"

I only look at him.

He sighs. "He was the blue-eyed fang who held us captive."

"The tower," I say, the word black as soot.

"Yes. I was fighting him, and losing handily, when you killed him." He purses his lips, watching me.

I look down, try to blink the blurriness from the edges of my vision. I cannot quite fathom this — that I have killed a man.

"You don't remember."

I try to focus on Val's words. "I remember ... fire."

"And before that? Do you remember where you came from?" I listen to the sound of my breath, try to think past the flash of heat and light, a wall of flames beyond which lies only ash.

"Karolene," he says.

"Yes."

"You remember your father's name?" When I do not answer, he continues, "Rasheed Coldeye."

"Yes."

"And your mother's name." I wait for him to tell me, but he does not. "Do you remember your mother's name?"

"Yes."

"What was it?"

We both wait then, I for the memory to crawl out of the flames, and he for my voice. Or perhaps he does not, for after a time he sets another log on the fire and rises and walks away, returning much later as I lie on my side watching the coals breathe white and red. He says nothing, and I have no words for him.

The snow begins to collect on the ground as we move higher into the mountains, little patches of white hiding in the shadows. I grow strong enough to keep my seat without help, though Val continues to lead my horse. We stop often for him to give me bread and cheese, or bits of dried meat to suck: provisions bought or stolen from a town I have not seen. Periodically, he leaves me at our camp and returns hours later with supplies. I notice that he does not eat, and it takes me some days to recall that this is because he is a breather. It seems strange, having remembered, that I could ever have forgotten.

"When do you eat?" I ask him.

"At night," he tells me. "I hunt animals while you sleep."

I nod and consider this carefully, adding it to the small store of things I now know: a breather might subsist on the life force of animals.

Every evening we sit before the fires that Val lights. He carves little pieces of wood with a knife, making foxes and owls and frogs that he tosses into the flames at the end of each night. I watch him throw them with sadness, wishing I could make something like them, or that he would not burn them all.

He will not tell me about himself, and I have nothing left that I remember. So, instead, he describes the places he has been. He has traveled to six of the Eleven Kingdoms. He has stayed with the desert tribes through the sun-bleached summer, and he has crossed the seas of ice with the northmen. He has even, he finally admits, visited Karolene, though he will not speak of it at all.

"I do not want to make your memories for you," he says, and will not be persuaded.

After I lie down for the night, my back to the fire, I try to remember the things he has told me: a tower room, a fang lord, fighting. It is as if I sift through the ashes of old fires, my hands blackened with soot, and only sometimes do I find something: a bit of misshapen metal, a singed scrap of cloth. I remember a woman rising from a dark pool, a man with a wolf's head, another woman dressed in silks. But I cannot piece these memories together, cannot be sure how one relates to the other, or how any of them relate to me. I remember reaching for sunlight so that I might kill. It is the only memory I wish I had lost.

We reach a high pass and see, stretching out before us, range upon range of mountains, indigo and amethyst in the fading evening light. We pause, Val allowing my horse to draw up beside his.

"Hotaru Brokensword," I say, finding a name for the woman in silks. Val looks at me. I laugh, the sound breathy and wreathed in smoke. "My mother's name."

"You remembered," he says, smiling. He seems very young to me. I cannot imagine why I ever believed him old.

The next morning, just as the sun climbs to its highest point, we reach our destination. I had not realized that we were going anywhere in particular. It seemed to me that we were only traveling, and that this was a thing that travelers do: move from place to place, never look back. But we take the little path curling down through woods into a valley, and come to a small stone cottage built on the edge of a lake. Together, they make a quaint picture: the single-story stone cottage with its wooden timbers, a small path leading to its front door, looking like a child's toy set alongside the wide expanse of the azure lake.

We tie our horses to a tree at the edge of the clearing that surrounds the cottage, and I follow Val to the house. The land around it is broken and muddy, with bits of plants and leaves sticking up, and I know that this must be the remains of a garden. While I cannot recall seeing gardens before, this feels familiar to me in a way that the forests and mountains we have travelled through do not. I hear the faint clucking of hens, and beyond the cottage I see goats grazing.

A woman opens the door when we are still some paces away, her pale hair pulled back in a bun, her face equally pallid. There are crow's feet by her eyes and lines of sorrow around her mouth.

For a long moment she merely stands in the doorway, looking at us. And then she says, coldly, "Breather."

"Shelter," Val says. "By the Laws of Old, we seek shelter."

I wonder if she will chase us away, or close her door on us, but then she says, "Three days and three nights, by the Laws of Old. Do not overstay."

Her home is a single room, with a loft above and a root cellar below. We sit at her work table and she brings me a bowl of hot stew and fresh bread. She brings Val nothing, sitting across from him in silence.

I adjust my cloak as I eat, and the hood slips off. I feel her gaze at once.

"This one is not well," she says, studying me. I pull the hood back over my head, clumsy in my embarrassment.

"No," Val agrees.

"Was it a fang?" She rubs her thumb against the edge of the table. "She is as pale and thin as one might expect, but," she pauses, then clicks her jaw shut, biting off the end of her sentence. "When did she lose her hair?"

"Near two months ago," Val says.

"There was a fang," I volunteer, but at Val's glance fall silent.

The woman watches us with only a slight crease of her brow. I think that she means to question me, but when she speaks she only asks, "Would you like more stew?"

"Please," I say, and she refills my bowl.

When she takes her seat again, Val says, "There are tales about you."

"Fools tell them." The words are abrupt, almost bitter. She sits stiffly, her back straight as a board, her hands hidden on her lap beneath the table.

"Your name is Brigit Stormwind, and you are a High Mage."

She shrugs, a slight twitch of her shoulders. "So much, at least, is true."

"Did you ever hear tell of a mage named Rasheed Coldeye?"

I look up, slopping the contents of my spoon onto the table. The woman, Stormwind, glances at me quizzically. "I have."

"Who was he?"

"The Arch Mage of Falinor. Anyone of the eastern kingdoms can tell you that."

Val places his palms flat on the table, studying the back of his hands. "What did you think of him?"

"He was a fool to trust the people he did, and a greater fool to make the enemies he did. He should have seen his death coming."

I swallow hard, setting down the spoon. She means that my father was murdered. I try to shake the thought loose, but it sticks in my mind like a prickly burr, catching on memories that lie just beneath the darkness.

Val considers Stormwind thoughtfully. "Could you see all that from your valley?"

"The waters of my lake are clear as crystal, breather. I do not need to leave to know what passes beyond these mountains." She speaks roughly, an old anger brushing at the surface of her words. I wonder who belittled her before. I wonder what drove a High Mage to live as a hermit hidden in a secret valley.

"Would you have given your support to Coldeye?" Val asks. "Or was he only a different sort of trouble?"

"There are many sorts of trouble in the world," Stormwind says, smiling thinly. "What are you asking?"

"If he needed help, would you have given it?"

"Where are your questions tending, breather? I do not trust your kind. If you want my help, tell me what you are about."

Val looks at me. Before he can speak, I say, "My father was Rasheed Coldeye."

"And she," Val finishes for me, "is a Promise."

Stormwind stiffens, her pale eyes fastening on me. "A Promise? That seems unlikely. Coldeye had no magical children." She hesitates. "If this is true, then an untrained Promise at your age is very dangerous. You should be reported, taken in to the High Council."

"You won't catch her," Val says, "as long as she is under my protection."

Stormwind looks between us as if she cannot quite fathom Val's words, what I am. "Why would a breather protect a wild Promise?"

"Because two months ago it was not a fang that touched her."

"Speak plainly, breather," she says, crossing her arms. She seems as tautly strung as a bow. I wait as well, my hands gripping the edge of the bench. I wonder if Val will tell her more than I remember.

"For the last year I have been the prisoner of the fang lord Kol — you have heard his name?" Val asks.

"I have," the woman allows. "He took Pren Castle in Gadon some years back. That is a land that has fallen into darkness."

"There is darkness everywhere," Val replies blandly. "Kol kept me in a tower room, delivering me an occasional human to breathe from." The woman regards him coolly, waiting. "Then he made a mistake. He brought me the daughter of Rasheed Coldeye. She promised to free me if I did not harm her."

"Why would a Promise—" Stormwind begins, but Val cuts her off.

"She called first to the birds, and a crow brought her a needle."

"Impossible," Stormwind snaps. "No wild Promise can do that."

"She took the needle," Val continues, unperturbed, "and cut herself. She used her own blood to break the enchantment that held me, a blood spell that had bound a woman's soul within it."

"A blood spell," Stormwind echoes. She gives me a long, measuring look, one that holds a certain amount of suspicion. I meet her gaze. Blood magic sounds rather dubious to me, too. But calling to a crow? That seems a wonderful thing. I wish I remembered how I did that.

"We escaped the tower but were recaptured in the hills. Kol was there, and he and I fought. The girl had already been beaten by him. She lay on the ground hardly able to rise." Val leans back, his violet eyes intent on Stormwind. "I had been starved for a year, and though I had breathed from the soldiers who chased us, I was hardly Kol's equal. I began to lose. Just as I thought he would finish me, he was struck by a bolt of lightning."

She pales, and it takes her a moment to find her words. "What you are saying cannot be."

"Kol," Val smiles, "turned to ash before my eyes. She burned like a blazing star and breathed smoke and still coughs cinders."

"A wild Promise cannot.... That is a working of the highest order."

"Perhaps," Val suggests, "she is not wholly untrained. I agree that her survival was miraculous. I thought her dead at first, and you know that I can scent life in every creature."

"Rasheed Coldeye," Stormwind mutters. She chews her bottom lip, her eyes roving over my features. "Your father trained you?"

"A little, I think," I say. Clearly Val believes it's true, so I must have told him so at some point.

"He did not take you as his apprentice?"

I glance toward Val.

"They hid her, taught her in secret," he says for me.

Stormwind looks back at me. "Your mother was also a mage."

"Yes. Hotaru Brokensword."

"How did she die?"

I meet her gaze, bewildered, remembering the woman dressed in blue silks. Why would Stormwind suppose my mother dead? I take a breath, pushing farther into the dark corners of my mind, knowing that the answers are waiting there for me.

And, suddenly, the memories blossom like flowers opening toward the sun. My father, lying pale and still on his bed, his eyes wide and staring, dead. My mother, her chest heaving in coughs that spatter blood on her kerchiefs, insisting that she and I travel to Karolene, seek help from a mage there. And, finally, Wilhelm Blackflame when I first met him, after my mother went to him and never returned. He looked at me as if I were a cursed thing, a piece of filth marring the perfection of his courtyard. His words ring in my ears as they did that first time, distant, hard. *Hotaru Brokensword is dead. Do not come here again.*

In the silence while I remember, Val speaks, his words half-mocking, "Did your waters not show you?"

"I did not look," she says stiffly.

"We went to Karolene to seek help," I tell her finally. "After my father died. But my mother disappeared."

Stormwind stares at me, her lips parted slightly, for the first time neither suspicious nor aloof. Instead, she appears to be struggling against mounting horror. "Karolene? Why Karolene?"

"My mother thought Master Blackflame would help her. He didn't — or perhaps he did. I followed after her, once she didn't return, and he told me she died. But..."

"But?" Stormwind asks, her voice sharp. Everything about her seems sharp, on edge.

"But she's still alive, and living in his home. I saw her." I glance toward Val, wondering why the memory feels empty, like an image painted on a backdrop of lotus flowers and blue skies, a picture I might have seen somewhere. How much of me was burned away with the spell I cast?

"I see." Stormwind drops her gaze to the tabletop. She breathes slowly, evenly, focused inward. After a moment, she looks back up and it is as if I never mentioned seeing my mother.

She says, "Your parents could not have taught you very much in secret. How did you make your lightning bolt?"

I don't recall my parents teaching me anything at all, but the spell — that I remember. "It wasn't lightning. It was sunlight."

"The sun was still rising," Val objects, then presses his lips together. He did not meant to contradict me, but he hasn't really. He doesn't know what I did when I killed Kol.

"I gathered it from where it slept in every creature around me, in every thing that had ever been touched by a ray of sunlight."

"Gathered it," Stormwind echoes. "But you didn't know how to channel such power."

I shake my head uncertainly.

"She has lost much of her memory, Mistress Stormwind," Val says. It seems he has finally decided to trust her with the truth of how damaged I am. "She knows only pieces of her life before she made her casting."

Stormwind nods. "I expect it burned its way right through her and took everything it touched. A fire requires fuel."

"I want to remember," I say.

Neither Stormwind nor Val answer me. Instead, Val rises from the table. "We will be pleased to stay with you these three days."

"Indeed."

"By the Laws of Old," he begins. She looks at him, her expression so cold and sharp it might have cut glass. He smiles as he continues, "I offer what help I can while I am here. Have you any needs?"

CHAPTER 13
A NEW PATH

V al spends the bulk of that day and the next on the cottage roof, fixing broken shingles and cutting out rot. I climb up beside him, though he doesn't let me do much beyond that. "Just sit," he admonishes me. "She'll give you work soon enough."

"But we're leaving after tomorrow," I point out on the second day when she still hasn't given me any chores.

"I am," he says. "We breathers have a rather dark history when it comes to mages. I dare not stay beyond the three days."

"You're not taking me with you," I say slowly.

"Not if Stormwind will keep you. She can train that Promise of yours."

"She wants to turn me over to the High Council."

Val hammers down a new shingle. I watch him, and it occurs to me that he is unexpectedly good at mending roofs. He sits back on his heels to look at the lake. Framed by the mountains rising around it, and unruffled by any wind, it looks like a mirror, perfectly reflecting the sky.

Val tells me, "Stormwind respected your father. She's now

thinking about what he meant to do by keeping his own daughter's Promise a secret. She's looking into who you were and where you lived and what happened to you. She knows that your casting was of a higher order than many mages ever achieve. She will take you on as her student despite her misgivings. Here, in this valley, you can learn from her and will be safe from prying eyes."

He turns back to the roof. "Nail."

I hand him another nail. Five shingles later, as he peels off a splintering scrap of wood and studies the touch of rot beneath it, I ask him, "Where will you go?"

"I have sworn allegiance to a prince of my people. I will return to serve him. He will want to hear what I have to tell of Kol." Val smiles grimly.

"What's his name? I've never heard of a breather prince." At least, not that I can remember. Which isn't saying much at all.

"Names have great power," he says, his eyes catching mine. "I will tell you that he lives in the Amara Mountains."

I have no idea how far the Amaras may be. "Will you come back?" I ask.

"I am a breather," he says almost angrily.

"So?"

He sets his hammer down. "Do you remember how I looked at you in the tower room? What you feared?"

I swallow. My memories of the tower have returned in patches, perhaps because they are the most recent ones I have. So I know what he means. "But you were starving then," I say.

"The more time I spend with you, the more I want to taste you."

"No," I say, my voice soft with shock. His violet eyes do not waver. He reaches out a hand and brushes the back of my wrist, his touch as light as a butterfly's wing.

"I am sorry."

I back away from him, his words, sliding a little on the shingles. "You can't. You're my friend."

"Mages and breathers cannot be friends."

"I'm not a mage," I cry. "You *helped* me. You brought me here. You kept me alive after I burned myself. You can't just toss all that to the wind. It means something, what you did for me."

"I was repaying my debt," he says. "You freed me from my chains and killed my enemy when I could not."

"A debt," I say in a strangled voice.

"Yes," he agrees quietly. I turn away from him and slither to the bottom of the roof, swinging down to the ground before he can see my tears. I don't want Mistress Stormwind to see me either, so I make my way to the trees.

He is the only person I know anymore, the only one who knows me — who knows the girl I was before I killed with a bolt of sunlight, and what I have become as I emerge from my ashes. And I am nothing more to him than a burden to be discharged. I feel as though Val has taken all the friendship he has shown me in the last weeks, all the quiet care and campfire conversations, and turned them into something hard and ugly. A debt. A thing to be repaid and forgotten. A bad taste in the back of his mouth.

I find myself heaving great, racking sobs that stir up the last bits of ash in my lungs and coat my throat in soot. I cough and weep in the shade of the winter-bare trees until I feel emptied out once more, and then I lie on my side, listening to the whisper of air in my lungs, the chirping of birds, the thrumming whistle of the wind through the branches overhead.

The ground is cold beneath me, a chill seeping through the clothes Mistress Stormwind gave me. She had pursed her lips at the soldiers' layered tunics and pants I wore, and this morning she provided me with a carefully mended skirt, a lady's long tunic, and a sweater. I realize now that they were meaningful gifts. One does not gift a convict good clothes before sending her to the gallows.

She will keep me on, and Val will leave without a backward glance. As much as I try, I cannot convince myself I am glad of it.

Above me, the birds fall silent. I turn on my back and see Brigit Stormwind standing five paces away. She is wrapped in a faded blue cloak, her bone-white hair tied back severely. She doesn't speak, but crosses the distance between us to sit beside me. I push myself up, wrapping my arms around my knees.

"He speaks truth, your breather," she says finally.

"You were listening?" I ask, furious.

She turns her hands over, her palms empty. "There is nothing of trust between mages and breathers. I had to be sure of him." I bite my lip to keep from saying something that will give her reason to throw me out. "I know of only one instance in which a breather sought shelter from a mage by the Laws of Old."

"One?"

"The breather was dying and wanted to pass on in peace; the mage granted her that."

"Oh."

"Your breather has trod on very uncertain ground, not only by letting you live but by offering you his protection — and by bringing you to me."

"He's repaying his debt," I say bitterly. "He said so."

"It is truth," she agrees. "But not the whole truth."

I look at her warily.

"He could have left you in the care of a village healer, with a pouch of coins to help you on your way. That would have cleared his debt. Instead, he spent the better part of two months nursing you himself and bringing you to someone who could train you."

"I don't understand."

"A breather does not help a Promise become a mage."

"He is a breather, and I am a Promise," I say, irritated. "So apparently it happens."

She chuckles. It's a warm, friendly sound that I wouldn't have expected from her. "You are beginning to see. I would not let his words sadden me if I were you. He is, I think, just trying to remind himself of the danger of what he has done."

"I wouldn't harm him," I protest.

"Not now. But mages are often called in to hunt down breathers."

"Maybe I won't be that kind of mage," I say. "And he isn't a rogue. He fed on animals on our way here."

Brigit Stormwind smiles. "I believe your father wanted you to be a very different sort of mage from the type we usually train. He always had a ... unique perspective on what we ask of our students."

"You knew him?" I cannot hide my excitement.

"We were apprenticed together."

"But—" I hesitate. She arches an eyebrow. "You're much older than he was."

"We were the same age. I was attacked by a breather once, and he took a portion of my youth from me."

That explains the way she looked at Val when she first opened her door to us. I can't help but ask, "What happened to the breather?"

"Another mage killed him before he could finish me."

"Val's not like that," I say quickly. But she heard his words as well as I; he'd said he wanted to breathe from me.

"Not where you are concerned, it seems," she agrees after a moment, surprising me. Had she not heard him? Or had she understood his words differently from me? I glance at her askance, but her expression is mild, thoughtful, telling me nothing.

I turn my gaze back to the trees, searching for glints of the lake beyond them. "I keep thinking about my mother," I tell her.

Stormwind waits for me to go on.

"I don't remember very much. But she might need help and..." I pause, then rush through the rest of my words. "She'll remember me. Maybe if I talk to her, I'll remember, too."

"It would be a death wish, to return to Blackflame's stronghold," Stormwind observes.

"Part of me feels dead anyhow," I say quietly. I don't know why I'm telling her this, except that I need to admit the words to myself, face the truth of them. "I don't know who I am. I only have bits and pieces of what I was. How can I grow if I have no past, no roots?"

Stormwind doesn't answer at once. When she does, it's with a measure of trepidation, as if she's not at all sure that what she says is wise. "The waters of my lake are crystal clear, Hitomi. I will teach you to look into them."

"To speak with my mother?"

"Yes."

I turn this possibility over in my mind once, twice, consider the angles. "What if she needs me?"

"She is Hotaru Brokensword. What she needs is for you to survive and learn, not to seek her out and endanger yourself. There is no other help you can offer her that would serve her better."

I don't answer. Perhaps she knows my mother better than I do right now. The memory I have of my mother is placid and still, not one of danger or distress. I suppose my plans can wait until I've talked to her. Even if Stormwind is wrong, I can see that I'm not much use as I am.

She still watches me, so I nod my head. She pushes herself to her feet, shaking out her cloak as if that has settled everything between us. Perhaps it has. "Come, then. There are chores aplenty, and I want to get out my books tonight. We should begin your training at once. You know how to read, I hope?"

I follow her back down to the cottage, answering her questions as best I can as she tries to assess just where she must start her lessons. My first chore is to wash out the clothes I wore. I haul water from the lake and scrub them in a tub by the fire, listening to the faint tap of Val's hammer overhead. It's a comforting sound in its way, and I am glad he still has one day left with us.

After I've wrung out the clothes and draped them by the fire to dry, there are the goats to milk. By the time I have gotten them into their pen for the night — no small task since I haven't a clue what I'm doing — it is nearly dinnertime. I trudge back to the house, my body aching, muscles I have not used in two months already protesting my afternoon's work.

I pause at the door of the cottage, surprised to hear voices coming from within. Val and Stormwind have barely exchanged a dozen sentences since their initial conversation. Even though Val has joined us each evening before the fireplace, both of them have directed their conversation to me, treating the other with careful distance. But now they're together, in the cottage, having a full-blown discussion.

I tilt my head, listening. The door has been left cracked open, and Val and Stormwind must not be far from it, for their voices are easily distinguishable.

"You've heard of the Shadow League?" Val asks now.

"Yes." The word is flat, emotionless.

"She was with them, helping a family escape Blackflame."

"I thought you were running from Lord Kol." Stormwind's voice remains cool.

"Blackflame caught her, thinking she was the Ghost. When he realized she wasn't who he wanted, he passed her on to Kol."

I close my eyes, trying to envision what he says. But I don't recall helping any family, let alone hearing of a Shadow League.

"Passed her from Karolene to Godan?" Stormwind asks.

"You are a mage," Val observes. "You know about portals. Blackflame opened one to Kol's fortress. I watched them arrive from the tower window."

Stormwind digests this news in silence. I stay still, barely daring to breathe. Val has never mentioned a word of this to me. I want to hear as much as I can before he realizes I'm listening.

"How do you know this when she doesn't?" Stormwind asks abruptly.

"Kol never knew when to stop talking. He told me her story when he brought her for me." Val's voice is tinged with contempt.

"But you didn't tell her."

I hear a faint creak of floorboards as Val shifts his weight. "If the details are wrong, they will reshape her memories. Maybe Kol didn't know the truth. If she remembers, she remembers. For now, I want her here, not searching for who she was." He sounds irritated, but I cannot tell if he is frustrated with me or himself.

"You think she'll leave if she knows?"

Val sighs. "I don't know. She has a strong sense of honor."

A silence.

"You seem quite certain that I'll take her," Stormwind says.

Val laughs, a humorless sound. "You are not the only mage living between Godan and this little valley."

"Then—"

"I brought her to you, Mage Stormwind, because Blackflame orphaned her and threw her to a fang and still has her mother."

I cross my arms over my chest, trying to feel something — shock? Anger? Confusion? But all I feel is a deep and unvarying grayness, as if the fire has taken a part of my emotions as well. I know what Val speaks of, but it is a knowing that resides in my mind while my heart beats steady and untouched.

Stormwind's voice is almost tentative. "And why would that matter?"

"Why *would* that matter to you?" Val replies, turning it into a rhetorical question. There is some secret here, I realize, some story of Stormwind's past that Val knows. A reason why he chose her of all mages to train me.

"You know a great deal about mages for a breather," Stormwind says.

"No," Val replies. "Breathers are always aware of mages and their politicking, if for no other reason than because we want nothing to do with you. It is you mages who know nothing of us."

"Indeed."

I hesitate a moment longer on the doorstep, but it's only a matter of time before I'm discovered. I shift my weight and put my foot down heavily, then push the door open. I stop abruptly, just inside, as if surprised to see them there. I can hardly bear to look at Val, remembering his words from earlier, realizing now how much more he knows about me than I do, how much he has held back from me. *You didn't have any right*, I want to snap at him. *It is my life, my history, that you're keeping from me.* But I can't say the words here, and then it doesn't matter anymore, because Val walks past me without a glance, leaving me alone in the cottage with Stormwind.

THE NEXT MORNING, having finished his work on the roof, Val goes out to the forest with one of the horses to haul in dead wood. Once he has brought in enough, he begins to chop it on the old stump behind the cottage, building up our wood pile to last the rest of the winter. Mistress Stormwind lets me off my chores in the afternoon, and I find myself watching him from around the corner of the cottage.

All the previous evening, as the three of us sat before the fire, I had turned over Val's words, thought about him, considered what he told me and what he kept back. While I don't agree with what he did, I can understand why he did it.

He will leave soon, and I don't want us to part on bad terms. Last night he barely acknowledged me at all, his attention focused on his carvings. I had felt awkward, too acutely observed to find a way to break the silence between us in Stormwind's presence. Now I watch him from the corner of the cottage, wondering how to begin speaking to him again.

He has taken off his cloak, his work having warmed him enough against the chill winter air. He moves methodically, the chips occasionally flying from the wood in little showers. I watch him split a short length of trunk in half and then quarter it. Then he sets his ax down and looks up, catching me peeping around the corner at him. I flush with embarrassment, stepping back.

"If you're going to watch me," Val calls, "you may as well make yourself useful."

So, while he chops, I stack the wood by the cottage wall and help him haul larger pieces over to be cut. The work is good, and while my muscles ache and my steps slow over the course of the afternoon, I am glad to be doing something.

"Would you just sit down?" Val finally snaps, pointing at a log he has yet to chop. "I don't want you falling over from exhaustion. Mistress Stormwind would have my hide."

I laugh. He smothers a smile and turns back to his chopping.

"You never told me your name," I say as he finishes the log he's on. He shrugs. "I started calling you Val because that's what Kol called you. Is it really your name?"

"It's close enough," he says, hefting another piece of wood.

"You know my name," I point out. "And both of my parents' names."

He doesn't answer until he has split and chopped the next log. As he tosses the pieces onto the pile beside the stump he says, "Valerius."

I hug my knees, grinning up at him. He pretends not to notice. "And you're about twenty-five years old."

He slides me a long look.

"Well, aren't you?"

"I'm a breather," he says with great patience. He seems to say that quite a lot.

"So?"

"Breathers age more slowly than humans. It has been a long time since I was twenty-five."

I chew my lip, recalling vaguely how he had called me "little one" at first. It's hard to reconcile those first images of him with the breather before me now.

He chops another log. "Did Mistress Stormwind say anything about your hair?" he asks.

I grin, unaccountably amused. "What hair?"

"That is, in fact, my concern."

"You haven't considered the benefits of being bald," I tell him. I list the advantages, ticking them off on my fingers, "No lice, no worries about how to tie it up, no need to dry it in winter, nothing for anyone to grab you by, and," I pause, trying to come up with one more reason.

"Nothing to keep your brain warm," Val supplies.

I laugh.

He returns to his chopping and doesn't speak again. I watch him, breathing in the scent of just-cut wood and letting myself rest in this moment, this new memory that I will be able to look back to once he's gone.

THAT NIGHT, while Val sits with his bits of wood, carving, Mistress Stormwind introduces me to the art of spinning, which she can do wonderfully and which I cannot do at all. She uses the wool she has collected from her goats, and I realize unhappily that she has three large bags set aside for her winter spinning, work that I must now learn to do as well. By the end of the night, I am able to produce spans of yarn as long as my hand and as lumpy as bad porridge. Val watches with great amusement.

"What are you grinning about?" I snap at him.

"Nothing at all," he says solemnly.

"I suppose you know *exactly* how to spin," I prod. "Why don't you show us how good you are?" I hold my spindle out to him.

Mistress Stormwind watches me with an expression of faint disapproval.

"All right," Val says and plucks the spindle from my hand. In the space of three breaths he has spun an arm's length of thread that even I can tell is as fine as any Mistress Stormwind has made that night.

"Good enough?" he asks with a wicked smile.

"Terrible," I tell him, snatching the spindle back.

"It just takes practice," he consoles me. "You should have plenty of time for that here."

"Thanks a lot," I grumble. He smiles pleasantly and returns to his carving.

Later on, as I lie in my little patched-together bed of blankets and straw in the loft, I wonder how a breather learned to mend roofs and chop wood and carve little creatures and, strangest of all, spin wool. Perhaps in all his traveling, he came across a land where the men did the spinning rather than the women. I fall asleep still musing over the possibilities.

In the morning, Val is gone.

I know it the moment I wake, an almost physical awareness, as if the air I breathe has lost its moisture, or a color has disappeared overnight so that, on waking, I find a world without amber or topaz, or amethyst.

I check for the horses behind the goat pen where we corralled them every night. They are gone, as is the gear we stored beneath the roof's overhang. I follow the path up to the woods, and then farther, watching for where the horses' hooves bit into the dirt or sank into wet patches.

At the top of the ridge, I stop. The trail continues, descending and winding through the trees. He must have left before the dawn, careful of seeing even a moment of the sun's light on what would have been the fourth day of his stay. I turn back to the cottage, wishing I had said good-bye last night.

Mistress Stormwind stands at the table when I enter, her hands dusted with flour, a round of dough before her.

"He didn't say good-bye," I blurt from the doorway.

"You'd better have your breakfast. There are plenty of chores to be done before we can get to your studies."

I let myself glare at her back for a moment before serving myself a bowl of oats from the pot by the fireplace. When I bring it to the table, I notice an object waiting where I normally sit.

"What's this?" I set my bowl down and pick up the piece of wood, turning it around in my hand. It's one of Val's carvings, small and compact as they all are.

"I suspect it's his farewell," Mistress Stormwind says. "He left it there this morning before you came down. I assumed he wished for you to see it at breakfast."

I set the carving next to my bowl and study it as I eat, running my fingers over the sleek head and rippling feathers, the wood smooth to my touch. It is a little crow with its head bent down against its breast, its beak holding a key. I can't keep from smiling.

I slip the crow into my skirt pocket when I am done, holding it tight in my hand. "What will you teach me first?" I ask Mistress Stormwind.

"Discipline." She eyes me severely. "Everything you have told me about your castings indicate sloppy use of energy. You will learn to be exact and careful in all that you do."

I find myself wishing I'd followed Val. Although, considering I nearly toasted myself with my last spell, I suppose she has a point. I push myself to my feet, "Yes, Mistress Stormwind."

"You have not fed the chickens yet, or milked the goats."

I almost laugh. Somehow, though her words are hardly gentle or loving, they have a comfortable ring to them that I can't quite place. It's like a memory that's more dream than real: beneath the scent of ash I catch a trace of a familiar place, a home I may have never had.

I cross to her and hug her quickly, before I lose my nerve. She stands stiffly, her brow creased in surprise.

"Thank you, Mistress Stormwind," I say, and go to see about the chickens and the goats.

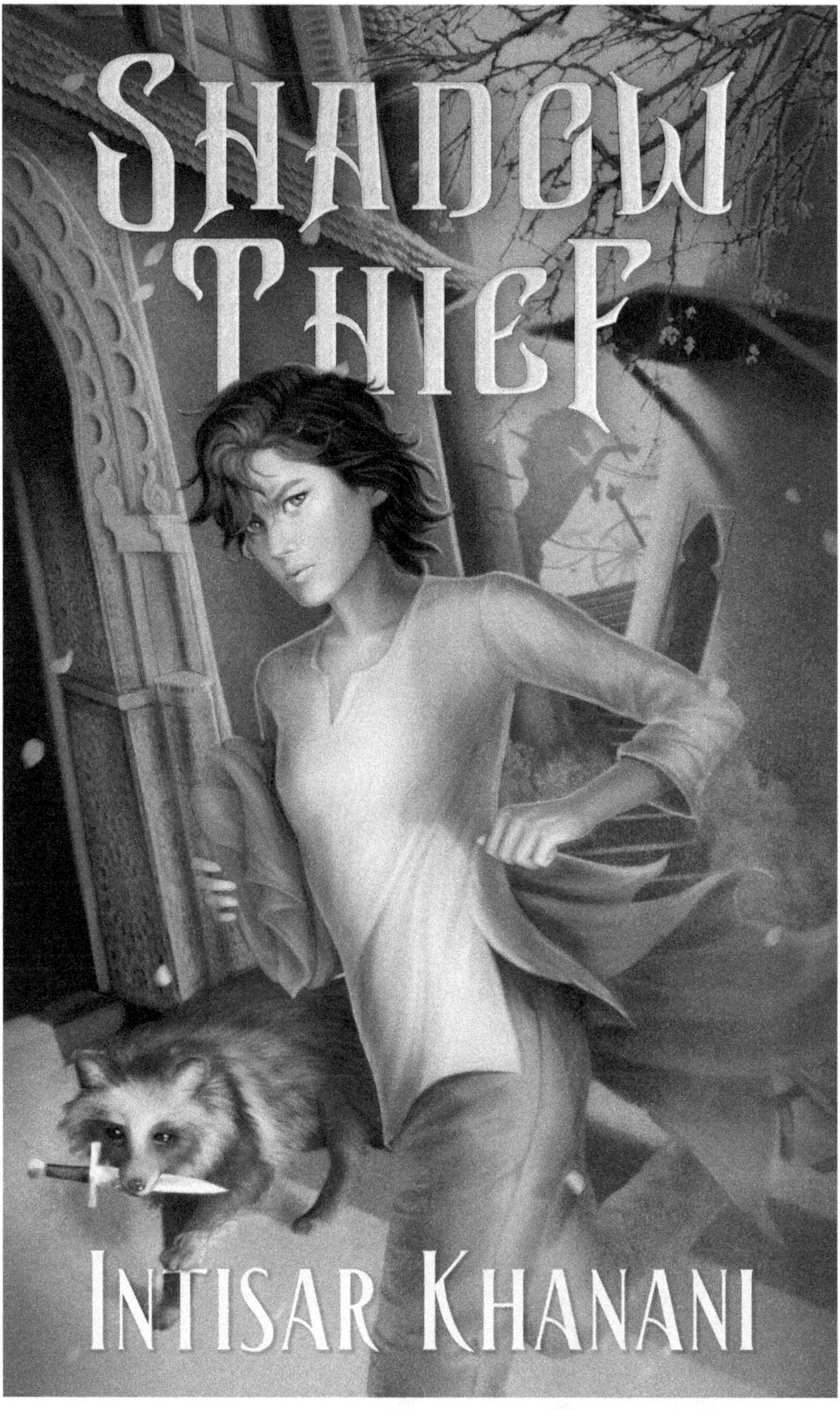
SHADOW THIEF
INTISAR KHANANI

A Sunbolt Prequel Novella

Shadow Thief

Intisar Khanani

Snowy Wings
PUBLISHING

I. TROUBLE

The scent of bread and pastries drifting through the back door of the Golden Cup makes my stomach growl. I pause in the kitchen yard, listening to the sound of voices and the clank of pots from within, wondering how likely it is they'll have work for me.

The Golden Cup is the last stop on my rounds of the various establishments that *might* be willing to trade a morning's work for a meal. I rarely come here. The Cup is a well-known teahouse that brings in some of the wealthiest merchants and even a few nobles. Three stories high, its tiled roofs curve up at the ends, supported by painted pillars. The geometric woodwork across the walls speaks of the owners' close ties to the eastern kingdoms. Perhaps that—the tenuous connection of a shared heritage—might tempt the cook into offering me a little work in exchange for food.

Enough dithering. Gathering my hopes, I cross the hard-packed earth to the kitchen door. As I raise a hand to knock against the doorframe, the cook turns toward me, a paring knife in his hands. He's new, and not of the eastern kingdoms at all, his skin the deep brown of the local islanders.

"I've no work for you," he says before I even open my mouth. "Better try the fish markets." He turns, calling an order to one of the kitchen staff.

But I've already been to the fish markets this morning. While the women who run the stalls know me, they're only two fists away from poverty themselves. There are few errands they can't send their own children on, though they'll sometimes keep a job for me if they can. It's a kindness I appreciate and try not to abuse too often. Nor did the docks have anything to offer, nor anywhere else I've tried.

I stand a moment longer in the doorway, but there's no point in staying, or begging. I rub my chest as I leave, as if I could rub away the disappointment, the terrible smallness knotted there. Which is no more possible than rubbing away my hunger.

I trudge across the wide square before the Cup and find a wall to sit beneath where I can't be charged with driving off customers. Those passing by barely spare me a glance, their minds on other matters. The morning is already turning muggy, spring easing into summer. Another season passed begging for odd jobs and trying to keep clear of trouble, and another season of the same approaching.

I lean my head against the wall and admit I'm tired. Wrung out by the daily scrabble to survive, with nothing but the worry of where my next meal will come from to carry me forward. I have friends, but it's awkward when your friends know how needy you are. It's uncomfortable, and sometimes the best way to keep them is to pretend you don't need anything at all. Or you only need little things—the occasional piece of fruit, or the odd job run. Except I don't like lying, and wish—how I *wish*—I had the sort of family that my friends do, always there in a wide network that makes sure each child is raised well, each person cared for. When someone falls down, a dozen people step in to help them because they are kin.

My hand comes to rest on the lump in my pocket, my most prized possessions, bundled up in a bit of fabric. We can't all have our wishes, after all. It's a truth I've come to terms with: my family is gone. My friends are kind, but they cannot do everything for me.

I still have to eat.

I've stolen before, but usually only small things, just enough to feed me for a day until I can find work again. But I hate it, hate taking from others who are only a few steps further away from poverty than I am. Nor do I want to get caught and thrown in prison for my transgressions. I've been there once before, and I don't ever want to go back. Most importantly, I don't want to disappoint those who have given me their kindness—people like Tendaji, who negotiated my release from prison when I was taken in for being homeless, and who still checks in on me every few weeks.

I look up, watching the passersby. Perhaps I'll see someone who needs help carrying their packages, or their shopping basket. Perhaps I'll see—I pause, blinking as I spot a familiar head of shaggy hair, chestnut streaked with black. There's no mistaking that mane, as unusual here as my own sand-gold skin. There's also no question that Kenta shouldn't be here—passing the Golden Cup and heading into the smaller alleys with their shoulder-to-shoulder buildings that house the poorer families of Karolene. Kenta works for his uncle's business back on the docks, dealing with the merchant ships, and it's still only morning. Yet here he is, striding into the cramped streets with a clear sense of purpose.

There's really only one reason I can think of that Kenta would slip away from his duties. And while I *know* the Shadow League—and Tendaji specifically—won't want me meddling, I

163

can't help the force that pushes me to my feet and after Kenta. It's a mystery, at least, and that's better than having to decide if I'm going to try to steal a bit of fruit, or if I can afford to wait until evening to search for a day-end errand to pay for it.

It only takes me a minute to catch up, and then I fall back into a walk. Kenta leaves the poorer neighborhoods via a cross street that cuts through the metalsmiths' road, then continues on, turning into the smaller alleys that run past the tanners' stinking wells of ammonia. A circuitous route. Either I've been less circumspect than I thought and he suspects he's being followed, or he's just muddying his path as a precaution, which would make perfect sense if he's doing something for the Shadow League.

I pause at the mouth of an alley, leaning against the white-painted adobe wall and waiting for Kenta to draw farther ahead of me. A broader road intersects with ours a little ways on. I frown as Kenta casts a sharp glance down the road and then starts walking faster, his head bowed.

Trouble, though what kind I'm not sure. I hurry ahead, not wanting to lose him. As I near the corner, the people around me change. Pedestrians move quickly away from the main road, their shoulders brushing the buildings as they walk, most of them quiet, although someone calls a word to the food vendor at his stall just this side of the intersection.

Their actions tell me everything I need to know. I risk a glance anyway as I reach the main road, keeping close to the opposite buildings. Down the center of the broad avenue stroll a group of five mercenaries. Their earth-brown skin is not that different from the locals', but these mainlanders are taller, and they wear black bands around their right arms proclaiming their service to Arch Mage Blackflame.

I keep walking. Kenta turns down a side road, disappearing from sight. If I want to catch him, I need to speed up, but I don't dare run and attract the mercenaries' attention. Better to cut down another alley and try to loop around to him. But the gaps between the buildings are too tight to squeeze through. Kenta has taken the first turn he can, and all I can do is try to get there myself.

I hurry toward it, the spreading quiet behind me making my skin prickle. From the back, my smooth black hair might set me apart, but at least I'm wearing the same short tunic and loose pants as the local boys. Hopefully they won't get close enough to spot me as a poor foreigner and easy game. I certainly don't want them to realize I'm not a boy at all.

Behind me, I hear a shout. I pivot on instinct to face the sound. One of the mercenaries stumbles sideways while the remaining four burst into raucous laughter. I watch, knowing I should make a run for the alley, but still unsure what has happened. The stumbler rubs his head, cursing. A lemon rolls to a stop some distance away from him, a second in the hand of one of the other mercenaries. He tosses it once and then lobs it at his comrade.

The lemon bounces off his chest, and the man snarls in fury, barreling forward to grab the perpetrator and slam him sideways into the small wooden food stall by the corner. A great pot of fragrant urojo soup flies off the counter as the whole structure topples, the supports splintering as they hit the cobblestones. The plate of lemons that once sat on the counter sends golden globes rolling across the road.

The vendor has already retreated: he stands plastered against the building behind him, hands pressed to his mouth, watching his livelihood being smashed to pieces before his eyes. My hands curl into fists. I might steal to survive, but I would never engage in such wanton destruction.

The first mercenary stands over the wreckage, laughing. His friend-in-arms scrabbles to right himself and he offers him a hand up, pretending to dust his adversary off. They're all laughing now. Then they look over, straight at the vendor. He drops his eyes, staring at the cobbles under his feet as if they might save his life.

It takes everything in me not to cross to him and help him pick up the pieces of what's left. But I can't afford to draw the mercenaries' attention—no one can. We all stand still in our places, waiting, like puppets whose strings are knotted past saving.

With a dismissive shake of his head, the first mercenary turns away, his friends following after him. The moment their backs are turned, three onlookers move toward the vendor. That's good at least. They'll have more to offer than I do. Though I might do some good through the Shadow League, if Tendaji will just allow me.

I turn, heading for the alley again, as if I hadn't been watching the mercenaries. I can hear them talking, voices loud and carrying at my back as I make the turn. But no matter that I'm facing away, I can't shake the sight of the food vendor, his livelihood destroyed. If he's lucky, the people around him will help him cobble together the wood for another stand, and the money to buy new ingredients. Neighbors might send over enough food that the family can get by for a few days, but no one in his circles will have enough to help him start over quickly and easily. It will be a struggle with no certainty that he won't slip into the same poverty I've grown used to. All because of a handful of mercenaries who shouldn't be here at all.

When I first arrived in Karolene three years ago, the mercenaries were as new to the island as I. There would be an outcry when they marched through the markets and down the roads and broke or stole things. Sellers would shout at them and passersby would chastise them. But now, no one dares. It only took a few dozen disappearances, broken bodies showing up behind the sultan's prison, for people to realize that opposing Blackflame's men would mean death, or worse.

There's only one group that has managed to oppose them with any success, and that's the Shadow League, an underground network of locals and the odd foreigner working together to undermine Blackflame's efforts. But even if I know both Tendaji and his son, the core leadership of the movement, that doesn't mean they want my involvement. They don't.

Doesn't mean I won't help if I can.

I scan the alley, but there's no sign of Kenta. I break into a jog, and take the first left on instinct—if the mercenaries threw Kenta off track and he was close to his destination, that's the direction he'll be heading. At the next intersection, I spot a bright-eyed boy playing a game with a set of colored stones and a stick.

"Did you see a young man come through here?" I ask. "He has big, shaggy brown hair streaked with black."

The boy grins and points to my right. "That way."

"Thanks," I say and head down the road. The buildings have grown close together, the roads winding and curving around them, occasionally passing right through them, the walls creating tunnels.

Another minute, and I spot Kenta ahead of me. He disappears into a darkened doorway.

I frown as I draw near, my sandals slapping against the hard-packed dirt. I don't know this building. Perhaps I'm wrong—perhaps Kenta came here on some errand for his uncle. Perhaps—

Kenta steps out of the doorway, arms crossed and chin raised. "Is there a reason you're following me?"

I come to a stop before him, panting slightly. "You're not at work."

His brows shoot up, and I catch the faint gleam of amusement in his gold-flecked eyes. "*That's* why?"

No, it isn't. I look down, shuffle my feet. He sighs, and I know he's about to shoo me away.

"I thought there might be something wrong with one of our friends," I say a little too quickly. "I thought I might be able to help."

He looks me over. It isn't an unkind look, just measuring and thoughtful, and yet I feel small before him, from the mess of my short-cropped hair, to the patched-up pants and tunic that are meant for a boy, to the tips of my dirty toes in their twice-mended sandals.

"Go home," he says finally. "This doesn't involve you."

"Home" is a vacant rooftop I rent the right to sleep on each night that I have a coin for it—which won't be tonight. There's not much shelter to be had there, regardless.

"It never does," I say, because it's clearly the Shadow League that's brought him out this morning. "But I can still help."

"Were you followed? There were mercenaries back there."

"I saw. They were too busy destroying a food stall to be bothered." I kept a watch behind me just in case, but there hadn't been a hint of anyone following me. "What's the harm in letting me come along?"

"It's not my decision," he says coolly.

I drop my gaze to the dusty hallway. I doubt I'll be able to follow Kenta after this—he'll be watching for me too closely—and even so, I won't be able to worm my way into the meeting, regardless.

Kenta sighs. "This is a small meeting. Hamidi just invited a handful of people."

"Hamidi?" I echo, my stomach tightening into a knot. Hamidi is only three years my senior, and I'm still treated like a child. He also doesn't usually call meetings; Tendaji does. "Has something happened to his father?"

Kenta stiffens. "It's not for you to worry about."

That's as clear an affirmation as I could ask for. "What happened?" I press. "Was he arrested? He was, wasn't he?"

Kenta shakes his head. "This isn't for you—"

If he says that again, I'm going to scream. "I've been to prison before. If they've taken him to the sultan's prison, then I can tell you what to expect. I've seen it. I can help you. You *are* planning to get him out, aren't you?"

Tendaji is the heart of the Shadow League. Without him, the small network of informants and activists could easily fall apart while Arch Mage Blackflame tightens his hold on the sultan and the islands as a whole. That's not something I'll stand idly by and watch happen. And as sure as the seven hells, I'm not going to let anything happen to Tendaji when he was the one who found me orphaned on the streets three years ago and stopped to help instead of walking on.

Kenta rubs his chin, looking away from me. "We're discussing what to do."

"Let me come. At least I can share what I know of how the prison works, how best to get to him."

I could wish, at this moment, that I knew Kenta well enough to convince him to take me along on the basis of our friendship. He clearly hails from the same land as my mother, but he's wealthy and I'm not. I might know him by sight, and have learned who he is, but I wouldn't call him a friend. I doubt he remembers my name.

"Fine." His tone is grudging at best. "But if Hamidi tells you to leave, you'll do as he says."

"Of course." I beam at him. "Thank you."

Kenta shrugs and gestures to the alley at my back. "Let's go."

2. DISAPPEARED

Kenta sets a brisk pace, but he's not much taller than I am. I can keep up without having to trot after him like a stray puppy. He doesn't speak and, for fear of losing my welcome, neither do I. We leave behind the tanners' neighborhood and cross into a wealthier district. Less than ten minutes later, we climb the steps to a pair of turquoise-painted double doors. They're lovely, the wood carved in a floral pattern and inlaid with bronze.

"Whose house is this?" I ask as Kenta knocks.

"Rafiki's," Kenta says, eyeing me askance.

"Oh," I say and shut my mouth. Rafiki is one of the oldest members of the Shadow League. I met him once, with Tendaji. Rafiki made it abundantly clear what he thought of me then.

A moment later, Rafiki himself opens the door. He's a thickset, broad-shouldered man with a head like a bull's and the temper to match. "Kenta," he says, making to step back. But then he sees me. "What's *she* doing here?"

"I asked her along," Kenta says, his voice cool. "May we come in?"

"I'll not have a thief looking through my house."

I bite back a sharp retort. If it weren't Tendaji's safety I'm here about, I'd be answering back already. But if I want entry, I have to ignore his words.

"I see," Kenta says. "Then please let Hamidi know I'll be sitting on your steps for the meeting."

I stare at him. Is he serious?

"*You* can come in," Rafiki says, glowering. "I won't have her."

"As is your right," Kenta agrees, and turns to sit on the step, one leg stretched out as if he were perfectly content to lounge there all day. "Have a seat," he says to me, patting the step.

"Get up," Rafiki snarls, glaring at Kenta's back.

I sit at once, fighting a smile.

"This is not a joking matter," Rafiki says. "You'll be wanted inside and she will not. I can't imagine why you brought her."

"You could ask," Kenta observes, resting an elbow on the step behind him. "But the truth is, she's been through the prison. We'll need that—"

"Of course she has! She's a thief and a criminal."

"I was put in prison because I'm an orphan and they didn't have anywhere else to put me," I snap, unable to help myself. I rise to face him, fury coursing through me. "That's what they do with the homeless children they pick up. They show us the prison to make sure we know we don't want to be there. That's not a tour you forget." I was there nearly a week before Tendaji found out where I was and came to negotiate my release.

"And you still thieve." Rafiki's voice drips with contempt. "Stupid enough to get caught, and still too stupid to stop."

"I can hear you halfway down the street," a voice says quietly. I twist to see Hamidi standing at the bottom of the steps. He looks up at us steadily. "This is neither the place nor the time for an argument, Rafiki."

"She's a *thief*."

"I can help," I tell Hamidi, struggling to keep my voice calm. "I've been inside the prison. If you're planning to get him out, there's a chance I know something that could help."

He considers me, and for once there's not a trace of laughter in his brown eyes. He's taller than me, with well-shaped lips and a sculpted nose. His hair, like his father's, has slightly looser curls than most islanders', falling in short ringlets that frame his face. He glances down at Kenta. "This was your idea?"

"I brought her with me," Kenta agrees, which is impressively generous of him.

Hamidi returns his regard to me. "All right, Hitomi. Come in and share your thoughts. But I don't want you more involved than that."

Of course he doesn't. He never does. I can't help an exultant grin.

"I don't think—" Rafiki begins.

"We can either come in or move the meeting elsewhere," Hamidi says, his voice cutting through Rafiki's protestations. "My father depended on you. His life is now in question. Will you let us in?"

He may be young, but he knows how to handle people.

Rafiki takes a deep, uneven breath, his lips pressed together in dislike, and then he steps back, holding open the door. "Come in," he says. And then, to me, "If even one thing goes missing from my house, I'll have you whipped."

I snort. "I wouldn't want anything in here anyhow."

Behind me, Kenta gives a single cough of laughter.

Rafiki slams the door shut behind us and stalks across the main hall, an exquisitely appointed space with woven cushions, thick carpets, and ornate octagonal tables inlaid with brasswork. We follow him up the stairs to a meeting room that contains a large central table surrounded by chairs. A trio of brass lanterns hang from chains above it, casting a warm glow across the room. The shutters remain closed.

A man sits at the table, tapping his fingers against the polished surface. Before him is set a silver-inlaid tray with a platter of fresh-cut fruit and a handful of small plates. Anywhere else, I'd sit down and help myself, but not here. Not with Rafiki watching.

"Abasi," Hamidi says in greeting at the same time as the man at the table says, "What is the news?"

Hamidi sits down at the head of the table. "A group of soldiers came to our home this morning. I was out."

"How long ago?" Abasi asks. I've heard his name before but never met him. Like Rafiki, he's been part of the Shadow League since its early days, and has donated more than once to help fund their operations.

I take a seat around the corner from Hamidi and keep my mouth shut. It's time for me to listen, try to learn what I can best do to help.

Hamidi hesitates. "About two hours ago," he says. "They came to the house and dragged him out. No explanation. My mother said they wouldn't tell her what they were charging him with. Just took him and left." He runs a hand through his hair, his fingers catching on his ringlets until he's pulled them back tight.

"But how did they find him?" Kenta demands. "Who could have betrayed his involvement?"

Hamidi lets his hand drop. "I don't know. I've already moved the rest of my family to safety, though."

I frown, staring hard at the table. Tendaji worked hard to protect his family, and even I know little about his life. His work-roughened hands suggest he has a trade not quite as genteel as Rafiki's—or Abasi's, whatever he does—perhaps that has helped to keep his identity from being discovered. Still.... "There are not

173

that many people who know who your father is," I say slowly. "I've known you three years and I don't know where you live."

Kenta sucks in his breath, but I'm not leaving this open to interpretation. "Whoever betrayed you knows you very well, which means they likely know other members of the League, too."

"We'll warn the League," Hamidi says. "We can't afford more disappearances."

It was precisely these kinds of disappearances that the Shadow League formed to stop. At first, Tendaji and his supporters tried to find the missing and free them, but that proved nearly impossible. So the League shifted to developing informants in a bid to learn who would be arrested next and warning those in danger. From there, the League has only grown, developing covert strategies to oppose each new change in laws the sultan has considered—and more often than not passed—all proposed by Arch Mage Blackflame. Laws that imprison anyone who protests, increase taxes on those who can least afford them, favor foreign traders over our own, and shut down schools that once stood as bastions of free thought and scholarship. Karolene is changing, quickly and deeply, and none of it for the better.

The Shadow League is the only remaining group protesting such changes, its secrecy the main reason Blackflame has yet to break it.

"What of your father?" Rafiki demands. "We must try to get him back. If the sultan's soldiers—or this conniving northland mage's mercenaries—manage to keep him, it could well be a death blow to the Shadow League."

"I don't know where he was taken," Hamidi says. "I've checked with our informants. No leads. Not one. My best guess is the sultan's prison."

"Then we try there," Kenta says.

"How?" Abasi asks.

That is the sticking point. The League hasn't attempted such a rescue since the first year of its inception because failure was nearly assured, along with the arrest of the would-be rescuers. At Hamidi's request, I describe the prison as I remember it, guard room by guard room and level by level. "They keep the most dangerous prisoners in the deepest cells," I explain.

"If we send someone to visit him," Rafiki says, "they'll bring him out, though, won't they? So we would only have to break him out of the visiting room, not his cell."

I shake my head. "No. That might work for a regular prisoner, but if they know who he is, they won't let him leave his cell. They would take his visitors to him. But they don't allow visitors to such prisoners anyhow."

"Then how do we reach him?" Kenta demands.

I don't know.

The conversation continues, one idea after another offered up before being dissected and found lacking. Hamidi's voice, usually so smooth and confident, is now alternately rushed and halting; he's clearly shaken. Was this all a game to him before? It never was for me, not since my mother disappeared three long years ago when she went to visit Blackflame, weak with an illness she couldn't treat, and never came back again. I've always known the risks, despite what Kenta thinks. Or how little Hamidi and his father have allowed me to do in support of the Shadow League.

I'm not going to let Tendaji disappear from my life as my mother did, not if I can help it. The prison won't allow visitors ... but what if we're not there to visit?

I look up. "I know how to get you in."

The conversation shudders to a halt.

"How?" Hamidi asks, watching me steadily.

"We claim your father has committed a crime—that we think he stole from one of you," I nod toward Rafiki and Abasi. "They

175

won't want to take him any visitors, but they'll be more than happy to have something else to blacken his reputation with, especially if someone of substance is making the charge. They'll take you in to see him. Alas, you'll discover he isn't the criminal you're seeking. But we'll have seen the location of his cell, and if I go with you, I'll know exactly what the locks look like."

"You think you can pick them?" Hamidi asks.

"Most likely. I'll need you to get me a shadow charm from a mage to hide me—and your father, if I can get him out. When the guards lead us out—whichever of you brings the charges against Tendaji—I'll follow them back in with the charm, work the locks, and help Tendaji escape."

"That simple," Hamidi says. I can't quite place his tone.

"Probably not," I admit. "But it's the best plan we have."

It definitely will not be that easy—having been inside the prison, I know there will be guard rooms to navigate, locks as well as bolts on doors, an open courtyard to cross with sentries posted, and only one gate to leave from, always guarded. But I have to at least try.

What I don't mention now is the one secret I've never shared with anyone here: that I carry another weapon in the magic I inherited from my parents. As old as I am, my Promise has become a burden rather than a boon—my parents never declared my talent when I was young, and now I'm past the age of training. If I'm caught, I'll either be bound to another mage as a source slave and forced to let them use my magic for their own needs, or it will be stripped from me altogether. That process often takes a person's mind along with their magic, leaving them a husk of their former self.

I use my magic sparingly and admit it to no one. But I would use it to rescue Tendaji.

Abasi rubs his hand over his mouth, then shakes his head. "We would have no reason to bring an unrelated boy in with us.

You're clearly not from our families. And frankly, petty theft is not an ugly enough crime for the soldiers to care to add that to his name. We'd need something worse, and a clear reason for *you* to go in."

"Worse like what?" Kenta asks.

A pause, and then Rafiki says, "Murder, but then we would need a body." Which, obviously, we don't have. And with the Shadow League's dedication to justice and overcoming violence, murder is certainly not on the agenda.

Abasi leans back. "There are only a few great crimes they might pay attention to. Murder and assault are the main ones."

"Then you have it," Rafiki says, his gaze cutting to me. "You say he assaulted the girl. She goes in to identify him, but it isn't him; then she goes back in and brings him out."

My stomach twists. No, no, no. That's easy enough for him to say, but I have no one to offer me their protection. If things go wrong, with a story like that, the guards might not stop with a beating. I want to be involved in the Shadow League, to help, especially now, but this ... this I don't know about.

"My father would not," Hamidi says, then shakes his head.

"It's a cruel slander," Rafiki agrees. "But, just as the girl said, when she sees him, she'll realize her imaginary assailant wasn't him."

That's not quite what I said, considering I was talking about theft and not rape.

"What girl?" Abasi demands, bewildered.

Rafiki jerks his head at me. "The street rat."

I give him a dirty look.

"Rafiki," Hamidi says, voice level. "We are sitting at this table together. Her name is Hitomi."

After a moment, Rafiki dips his head. "Right."

"She hardly looks like a girl," Abasi says, as if I wasn't sitting right across from him.

"It's safer on the streets when you look like a boy," I say. "Doesn't change what I am."

He eyes me with concern, then seems to steel himself as he turns to Hamidi. "It could work. The story is sordid enough to please them. Even if she does not break him out, if we know where he is, we will have gained something."

"Perhaps," Hamidi says, his gaze settling on me. He's as aware as I am that I haven't agreed to this yet.

I wonder if he's seeing something different from what he's used to expecting. He and his father found me when I was a child of eleven, hungry and alone on the streets, grief-stricken by the disappearance of my mother. Tendaji found me a place to stay and checked in on me with Hamidi as I learned to survive. I may not have stayed long with the two-faced woman who took me in and beat me every time the floors weren't clean enough, but I haven't forgotten their kindness in trying to help. Both then and over the ensuing years—from meals to odd jobs that might last a season. Unfortunately, they've always thought of me as that lost little girl from the street.

But Tendaji has always been there for me. Perhaps the risks were different for him when he came to get me out of prison, but the risks were certainly there. If he'd been recognized as part of the Shadow League, he would not have escaped with his life. He still came, and I'll do the same for him.

"We should try it," I say, meeting Hamidi's gaze. "But I don't —I don't like going in with them with that sort of story."

Abasi shifts, his brow furrowed, but he doesn't speak.

I take a breath. "If someone's with me, there's not much danger in claiming we want to verify the identity of a criminal. At worst, the guards will turn us back. At best, we'll walk into the prison, see your father, and walk out. If you don't want me to go back for Tendaji after that, I don't have to. If I do go back, it will be as a boy." And we both know there's no one else in this group who can pick a lock; these men are all better born than that.

He nods once, turns toward Kenta. "What do you think?"

"I think," Kenta says slowly, "that I would have to be the one to go with Hitomi." He glances toward me, and I find myself desperately grateful for his words. "If I pose as your stepbrother, no one will question it. And you'll need someone who has clear ties to you in order to get in and out."

Of the men in the room, Kenta is the only choice that won't raise interest or suspicion. The two of us are clearly wageni—foreigners—from the comparative paleness of our skin to the smoothness of our hair, to the shape of our eyes. What differences we have can be explained away through a claim of being only half-siblings, if that. It is a perfect deception. And I'd much rather have him with me than Rafiki or Abasi. He's already stood by me once.

"Agreed," Hamidi says. "But are you willing?"

Kenta shrugs. "I can't think of another plan to trick our way into the prison. So, yes."

"Then we do this as soon as we can," Hamidi says. "Let's work out the details."

3. THE SULTAN'S PRISON

T he sultan's prison was originally built as a fort to stand against the looming threat of invasion from the mainland. As the danger waned and peace was established among the Eleven Kingdoms, the soldiers transferred to newer buildings with wider practice fields and closer to the sultan's palace. The fort sat unused, the story goes, until a great fire destroyed the old prison. The sultan then gave permission for the fort to be converted into a replacement.

We stand before the massive gates, the walls rising easily four times my height, huge round watchtowers looming at either corner. The tops of the towers are crenellated in a manner that is as distinctly pretty as it is practical, as if it were topped with flower buds to protect its long-ago warriors. Now the battlements lie empty, at least where they look out over the city. I know from my time within those walls that there are sentries stationed looking inward instead. The white paint that once coated the walls has worn away completely at the ground level, and remains only in patches higher up, giving the whole structure a grim, dilapidated aspect. Behind us, a row of slender palm trees stand, their fronds rustling in the breeze high above.

"Ready?" Kenta murmurs, glancing at me.

I look back to the great windowless walls and imagine Tendaji behind them, locked in a cell. "Let's go."

We cross the road, threading through the crowds of pedestrians, pausing to allow a man with his handcart full of coconuts to pass. The gates are a pair of huge wooden doors, only one of which is open. A handful of uniformed guards stand before them, swords and daggers at their hips. They watch our approach with disinterest.

"We're here about a prisoner," Kenta says.

"Any weapons?" one of the guards asks.

"No," Kenta assures him. Neither of us wears a belt for a sword or dagger, nor do we carry any bags. I left my own package safely stashed behind a pile of discarded furniture on the rooftop I borrowed my clothes from. The only things I carry are the two shadow charms Rafiki procured for us, wrapped snugly in the folded waistband of the long, brightly patterned skirt I took. The charms are ugly little things, crudely made, and I'm not sure I trust them to do the job, but that's a worry for later. Now I nod solemnly, keeping my eyes downcast.

"Go on, then," the man says, gesturing us through.

The gates open into a small interior courtyard with no way in but a single door into a large, brown brick building. It's as crudely built as the walls, and no more welcoming. A number of men and women wait in the courtyard, leaning against the wall to our left to keep out of the sun. This is where Tendaji met me after negotiating my release.

I remember him as he stood waiting for me, a small, slim man—shorter than Hamidi—with close-cropped tightly curled hair that was edged in gray even then. I can still feel that first burst of gratitude tinged with the despair that had wrapped around me in my week's imprisonment. And I remember how his gaze flicked from me to my soldier escort and back, and his normally gentle expression hardened to furious. I dropped my eyes at that, so ashamed I was here, still afraid I would have to stay, that he would see me in my ragged clothes and unkempt hair and decide I wasn't worth the trouble I caused him.

I remember how he crossed to me, shooing the soldiers away with a wave of his hand. "Hitomi," he said. "Child, look at me."

I looked up, holding myself tight, tight, tight, so he wouldn't see my desperate need.

He lifted a hand to cup the back of my head as if I were his own child, beloved to him in some inexplicable way. "There is no shame in being afraid."

I only stared at him, the taste of ash on my tongue. Because I was afraid, and because he was wrong. I had been brought here like so much trash, and if he had not come for me, I might have spent years here, racking up a debt for my keep that I wouldn't be able to stay ahead of, no matter if they allowed me to work or not.

Tendaji sighed, dropped his hand to squeeze my shoulder, and led me out without another word. I have done my best to never come back here—until now. For Tendaji.

Kenta guides me across the courtyard to the far door, one hand on my elbow, for all the world like a concerned elder brother. He catches my sideways glance and frowns at me. "Play the part," he murmurs.

I am, aren't I? But perhaps not well enough. I drop my head and pull a little closer to him as I count the steps to the other side. With Kenta still attached, I step through the open doorway into a darkened room, blinking to make out the interior. A window has been cut into the wall to my left, a brightly colored fall of cloth keeping the sun's direct rays out.

"What do you want?" A soldier—or perhaps a clerk of some

sort—sits cross-legged on a cushion against the wall to the right, facing us across the room. On the low table before him lies a thick ledger, a small pile of papers beside it.

"Wait here," Kenta tells me, and crosses to kneel before the table. He speaks quietly, as if he does not want to disturb me. I try to look a mix of frightened and sickened.

How would a girl being asked to verify the face of her attacker really look? I think I would be angry. Not just angry, but filled with a wrath that boiled in my blood. I would be ready to find such a man and demand justice be done—only I wouldn't expect that either, would I? Is it possible to be big with rage and still feel small? To vibrate with fury and yet know your own helplessness? I swallow hard, aware that I've started to shake with the anger streaming through me. Because whatever I might feel if this were really me, that looks nothing like the timid creature I'm projecting, one who not only has the support of her stepbrother but also waits meekly upon his aid and protection. No, that's not true; such a girl would feel that same inability to protect herself that I fight every day of my life. So I wrap that smallness around me—the utter helplessness I know too well—and it fits me like a glove.

A faint clink draws my attention back to Kenta in time to see a glimmer of silver disappear beneath the clerk's palm. He slides the coins off the table and into his pocket in a smooth, practiced move. Then he makes a show of making a notation in his ledger. "I don't think it will be a problem. You are not a *visitor*. If a prisoner here has done more than we know, well then, it is our duty to find that out."

Fine words for someone who requires a bribe to consider their duty.

Kenta dips his head, murmuring his thanks, and they rise together, walking back toward me.

"I'll inform Captain Saka," the clerk says, his eyes slide over me, making my skin itch. I look away, biting back an angry word, one that I would never dare speak. Helpless, I remind myself. Just as I have been, but acknowledging it this time. It feels shameful, this act. An embarrassment to admit the truth.

Kenta steps between us, turning to block the man's view of me. "I thank you."

We wait as the clerk disappears through the connecting door into a lamplit room. "We might make it through," Kenta murmurs, keeping his gaze on the half-open door.

"Of course we will," I whisper. "They have their duty, don't they? And you have a few more coins to remind them of it?"

His lips twitch. "A few more," he agrees.

I'm glad of it. The pouch Abasi gave Kenta is small but, I'm relatively certain, filled with silver ryals. Given that I haven't touched more than a copper pysa since my mother disappeared, there's a fortune riding in his pocket.

The door swings farther open, and a man enters, his uniform crisp and clean. The embroidered rank marks at his collar make it clear he is a captain. The clerk follows behind him, speaking quickly. "I told them it might be possible, but of course I gave no promises."

Captain Saka raises a hand, his fingers flicking away these words and effectively silencing the clerk.

"I understand a crime has been committed against the young lady," he says, his gaze coming to rest on me. I drop my eyes, and this time I'm grateful for my act. He has a shrewd gaze. It's not one I particularly wish to meet. I draw closer to Kenta, as if I could hide behind him from the terrors of the world. Though I don't think that really works for anyone.

"If you will, sir," Kenta says respectfully. "We are not sure of the criminal's identity. I believe it was a man who was arrested this morning on other charges—but until my stepsister sees his face, we can't be sure. I want the man brought to justice, but it must be the right man."

"Indeed," the captain says. "If it is the man you seek, there's no need to worry about justice being done. He's been found a traitor already."

Kenta hesitates. "But if it isn't," he says, "then the man who attacked my stepsister might still attack another girl. We need to know. To stop him."

Saka doesn't answer at once. Instead, I feel his knife-sharp gaze on me, measuring me, looking for what lies beneath the surface.

"Please," I say into the quiet, my voice small. I don't even have to pretend.

Kenta doesn't glance at me, but I can sense his tension, the tight line of his shoulders clear through the fabric of his tunic. I'm sure the captain has noticed as well, but it may still work in our favor.

"I see," Captain Saka says. "Follow me."

He turns and steps through the door, holding it for us. The clerk bestows a self-satisfied smile upon us and moves back to his desk.

We follow Saka through to the connecting room, another office of sorts. A second captain lounges on a cushion with a cup of tea in his hand. He ignores us, gazing moodily at the worn carpet beneath his feet.

"This way." Saka strides ahead to yet another door, this one opening into a wide courtyard of hard-packed dirt. One side of the yard is walled off for the prisoners, the wall sporting a series of small windows that allow us glimpses of the score or so men within. I look away, remembering the barren yard on the other side. My breathing unsteady, I force myself to focus on the moment. The sun is edging to its zenith, and without the sea breeze blowing through this space to cool it, the heat is oppressive. Nor are there many shadows here.

I count my steps to the next doorway, increasingly aware of how little help a shadow charm will be in sunlight. Even if the charms are strong enough to hide Tendaji and me, the shadows themselves will be terribly out of place both here and in the smaller courtyard we first passed through. We could wait for evening, but it's a gamble to spend that long inside the prison trying not to be found. And we would still have to get through the rooms with their closed doors without drawing attention. Shadows do not open doors.

The next room we enter is a genuine guard room, the door locked from within. The soldiers stand at attention as we enter, saluting their captain, and move to open the next door with alacrity. It bears not only a lock but also a bolt. I breathe slowly, trying to ease my anxiety. I can pick the lock—from the shape of the key Saka uses, it's clear it's not complex. But that bolt will be a problem. Either we'll have to follow someone else through, or I'll have to use my magic to open it. Both options have their risks.

Saka orders a pair of soldiers to accompany us. Then he unhooks a lantern from beside the door, lights it, and guides us down the darkened hallway, the soldiers falling into step at our back. "When they converted the fort into a prison, they bricked over the windows," Saka tells us. "It will be dark from here on."

The darkness closes around me, stinking of unwashed bodies and despair, as familiar as an old nightmare. I focus on our path, committing each turn to memory, the steps in between. We descend to the lower level of the fort, passing through a hallway lined with cells. The walls are stone, but the doors are metal grates, and through them we see the faint shapes of people, the gleam of eyes looking back at us. There are too many in each cell, far more than the four or five I shared my cell with two years back. How can there be so many prisoners, so many criminals for so small an island archipelago as Karolene?

But I already know the answer to that—these are protesters as well. Men and women who have spoken out against the changes on our island, who pointed their fingers at Blackflame. These are people not unlike Tendaji, though perhaps they did not organize as he did.

"He should be in here," Saka says, stopping at the last door in the hallway. He bangs against the grating with the side of his fist. "Get back!"

The two soldiers enter first, short swords drawn. They herd the dozen or so prisoners against the far wall.

"Where's the one named Omari?" Saka barks, stepping into the room. It is strange knowing Tendaji's real name, hearing it ring out in the dim confines of the cell.

The prisoners don't answer, their eyes squinting against the lamplight. One of them, hidden at the back, begins to whimper.

"I said, *where is Omari?*"

The men press against the wall, all but one. He's tall, his face badly bruised and his clothing tattered. He waves a hand toward the far corner. "There's a man there. Your soldiers brought him in a little while ago. Maybe that's him."

I stiffen, staring at the sprawled figure where it lies in shadow. Saka turns to glare at the figure, then strides over and lands a brutal kick in the man's side. "Get up, man."

The man doesn't respond, not even to cry out or moan or huddle tighter to protect himself. He doesn't move. Bile burns in my throat. He's either dead or unconscious. Regardless, Saka's violence is sickening.

"Get *up.*" The boot connects again.

"Stop," I cry, before I can help myself.

Saka glances over his shoulder, dark eyes fastening on me. He raises his brow.

I press my hand to my mouth, make myself drop my gaze, but I'm shaking now, shaking with fear and fury. The man on the ground *can't* stand—surely Saka can see that? This isn't justice but cruelty, through and through.

"You would protect your attacker?"

I swallow and shake my head as I look back up at him. "Is that him?"

"You tell me," Saka says, jerking his head toward the figure.

Kenta grips my arm. Together, we cross the room to Captain Saka. I stand above the slight frame of the fallen figure, the lamplight shining on a tangle of limbs. The hands are bloodied and broken, the tunic soaked in blood. The man's face is swollen and bruised, the nose broken, and the jagged edge of broken teeth gleaming through torn lips. It's his hair I recognize, the same ringlets as Hamidi's, coated in blood and muck, but the black and gray still showing through. I stare at him, my breath coming in quick, hard gasps.

"Is that the man?" Saka demands.

Looking down at Tendaji, I shake my head.

Saka turns to the remaining prisoners, but I can't tear my eyes away from the man who once saved my life. He lies so dreadfully still, not even his chest rises with breath. "He's dead," I whisper, my voice small. I so desperately don't want it to be true.

"Of course he isn't," Saka says, without looking. "He was interrogated this morning, but men don't die that easily."

They do. I've seen a few bodies in my years on the street and it doesn't always take very much to kill a man. A man can die from wounds that are hidden from the eye, things gone wrong deep inside. I've seen it before—men as strong as lions curled up and cold as stone from a beating that hit them in the gut just so. But just to be sure, I stoop down and touch his wrist—it is cold and limp. There is no pulse at all. Kenta has to steady me as I straighten. The look on my face must answer whatever doubts he had, for he does not speak, his expression tightening with grief.

"Which of you is Omari?" Saka demands of the prisoners, stalking up to them.

I force myself to shift, keep my focus on Saka. Kenta is shaking beside me. Or maybe that's me. It's hard to tell.

The prisoners mutter denials, pressing away from Saka. He frowns at them, and in a moment he will grab one and demand their identity. Perhaps he will kick them, or use his fists to get the answer he wants. All because of me, my plans.

"They're not," I begin and stop, the words catching in my throat. I don't want him to look at me, to guess that my story is a lie, or suspect me of deception. But I can't remain silent when I might spare these men the same violence I fear.

"What's that?" Saka demands.

"Let me just look at their faces," I say, my voice rasping. "I'll know him if I see him."

Saka considers me, then nods. "All of you, turn your heads toward the young lady. Keep your eyes down, hear me?"

The prisoners obey. I stare at their faces, noting the bruises and cracked lips, the set of their shoulders—some slumped in exhaustion, some strung tight in anger or hunched in fear. Kenta walks me along the line of prisoners as I look each one in the face. Whatever they've done or haven't done, they don't deserve this. Justice isn't being beaten to death in a dark room. It isn't terror and pain and confusion. It can't be. They have a right to something better than this; a justice that still sees them as human. These men will either be broken in here, or come out something darker than they were before. It is the rare man who can face such horrors and come out a better person.

"Do you see him?" Saka demands.

I turn toward him, say woodenly, "He's not here."

He sighs. "I am sorry to hear that."

"We thank you for allowing us to check," Kenta says, his voice slightly uneven.

Saka gestures us out.

I cast one last look at Tendaji, lying broken on the floor, and then step into the hall. The guards close the door behind us.

It no longer matters if I can pick its lock.

4. DISMISSAL

Outside the prison, Kenta vomits into the dirt next to a coconut palm. I stand beside him, my stomach roiling, and stare down the road toward the distant blue of the sea. But no matter where I look, I can still see Tendaji's face, bloodied and grotesque in death. I am aware, distantly, that my hands are trembling. I press them against my thighs so no one will notice.

Kenta spits into the dirt one last time, then straightens to lean against the palm. "How are you not ill right now?"

My hands curl into fists. I take a slow breath, answer, "I've been in there before."

He regards me for a little too long. Then he pushes away from the palm and starts walking. My heart drops as he keeps going, his back to me. Somehow, I didn't think he'd walk away like this. But he never offered me anything more than the chance to help, and now I'm no longer needed. Kenta also knows more about me than maybe I should have allowed. Perhaps it's better I only see his back now so I won't see the contempt in his eyes.

He pauses twenty paces on, then glances over his shoulder,

half turning until he catches sight of me. His brow is furrowed. "Aren't you coming?"

I hurry to catch up with him, my heart tapping a lighter rhythm.

"What are you happy about?" he asks, eyeing me strangely.

"Nothing," I say, embarrassed. "Just thought you didn't want me anymore."

The wrinkles in his brow deepen. "You used to people walking out on you?"

I start forward, struggling to hold on to that moment of happiness, but it's already trickling through my fingers like water. Why do so many things have to hurt? Kenta falls into step with me, but he's still waiting. "My mother didn't," I say finally. "She meant to come back. She just died before she could."

He doesn't answer.

We take a long, convoluted way through the city to ensure that no one has followed us. Halfway through, I lead Kenta aside, down a side street to a small square where a wealthy merchant built a fountain, providing water to any who need it. We take turns drinking from the tin cup on its thin chain.

"How do you do it?" Kenta asks as I set the cup down.

"Do what?"

"I understand you've seen violence before, but—that was Tendaji. He was kind to you."

I look away, then back at him, anger sparking in my breast. "What should I do? Fall apart while the guards watch? That would only attract their attention, and I can't afford that. I don't have the privilege of knowing I'll be safe from them—ever. So. I hold myself together."

"And now?"

"And now, what?" I demand. "I haven't eaten since yesterday. Whatever I have in my stomach needs to stay there. I am holding myself together, Kenta, because no one is going to pick up the pieces for me if I don't."

The gold in his eyes seems to waver, disappearing into the brown. He dips his head and gestures to the road. I fall into step with him silently, and somehow, it's comfortable rather than awkward. As if I hadn't just snapped at him for asking how I can look at horrors and still keep myself together. Perhaps I should have mentioned the men I saw beaten when I was held in the prison, or the women who were taken away and brought back hours later, weeping and bleeding. Perhaps I should have mentioned the boys I've seen cut down in the street, the bodies I've helped carry from the back of the prison to the graveyards. But really, it's probably better that he doesn't know so much about me.

"You didn't eat at Rafiki's," he observes after a few streets.

"After the welcome he gave me? I'll eat somewhere else. You don't need to worry about me," I add. "I always come out all right in the end."

It's a lie, or at least, it's not wholly truthful, but it's the sort of thing people take comfort in hearing. This way, Kenta won't feel like he needs to be responsible for me, and I won't become a burden to him.

He makes a noncommittal sound, and we continue through the heat to the old bridge over the river where we promised to meet Hamidi. By the time we reach it, I've forgotten our conversation, my mind circling back to Tendaji, bruised and broken and *gone*. And Hamidi, waiting to hear what we learned at the prison.

We clamber down the bank and step beneath the arched stone abutments into the shade. Hamidi waits there, his clothes blending with the deeper shadows. He rises, hurrying toward us, and I find I don't have any words for him. Kenta will have to tell him.

But Kenta bends over, hands on his knees, his face pink from heat.

Hamidi's gaze fastens on me. "What happened? Did you find him?"

"We..." I swallow hard, can't seem to find the words.

Kenta straightens, shakes his head, and I realize he doesn't want to say the words either. That he's avoiding it as much as I am.

"What?" Hamidi asks, his voice taut.

I take a breath, wishing Kenta would speak. "I'm sorry," I say into the waiting quiet. "We saw him. They—they must have interrogated him right away."

"You spoke with him?" Hamidi asks.

I hold myself tightly, say the words I must: "He's dead."

I watch the disbelief flicker in his eyes, the slow shake of his head. Was this what it was like for my mother to tell me, her own heart bleeding as I stood beside my father's deathbed not understanding?

"But he was *home* this morning." Hamidi's voice is that of a young boy's, half his age. It is the voice of an orphan.

"I know."

"You couldn't have been mistaken?"

I shake my head, and finally Kenta speaks. All he says is, "No."

Hamidi turns, walking blindly away from us. He comes to a stop where the sunlight streams over the other side of the bridge. I wait, watching his back, willing him to survive this. It is hard enough when a parent dies. To have them taken from your house and tortured to death—that is another kind of sorrow. Tendaji's bloodied face floats before my vision, and behind it the battered faces of the men who shared his cell, and I find myself shaking with horror and grief and, as I look toward Hamidi's bent head, *fury*.

I clench my fists, staring at his back. Tendaji's death is not going to break Hamidi. It's not going to destroy the Shadow League. *I won't let it.* Hamidi needs to focus, needs to keep moving. He cannot let his father's death spark the fire of revenge within him. Nor can he drift as I did, for days, weeks, lost in a tide of grief.

"They interrogated him," I say, pitching my voice to carry. "We don't know how much information they were able to get from him."

Hamidi turns around slowly, stiffly. With the light falling behind him, he's nothing but a dark silhouette.

"We can't help your father now," I say. "But there are others who haven't been picked up by the guards yet. You know all his informants, you know how many people's true identities he knew. Is there anyone you haven't warned yet?"

He shakes his head. "Rafiki and I have already informed those members most closely connected to the League—people who also might have been betrayed."

That had been their task while Kenta and I infiltrated the prison.

Hamidi rubs his mouth, thinking. "But you're right. There are some I should have realized I needed to warn. Informants only my father and I know."

"Your father was training you, wasn't he?" I ask.

He nods. "Everyone he knows, I know. I'll make sure they're warned." His focus shifts to Kenta. "I'll need your help with that. We'll have to work fast."

"Be careful," I say.

"I know," Hamidi says, and one corner of his lip pushes upward for just a moment, a feeble attempt at a smile. I'm grateful at least that he's beginning to sound like himself again, steady and focused. As much as he will need time to grieve, he'll also need to keep that focus to get through his father's death, and to get the Shadow League through it.

"What about the traitor?" I demand. "Have you thought of who it might be?"

His expression stills. "There are only three members who know my family."

"Who?"

He considers me and then says with careful deliberation. "Kibwe and Abasi."

He's choosing to tell me, to trust me with this. I try not to let the flutter of hope I feel get away with me; just because he's willing to tell me this much doesn't mean he'll let me continue to help. I'll still have to make that happen. "And the third?" I press.

His features tighten as he looks at me. I cannot quite read the expression in his eyes—dawning horror? Guilt? "The third is an informant of ours who lives in Blackflame's household."

Kenta frowns. "If he caught this informant, then it might not have been betrayal, per se. He may have tortured the truth out of them."

"I'll look into it," Hamidi says. "My father may have given up their identity during his interrogation regardless. If they aren't the traitor, they'll need to be warned."

"What about the other two?" Kenta asks. "Abasi seems unlikely—he would hardly have encouraged us to break your father out if he's the traitor. And he's always been there for us. What of Kibwe?"

I cross my arms against a creeping chill as Kenta and Hamidi discuss Kibwe. I don't know him, can hardly weigh in on his guilt. So I wait, listening, my sweat-soaked clothes clammy against my skin. He's a fisherman, it seems, and won't depart for his night's fishing until dusk. He has helped more than a few people escape Karolene by granting them passage to the mainland on his dhow.

Soon enough, they agree to a plan: Hamidi will check in on his informant in Blackflame's house and then go on to warn the Shadow League members most at risk who haven't been contacted yet. Kenta will investigate Kibwe as well as he can.

"What about Abasi?" I ask.

Kenta shakes his head. "He was with us this morning. He was the first to argue for your rescue plan—and we weren't caught at it. If it was him, he would have told the guards to hold us."

"Then you're sure it's Kibwe? It couldn't be this informant of yours?"

Hamidi clears his throat. "No. They entrusted us with something of equal value to themselves when they learned my father's identity. They would not risk it. As for Abasi, he's been a family friend since I was a child. I'd rather not think it was Kibwe, but I can't imagine it was Abasi."

It doesn't seem at all likely, I have to grant him that. He seems too well dressed to take a bribe in exchange for his honor. Still, appearances can be deceiving. "What does he do for a living?"

"He's a silk merchant," Hamidi says.

So he isn't desperately needy. Which does make Kibwe the more likely suspect.

"We'd better go," Kenta says. "There's no telling how quickly the guards will act on their information."

Hamidi nods, turning toward the path up to the road. Walking away.

"What about me?" I ask, taking a step after him. "What would you have me do?"

He pauses as if gathering himself, turns to face me. "You've done enough. I'll send word if I need you."

His words hit me like a slap in the face. I stiffen, staring at him, but he's already leaving, striding to the bank and calling for Kenta.

You've done enough.

Tendaji is dead, the Shadow League on the precipice of an abyss, and I've spent my usefulness. I knew better than to hope, and yet I did anyway.

Kenta pauses before me. "Hitomi?"

I shake my head. I don't want to talk to him, don't want his pity or his kind words right now.

"Stay safe," he says finally.

I don't answer.

He hesitates, as if there's something more he wants to say, but he must not find the words. He continues on, following Hamidi up the embankment and into the city.

EVENTUALLY, I leave the bridge and make my way back to the rooftop where I hid my old clothes and my package of belongings. This neighborhood is a few blocks from Rafiki's house—it seemed wisest to borrow from a less-wealthy building that housed many families and had a staircase up to the roof. I change behind a screen of clothes, carefully fold the now decidedly not-so-clean clothing I took from the clothesline, and go down the stairs to the street.

It's heading into late afternoon and the markets will be reopening now that the worst of the heat of the day is past. There will be women with heavy shopping baskets, some of whom would hire a boy to carry their groceries home for them. There might be errands the vendors want run. There might even be another possibility of work at the docks.

I lean against the building behind me, then slide down to sit, the dirt warm against my legs. Leaning my head back against the low wall, I let my eyelids sink shut, my whole body aching with hunger. If I don't start thinking about my next meal soon, I won't manage anything until tomorrow. But I want so much more than a meal.

It doesn't matter, though. This is what I have: an empty belly and *you've done enough.*

I cross my arms to hold myself in. But in the dark behind my eyelids, there are other truths I cannot escape, flickers of images that I wish I could unsee: Tendaji, his body broken and his breathing still. I can remember the way his face lit up with a laugh; the feel of his hand resting on the top of my head, as if he were my uncle, as if I were a child of his heart. He helped me when I was lost, and even if he could not find me a home with sheltering walls, it was he that made these islands another home to me. Through him I found myself here, sank into the language and adopted the clothes and learned to live again. And now he is dead.

Nor can I escape the memory of Hamidi's gaze, the hollowness I saw when I told him of his father's death. I press the heels of palms against my eyes, try to rub away the memories. It doesn't help, of course. Such things don't disappear so easily. It's been three years since my father died and my mother disappeared, and I still remember them as I last saw them: my father, thin and wasted and deathly still in his bed, and my mother clutching her bloodied handkerchief to her lips, bidding me wait for her return. I waited until the innkeeper turned me out, and then I followed after her, only to be turned back. So I returned to the streets around the inn, and waited and waited until I became a fixture, and the locals began giving me errands and chores in return for food, so I would not die there on their doorstep.

I waited until Tendaji found me and offered to help me find a place to work. He spoke with the innkeeper, obtaining his promise that he'd send word if my mother returned. I remember Tendaji leaving me to go into the inn, and Hamidi, as old as I am now, squatting beside me to keep me company in his father's absence. He didn't say anything then, but his eyes held a wealth of pity in them. I was grateful for his silence.

And now I've seen Tendaji dead as well, and I cannot wipe the image from my mind, nor can I ever undo the pain of the news I brought my friend.

Abasi or Kibwe.

Kibwe or Abasi.

I don't know the one, but I can find the other. Hamidi shouldn't trust either until he knows. The rest of his family is still alive. He shouldn't trust *anyone* until he knows.

I push myself to my feet, turn to face the business district.

Hamidi may not want my help, but that doesn't mean he won't get it.

5. INTUITION

W hile by no means one of the biggest families in the silk trade, Abasi's name is known among the street merchants, and it's laughably easy to beg directions to his house.

He lives in a steady, older neighborhood, composed of two-story buildings that often house two or three generations together. Abasi's home is a good size, with the traditional double wooden doors painted a vibrant blue and set within an ornate frame with a central divider. A gorgeous latticework balcony graces the second story. Two other homes sit in close proximity on either side, leaving only the front door as a point of entry. I follow the houses along and turn at the end of the road to see what alternate entries and escape routes I can find. Just as I hoped, a narrow alley runs behind the buildings, providing easy access to the small, walled yards.

I walk the alley, inspecting each of the houses in turn. From what I can tell over the tops of the high walls, the houses are all about the same in terms of wealth. Chickens cluck behind the walls of a few, a goat bleats somewhere to the right, and twice I catch the sound of women talking, perhaps washing dishes or hanging wet laundry in the yard. My mage sight shows me nothing of concern—no wards, no protections, no niggling little spells I don't want to meet. Nothing. All I sense is the faint flow of magic in the world itself, nothing more than a glow permeating the earth, whispering on the wind, which is nothing to worry about.

The second house down, adjacent to Abasi's, sports a row of mango trees growing against the inner wall, their fruit still hard and green: the perfect place to hide my valuables. I make a running jump for the top of the wall. On my second attempt, my fingers close over the edge, and I haul myself up. I crouch there a moment, rubbing the grit from my hands and inspecting the raw tips of my fingers. Then I take my package from my pocket and hide it among the branches, snugging it tight so that it won't fall.

Satisfied, I drop to the alley and return to Abasi's house, rapping on the back door. Eventually, a tall woman in a lovely yet well-worn orange and yellow day dress opens the door. Her hair is wrapped in a matching swatch of fabric, and her hands drip soapy water.

"Ehh, boy, what do you want?"

I dip my head meekly. "Please, auntie, would you have some work I could do in return for a meal?"

"Not today," she says firmly, stepping back to shut the door.

"I haven't eaten since yesterday," I say in a small voice, hoping to stir her pity. "I know it's hard to trust a boy you don't know, but I'm small and quick and can work hard, if you might spare a bit of bread for me. I can scrub, or shell peas, or wash clothes, if you wish."

She hesitates.

"Just a bit of bread, auntie," I say, hating that I have to beg.

She heaves a sigh and steps to the side. "If you try anything,

I'll have Jelani whip you. No stealing, no wandering around. Understand?"

"I understand," I say somberly, though I want to protest. When I ask for work, it's because I'm trying to *avoid* thieving. And yet these are almost always the words I'm welcomed with.

She grunts and leads me over to the washing tub. I push up my sleeves and set to scrubbing the clothes while she brings out a basket of corn and a metal bucket for the husks. Her name, she tells me, is Chiku, and she has been working in Master Abasi's house for twenty years.

"Twenty years," I marvel, wringing out a pair of pants. The water dribbles down my elbows, soaking my own pants, but they will dry soon enough in the island heat. "I've only been in Karolene three years."

She eyes me askance. "Is that so? What brought you here?"

I keep my eyes on my washing. "I came here with my mother. She was ill, and we were seeking a cure. She went out one day and never came back."

Chiku pauses in the act of husking an ear. "She disappeared?"

I'm running a risk sharing this, but if she doesn't sympathize with my words, that will tell me a lot. "I don't know. My mother wasn't so ill that she could have died that day. She left to meet with Arch Mage Blackflame and didn't return."

"Oh, child," Chiku says, her voice soft with sorrow. "Have you no other family here?"

I look up, a pained smile on my face, as if it were an easy truth when we both know it is not. "No."

Families in Karolene are big and connected. They take care of each other. It's rare for a family feud to progress so far that a complete split results, and almost unheard of to have no family at all. Without a family, you have nothing—no support in times of need, no safety when trouble comes knocking.

Chiku returns to husking her ear of corn, frowning. I've

managed to gain her sympathies on a deeper level than I did at the door. Now I only need to work into the conversation the questions I want answered without arousing her suspicions.

I sort through the remaining clothes, thinking quickly. I need to find a way to ask about Blackflame, but jumping in directly after what I just shared will look suspicious. My hand closes on a child's tunic. Perhaps establishing the family's connection to the court will help—that's where Blackflame is most active, and where much of Abasi's custom will come from. But to get to that, I'd best start with Chiku.

"Does your family work with you here?" I ask.

She shakes her head. "No, I go home to my family at night."

I look at her in surprise. It's relatively common for at least a smaller family unit to work together for the same master, or even live in attached quarters. "But—do you take care of this whole house yourself? Master Abasi and all his family, too?"

Chiku reaches for another ear of corn. "There is Jelani. He does the cleaning and driving. I only have to cook and wash."

"Driving?" I echo.

She catches my quizzical glance about the small yard and smiles. "Oh, the master rents space at a stable down the road."

I wring out a child's soapy tunic, drop it into the tub of clean water, and start rinsing. "Cooking and washing can be big jobs. Is it a large family that lives here?"

She clicks her tongue. "No, just Master Abasi and his wife, their daughter and her husband, and their two children. I started here back when Master Abasi was planning his wedding. His parents both lived with him then, of course."

"Ah," I say. "He has only one daughter?" That's a small family, by any standard.

Chiku sighs and sets aside the last ear of corn. "He has a son as well. Young master Kito was invited to court by a friend among the nobility."

I brighten. "How fortunate for the family!"

Chiku gets to her feet. "It seemed so at first. But lately," she shakes her head. "I would not speak ill of the boy. Why, I half raised him myself!"

"But you are worried?" I ask, willing her to stay. "It seems like a closer connection to court could only benefit the family."

She studies me a moment, and then says, "Last month he negotiated a bit of ongoing business on his father's behalf with the Arch Mage himself."

"The—Arch Mage Blackflame?"

"There isn't another arch mage on the islands, is there?"

No, there isn't. "How fortuitous," I manage, my mind racing.

"Your mother disappeared," she says, voice sharp. "You need not pretend, child. I have been thinking all this last month that I should find a different house to work for."

"But ... if it is just business," I say hesitantly. Abasi seems wise enough not to refuse a business deal with someone as powerful as Blackflame when anyone who crosses the man disappears. Did he tell Tendaji, though? Or is there more to it than business?

"My cousin disappeared three months ago," Chiku says, voice hard. "And I've had to serve tea to the man myself."

"He came here for tea?"

"And to discuss their business," Chiku says, flicking her hand dismissively.

I don't believe it. Nobles don't visit their silk merchant's house to discuss what they want; they expect merchants to bring sample wares to them. While not actually a noble, Blackflame would count among the aristocratic class that expects house calls. If Blackflame came here, he had a very good reason to do so.

"I'll not serve him again," Chiku says. She stares across the yard, her gaze focused on the middle distance, but her voice firm.

"My cousin, your mother ... I won't support the man, and I won't support anyone who does."

"Careful," I say before I can help myself.

She blinks, looking down at me, and nods, accepting my word of warning for what it is. If someone overhears her—well, it's better not to say such things aloud.

She turns toward the door.

"When you're done, hang the clothes on the line there. I'll get a plate together for you."

I quickly finish the last of the washing and haul the heavy basket of wet clothes over to the clothesline. By the time I'm done hanging them, Chiku has come back out from the kitchen with the promised plate.

"You may sit on the step to eat, and then off you go," she says, handing the plate to me. "And remember, that's all the work we have for you. No coming back tomorrow."

"No, auntie. Thank you," I say, reaching for the plate. In addition to the bread, she's given me corn mash and a generous spoonful of curried vegetables. I look up at her, beaming. She turns away as if she hadn't seen my smile, but I catch the faint crinkle of crow's feet by her eyes.

"Go on, eat," she says, and returns to the kitchen to work.

I eat quickly, the food delicious and gone all too fast.

"It looks cleaner than if I'd washed it," Chiku says, taking the empty plate from me as I stand in the kitchen doorway.

"Thank you, auntie." I don't have to pretend my gratitude. "It was wonderful."

"Off with you then," she says, and shoos me out the back door and into the alley.

I walk along with a bounce in my step, my stomach comfortably filled. As I near the wall below the mango trees, I slow with surprise, for there, watching me, sits an adorably rotund golden dog. Its ears are twin triangles poking up from its ruff, and a dark mask of fur lies across its eyes. In similar contrast to the honey tones of its shaggy coat, its legs are slim and dark-furred. It also looks decidedly unfriendly.

Perhaps my package can wait until later.

"Good dog," I murmur and shift course to walk along the opposite wall, keeping as far away as possible from its small, sharp teeth.

It turns its head, watching as I pass, its thick, dark tail curled around its haunches. Just as well to keep away from it. I continue on, listening for the telltale sound of claws clicking against the cobblestones while hoping to God the dog stays put.

"That was stupid of you," Kenta says from behind me.

I twist around with a cry, staring. Where the dog sat moments before, Kenta now stands, his eyes blazing with anger.

I stare at him, stunned for the space of a heartbeat, and then realize what I'm looking at and clap my hands over my eyes. "Where are your *clothes?*"

A brief silence follows, in which I wonder if I should attempt to peek at him over the top of my hands or if that will still show me too much.

Then Kenta lets out an exasperated chuckle. "I *am* wearing pants."

"Tight pants!"

"They're still plenty—"

"*And* you're a dog," I add, risking a glance at him over the tips of my fingers. It's just enough to see him from the shoulders up.

"Tanuki," he clarifies.

Unfortunately, that word means nothing to me. I've met a lycan before, able to shift into the form of a wolf, but I've no idea what a tanuki is other than the fluffy black-masked dog I saw a moment before.

"What were you doing in there?" he demands. "Hamidi told you to stay away."

"No," I say, careful to keep my view of him blocked with my hands. "You told me to stay safe, and he said he'd let me know if he needed me. I was perfectly safe earning my dinner." It's hard to smile smugly when hiding behind your hands. "I also found out something."

"Found out what? And what were you doing to earn your dinner?"

What does he think I was doing? Turning cartwheels? "I was washing clothes. The housekeeper told me Abasi is conducting a business deal of some sort with Blackflame. I'm not sure what, exactly, but his son negotiated it for him."

"How would she know that?" Kenta shakes his head. "Are you sure she wasn't making it up to impress you?"

"She didn't need to impress me," I assure him. "Blackflame stopped in to discuss their supposed business, and she had to serve him tea. Which, I might point out, is *not* how most wealthy folk conduct business with their merchants. But a business dealing isn't really proof of betrayal, is it? Hamidi will want more."

"Not from you, he won't."

I throw up my hands in frustration and get a clear view of Kenta, bare chested and in tight leather pants that start below his navel and certainly don't reach his knees. With a yelp, I whirl around, clapping my hands over my eyes again for good measure.

Kenta makes a choking sound.

"Are you all right?" I ask, not daring a look.

"Fine," he says, his voice not quite steady. "Give me a moment and I'll get the rest of my clothes."

"You have more clothes?" I demand. "Why in the Eleven Kingdoms haven't you put them on yet?"

"Just wait," he says.

I hear the distinct sound of Kenta scraping his way up the wall and then jumping down again a moment later, followed by the rustle of clothing.

"All right, I'm clothed now. Though really, it's not anything you haven't already seen among the fishermen and dockworkers."

I fix him with a glare as I turn around, glad to see him in both a tunic and a pair of pants. "They wear *loose* pants. *Past* their knees." His pants had been so tight they didn't leave much to the imagination, and I have no interest in imagining such things in the first place. "And they don't turn into dogs."

"Tanukis," he says, still looking entertained. "Here, catch."

He tosses my package to me. I jump to catch it, my heart giving an unpleasant thump. "How did you find that?"

He taps his nose. "I tried tracking you once I'd been to see Kibwe. I wanted to make sure you were all right after this morning. I lost you after you returned your clothes."

Must be convenient to have a dog's sense of smell, at least when it comes to finding people. "What did you find out about Kibwe?" I ask.

"He's been ill the last five days or so, unable to leave his bed. His wife's been worried about him. The neighbors haven't seen any unusual visitors stopping by to see him."

"Not even a healer of some sort?" I ask, half-worried even though I don't know the man.

"They didn't have the coin for one. I gave them a bit from that pouch Abasi gave us for the prison guards." Kenta pauses, as if regretting having shared that much.

"I'm glad," I say. "If he betrayed Tendaji before he got ill, it wouldn't have taken the soldiers this long to make the arrest."

"I know," Kenta says. "It wasn't Kibwe."

"So, did you come here to look for me or check on Abasi?"

"Both," he says. "Once I got here, I scented your bundle of

things and heard you chatting in the yard. I decided I'd better wait and make sure you made it out safely."

At that point, he must have stored his clothes and shifted into his tanuki form in the hopes of remaining unnoticed while he waited. To make sure I got out all right. "Thanks," I finally say, warmth filling me. "For waiting and trusting me to get out on my own." And trusting me with his ability to shift, though I'm not yet ready to say that last out loud.

He shrugs. "What else was I supposed to do? Now that you're out, though, we should leave before we're noticed."

I purse my lips, studying him. He's intent on getting me away. No argument I could make will sway him. Just like Hamidi. Well, what they don't know, they can't argue with. So, I merely sigh and nod. "All right," I say.

"All right?" he frowns, taken aback.

"Yes, all right." I turn toward the main road. "I've got to move if I'm going to have somewhere to sleep tonight. You'll let Hamidi know what I found out about Abasi?"

"Yes, but aren't you...?"

"I've got my own affairs to take care of," I say coolly. "Hamidi can let me know if he needs me."

6. A THIEF IN THE NIGHT

Three hours past sunset, with darkness full and heavy upon the city, I turn the corner into the alley behind Abasi's house once more. At the familiar wall with its mango trees, I climb up to store my package, then take stock of the night. The moon is half-full, glowing high and bright. By its light, I can just make out the alley lying empty and still. The houses are quiet, only a few windows lit from within, cracks of lamplight peeking through shutters and lattice boxes.

It's not quite late enough to get to work, so I sit hidden among the leaves and soak in the quiet. I'm being stubborn and perhaps a bit reckless, but I'm not going to get any rest until I know for certain who sent Tendaji to such a horrifying death. Maybe it wasn't Abasi—I'll be glad if it isn't. But we need to know. The longer the traitor goes unidentified, the more likely they will take down the Shadow League, and not just its leader. It will be hard enough for Hamidi to keep the League together because of his youth, but he's the only one who knows every part of it. He was trained for it as no one else has been. And he'll be as much at risk of betrayal as his father.

I sigh.

"I hope that sigh means you're going home again," Kenta says from below me, nearly scaring me off my perch.

I grab the edge of the wall, gasping. He can certainly walk with the silence of a predator, however cute and fluffy his tanuki form might be.

"What are you doing here?" I demand, keeping my voice low. The last thing I need is for someone to hear us. It would be handy to have a silencing charm of some sort right now, but I haven't the money for one, nor do I know how to make one myself.

Kenta grins up at me, his teeth gleaming in the moonlight. "I could ask the same of you." At least he's lowered his voice as well.

I consider lying, but I wouldn't even believe myself. "I asked first," I retort.

"You gave in too easily," Kenta says. He stands beneath the wall, hands on his hips. Thankfully, he's fully clothed. "And you walked away."

"Great," I grumble. "Next time I'll argue more."

Kenta shakes his head. "You know he doesn't want you too closely involved."

He would be Hamidi, of course. "Because he still thinks I'm a child," I grouse. "I'm as old as he was when he and his father first found me on the streets, and I've learned a good deal in the meantime."

I hop down from the wall so I can glare Kenta in the eye instead of looking down at him. Although I'm shorter than him, so I'm actually looking up. But it will allow us to lower our voices further, and that's more important than not wanting to feel small before him.

"For example," I continue, "I know that merchants have to keep meticulous records of all their transactions for reporting to the sultan. If Abasi really has entered into business with Black-flame, there'll be a record of it."

"In his house?"

"His library," I say. "He doesn't keep an office at the warehouses he rents space from. All his business is done out of his house."

"How do you know?"

"I walked over to one of his warehouses and asked."

Kenta stares at me. "You just *asked?*"

"I said my mistress wanted to check the record ledger for her last five purchases because she thought there might be an error. I was to find out where she should go to look them up. They told me it was all at his house."

I can't be sure, but I think that glint in Kenta's eyes might be respect. "I see. And what are you planning now?"

I slip my lockpick set from my pocket and lay the picks and torque wrench on my palm. "I'm going to check his business ledger to see what he's actually done, see if I can find any indication of why Blackflame would visit him at home."

He eyes my tools. "You think you can get in?"

"I know I can." I keep my voice steady and casual, but I must still sound a touch arrogant, for he frowns. I grimace. "All I want is to get into an unoccupied room. It's not that hard."

"So you say. You're not going to give this up, are you?"

"No," I agree cheerfully, pocketing my tools.

"Fine. I'll keep watch for you. Just don't do anything stupid."

"Do I look stupid to you?" I demand, so insulted it takes a moment for his first statement to sink in. He's going to keep watch?

"You *look* like a boy. I'm talking about what you're planning to *do.*"

"I'm not a boy," I say, further aggrieved, even if I am wearing boys' clothes. "And considering my plan got us in and out of the prison this morning, you ought to have more faith in me. I do know what I'm doing."

"Good, because I don't want to have to explain to ... our friend how you got yourself caught while I stood by watching."

"You don't trust me to do anything right either, do you? The both of you are so *annoying*."

Kenta coughs with laughter. "I'll be sure to tell him you said that."

"I hope you do," I return, unamused. "He could use my help, as little as he seems to want it."

Kenta doesn't answer, but I get the distinct feeling he doesn't disagree either.

SOMETIME PAST MIDNIGHT, I step down from my branch to balance on the wall.

"Kenta," I whisper. I don't look toward him, not wanting to push his shadow charm to its limit. My own chafes against my finger. Given that Kenta spotted me so easily earlier, it seemed wise to use the charms I was given for the prison.

Now, Kenta climbs down from his perch to join me, a deeper shadow within the moon-speckled darkness. I lead the way along the top of the wall in my bare feet, stepping over or ducking under the branches that extend over the wall. The next house's wall is slightly higher—a step up from the wall where we started. Grinning, I grip the edge of the wall and swing down into Abasi's backyard, Kenta behind me.

I stand for a moment, breathing slowly, relieved that our shadow charms are still holding. They're poorly made, but I don't have the knowledge to fix them. Logic tells me there shouldn't have been anyone looking out their window in the dead of the night anyway, but logic also tells me that you can't trust people to stay in their beds all night. The shadow charms are a nice safety.

While Kenta moves silently to stand in the shadow of the house, disappearing altogether, I hunker down by the door to the alley and quickly work the lock. If we need to run, I don't want to have to scramble over the high wall. Thankfully, I've practiced enough that I can manage this lock without much trouble. The darkness makes no difference; most of lockpicking is working by feel anyway.

Finished, I cross to the kitchen door.

"Any sounds?" I whisper, my voice barely audible. I can't tell where Kenta is.

"No," he says from my right. I kneel by the door, rest my ear against the wood. All remains quiet on the other side. My stomach is knotted tight with tension, but my fingers work the lock without the slightest tremor. The door swings open on well-oiled hinges, bless Chiku. The room within lies empty.

I step in, leaving the door open only a crack. Anyone checking on the kitchen shouldn't notice anything amiss, but I'll still be able to get through at speed.

I wait a few minutes in the darkened kitchen, hoping my eyes will adjust. When I returned my dinner plate to Chiku earlier, I'd looked into the room, so I have a general sense of the layout. Still, being able to see in more detail would help me avoid banging into something noisy and rousing the household. All I can make out is the paler rectangle of the far door. Short of lighting a candle or using a glowstone, though, there's not much to be done.

I pad through the kitchen one step at a time. The hallway lies dark, but the stairs at the end are half-lit by the steady white light of a glowstone. It takes a well-off man to leave a glowstone lit all night while the household sleeps. Money, or a mage in the family who can easily recharge the charm as needed. I frown, pausing to study the stairwell and walls, opening myself to my mage sight. I can see the faint flow of the spell wrapped around the glowstone, bright as a star in my mage sight, but there's no sign of magic anywhere else. No wards, just as I thought earlier today. If there were a mage in the family, there'd be at least a few protections and charms at work.

Exhaling softly, I take the stairs up, listening for any sign of movement. It seems too easy to walk into a house like this. For all my bold words to Kenta, I've never broken into a house before, just storerooms or darkened shops where I might find something to eat. It's disconcerting how simple this seems.

The stairs open into a carpeted room, cushions lining the wall. It's built along the front of the house, with a door and a window leading onto the latticework balcony. I cross the room to the tiled hall and kneel before the first door, listening for any sounds. I can't make out anything, but that doesn't mean there isn't someone sleeping within—and if I walk into the wrong room, I doubt Abasi will be pleased with me. Even my shadow charm may not be enough to protect me.

I'll have to make sure I find the library, empty as it should be of all occupants. If I can't trust my ears, I'll have to rely on magic. I may not be quite sure what I'm doing, but there's not much to do other than try.

I place my palm on the tiled floor and reach out with my mage senses. There aren't any spells here, but I can sense the latent magic in everything around me, can feel its gentle flow from the sunbaked bricks that form the floor and walls, to the heavy wood with its memory of sap and growth, to the faint touch of lifeblood pulsing through the sleepers within. Smiling faintly to myself, I move on to the next door.

Of the four rooms composing the upstairs, only one does not contain any sign of life. Crouching before the door, I ease it open. The room within lies still and dark, the only light that of the glowstone filtering down the hallway. The shutters are closed.

I wait until my eyes adjust to the gloom. A carpet darkens the floor. To one side stands a small writing table, its surface clear but for a single ledger. Probably the best place to start.

I ease the door shut, searching the room with my mage sight. If Abasi has a glowstone burning in the hallway, chances are he keeps one in the library as well. The charm isn't readily visible, but most charms that aren't in use are hard to spot. Sighing, I cross to the shutters only to smack my knee into something set beneath them: a large wooden trunk. Breathing in a curse, I wait till the pain passes before opening the shutters to allow in the moonlight. Then I begin a quick search of the room. On a shelf behind the desk, I find an old oil lamp. I set it on the desk, skim my hands over the shelf again, and grasp a small box. Tucked within it is a simple firestarter charm. Two clicks and I have a flame to light the lamp, bringing the library into view.

The shelf behind me holds at least two dozen books, as well as a shelf full of old ledgers. Beyond the desk, there is little else in the room—a hookah in the corner, imported from the desert lands, and a few cushions along the wall. I can now see the great wooden chest I encountered beneath the window, decorated with a floral brasswork pattern. The heavy lid has a metal latch that hangs down, fitting precisely over a loop built into the body of the trunk. A nice, thick lock hangs from the loop, holding the lid shut.

Crossing the room, I take a pair of cushions and cover the crack at the bottom of the door. Then I sit at the desk, open the ledger, and begin reading. Abasi's hand is even and clear, and it is no trouble to skim over the entries. The trouble is that, no matter how far back I go, I find nothing—no indicator at all that he's been in contact with Blackflame, or when such contact might have begun. Perhaps he wouldn't record his dealings as being directly with Blackflame himself. Does the arch mage have a man of business to handle such transactions? I have no idea. Or perhaps there is some other way Abasi could change how he records his business.

It doesn't seem likely that Chiku would have lied about serving Blackflame tea—her anger seemed too real, as did her grief at her cousin's disappearance. Perhaps there is no record because Abasi hasn't finished and delivered what he promised. But that makes no sense—there would be an order recorded, at least, unless the only business they are engaged in is destroying the Shadow League. If that were so, then the ledgers would hold no evidence of that. But then where would I find what I need?

I bury my face in my hands, trying to think. I'm tired, the day is too long by far, and I can't make sense of this anymore. No doubt it was too simplistic to hope that if Abasi was the traitor, he'd have some proof of it just waiting to be easily discovered ... unless he's locked up what proof there is. I turn to gaze at the trunk beneath the window.

A lock I can deal with.

Closing the ledger, I squat before the trunk and work as quickly as I can. The silence in the house weighs on me, heavy with foreboding, but there's nothing to be done about that. I can't leave without checking the trunk or I'll always wonder what I missed.

I heave the lid up, resting it against the wall. The interior contains disappointingly little: a packet of letters bound with a string set atop some sort of cloth-wrapped package, and sitting beside them, three bundles of silk fabric samples corded together. I lift the letters, turning the packet over in my hand. The topmost envelope is addressed, *For my father, Abasi Chui Kondo.* I slip out the loosest envelope, from somewhere in the middle of the stack, and extract a letter.

Dear Baba, the letter reads. *I cannot understand your refusal to enter into this opportunity. Indeed, I believe Arch Mage Black-*

flame quite aggrieved, and I am worried that his anger at your ill use will have other ramifications for us. How can you be so short-sighted? You have ever been the keen businessman. I grew up beneath your tutelage, and I tell you now, you are making a mistake. Have you not considered how your actions might impact me? Or, if you care nothing for me, saying I have brought such troubles upon myself, then what of my sister?

Frowning, I fold the letter and put it away before I check both the topmost and bottommost letters. They all appear to be from Abasi's son. The topmost letter is dated even earlier than the one I read. The bottom one is short but desperately grateful: *Arch Mage Blackflame is pleased to hear that you will bring a sample of your silks for his consideration. He expects you tomorrow evening. Thank you, Baba. I assure you, I will always speak with you in advance of negotiating other opportunities.*

Much good may it do him.

I return the letters to the trunk. Perhaps our traitor isn't Abasi—at least, it seems as though he was displeased by the situation his son brought about, and that he looked at it only as a transaction and not an alliance. Perhaps Blackflame stopped here regarding the silks and nothing else. Perhaps he never even put in an order, and so there was nothing to record in the ledgers.

All I have is my gut telling me that all is not as it seems. Without a real reason to suspect Abasi, I'm breaking into his house for what? I rub my mouth, still staring down at the trunk. I should have gone back to Hamidi, laid out my concerns, and let him decide what he wanted to do, even if that meant I'd certainly not be invited to help.

Sighing, I reach down and poke the cloth-wrapped package, intending to shut the trunk and sneak back out of the house. The package rustles, the crinkle of paper barely audible. I glance toward the door, then quickly lift out the package, balancing it on the edge of the trunk to open it. Beneath the sturdy cotton wrapping I find a letter and more fabric, folded carefully—a garment of some sort. The letter says only, *I am glad we have come to an understanding. Here is a token of my appreciation. If you require entry to my home, wear it.*

I stare at it, but that's all there is, no name, no further explanation. It's as strange a note as ever I've read. Whatever this is, it's—

From the hallway comes the distinct patter of feet.

I'm caught. I know it as the footsteps come to a stop before the door. I drop the half-wrapped package into the trunk and swing the lid shut, catching it at the last moment so it doesn't thud as it closes.

"Babu?" a young voice asks, and a boy of eight or nine years pushes open the door.

For a moment, my shadow charm holds as the boy casts about the room. Then, as he frowns at the shadow that should not be before the window, the dratted thing fails.

His eyes widen as the shadows drop away from me. If I get out of this alive, I'm teaching myself how to make a charm that will actually hold together.

"You're not my grandfather," he says.

I shake my head, offer him a mischievous smile. I have only a very slim chance of walking away from this now. "No, I've just popped in for a visit."

If there's one thing I can say for Abasi, it's that he's taught his family well. "You're a thief," the boy says, brow furrowing. "What are you stealing?"

"Nothing. I've come to make sure—" I break off, for there is the click of another door, and then Abasi's voice filters in from the hallway.

"Are you talking to someone?"

"There's a boy stealing things from your library," the child says. "Well, he *says* he isn't stealing, but your chest's lock is gone."

There is no way out—I don't dare jump from the window, nor can I climb to the roof from it. The only way out is through the door. I shift to sit on the lid of the trunk, thread my fingers together as casually as I can, and watch as Abasi steps into the room. He stares at me, his expression darkening, and then he turns to the boy and says, "Go tell Jelani to bring a rope."

My chest tightens with fear, but I'm not dead yet. I doubt I could shove my way past Abasi and all his family, but that doesn't mean I can't escape before ... whatever it is he plans to do with me.

"Yes, Babu," the boy says, and departs at a run, his feet pattering down the tiled hall.

Abasi wears a long loose tunic of simple white cotton and a matching set of pants, rumpled from sleep. But he's wide awake now, his gaze flicking around the room, taking in me, the window, the lamp on the desk, and the trunk beneath me, its lock on the floor beside my feet.

"Hamidi's street rat, aren't you?" he says, stepping all the way in and shutting the door behind him. "What are you doing here? How did you get in the window?"

"I climbed," I say, though really I only climbed the stairs.

He angrily waves this away. "What are you doing here, girl? How did you get into the trunk?"

"Easily," I say, amused that he can't seem to ask one question at a time. If I can only convince him that I'm not afraid, that he would do better to deal with me than turn me in, I might even be able to walk away from this. "The lock was no trouble to pick. If you want to keep things shut, you should get a ward put on the trunk, or pay for a better lock."

Abasi bristles. "For the last time, what are you doing here?"

221

He stands with his legs braced, as if expecting me to try to run through him.

"Looking for evidence," I admit. "There was a rumor you had some dealings with Blackflame. I had to know."

"A follower who disobeys their leader is not much good at all," he says.

"Our leader is dead," I say, my voice shaking slightly as Tendaji's face resurfaces in my memory. "I didn't disobey anyone." Well, not precisely. In a manner of speaking.

"Dead?" Abasi stares at me. He doesn't know. I open my mouth to tell him, and then shut it again as he spits a curse. "Those stupid soldiers were supposed to keep at least Hamidi alive."

My hands curl into fists, my breath uneven. He knows Tendaji's dead, even though only Hamidi, Kenta, and I should have known. Which means he knows it from the other side. I need to get away, warn Hamidi before he's found—caught by the soldiers set on him by his father's oldest friend. And then tortured and killed, as he will be. Because of Abasi.

"They killed Tendaji," I say tightly. "Why would you think they'd treat the rest of us any better?"

"Because the two of them had all the names," Abasi snaps. "Are you really that dense, girl? With Hamidi dead..." He shakes his head.

"But you were—you've always been a part of the League," I say, knowing that I'm being as stupid as he thinks, but I can't understand this. "I saw what they did to Tendaji. He was your *friend*. They broke all his fingers and his teeth. He was covered in blood and bruises and burns—"

"Shut up," Abasi snarls, striding across the room toward me. "I do not want to hear such things!"

I'm on my feet and three steps away from the trunk in a

heartbeat, but there's nowhere to go, no way to get away from him.

"Master Abasi?" A tall, heavily muscled man steps in, a length of rope in his hands.

Abasi stands five paces away, his nostrils flared. "Jelani," he says, never taking his eyes from me. "We've caught a thief. Tie her up and then go get the carriage. I'm taking her in myself."

7. A TWIST OF MAGIC

T he carriage is simply built but comfortable, with cushioned benches, a curtained window, and a glow-stone set inside a colored-glass lamp. There surely must have been a glowstone in the library, not that it matters now.

I perch on the edge of one of the benches, my wrists tied behind me, listening to the indistinct sound of Abasi addressing Jelani. I can't imagine why he'd need to give directions unless we aren't going to the sultan's prison at all.

I wriggle my hands, trying to work my way out of my bindings, but Jelani has done his work well. Wherever we're going, I have to make sure we don't get there. Thieves aren't looked kindly upon, and if Abasi mentions my connection to the Shadow League, I've no hope of surviving imprisonment. The soldiers' treatment of Tendaji is proof of that.

I glare at the floorboards. I will get out. Escaping two men in a box on wheels is nowhere near as difficult as the second floor of a stone house filled with people. I can do this.

Abasi climbs up into the carriage, something bulky tucked under his arm. Jelani shuts the door, but Abasi doesn't sit down.

Instead, he shakes out the fabric, swinging it around his shoulders.

"That's a *northland* cloak," I blurt, staring at him. It's a deep red, giving the impression that Abasi is bathed in old blood. I'm certain it's the same material I found in the trunk with the note. I just hadn't recognized it for what it is. No one in Karolene would have such a cloak, or need one—except for Blackflame, who hails from the northlands himself, even if he was trained in the Eleven Kingdoms.

"If Hamidi is, in fact, dead, we have very few people to question. You do know a few of the Shadow League, don't you?"

"No," I say, feeling ill. "I hardly know anyone. Not as many as you do."

Abasi shakes his head and sits. "I doubt that. I'm afraid it must be done."

He's lying, and he knows it. I can tell it from the self-satisfied little smile on his lips. Does he not want to be the one to directly betray his other contacts? Or perhaps he's just afraid of being taken in for interrogation himself if he admits how much more he knows. Perhaps to our enemy he pretended that knowing Tendaji was a happy fluke, a chance discovery, and so he had no other names to share.

"What must be done?" I ask.

He leans against the cushions as the carriage rattles forward. "Tendaji was supposed to be sent to Arch Mage Blackflame, but the fools at the prison killed him with their interrogation. Hamidi would be the next choice, and he should have been caught while you and Kenta were poking your noses into the prison. But you're telling me he's dead already. Blackflame will be angry, and I don't want that anger turning on me or my family. I'll give him you to question instead; you know at least two others who know most of the League between them. And don't imagine

Blackflame will believe you if you name me—he'll expect you to try to frame me."

"That's very strategic," I agree caustically, then pause. "But why didn't you alert the soldiers to arrest Kenta and me at the prison?"

"You wouldn't have succeeded."

"If you wanted people with names, though—"

"I am not a *monster*," Abasi snaps. "You were right—your going in there with such a story—if they'd arrested you, thinking you'd already been violated, they would have had no qualms using you themselves. I don't want anyone hurt, you understand. I am doing what I have to."

"Did you not think Tendaji would be hurt? Or Hamidi?"

"Shut up," Abasi says, one hand fisting in his cloak. I study the way his knuckles stand out, the thick cloth of the cloak itself. That's a mystery right there, and perhaps all the evidence I need, should I survive this.

I clear my throat. "Does the cloak guarantee you entry to Blackflame's house in the middle of the night?"

"I can hardly imagine that has any bearing on you."

"I'm curious," I say, certain beyond a shadow of a doubt that the cloak is irrefutable proof of Abasi's treachery. "But more than that, I want to know why. They were your friends. You clearly have some sense of honor. *Why*?"

Abasi looks toward the curtained window, and for the first time I see something akin to shame on his face. "When I joined the League, Tendaji insisted it would not endanger my family. He was wrong."

"Coward." The word breaks from my lips before I can stop it.

"You've no idea what it is to protect your family," Abasi snarls.

"The Shadow League could have protected you! They could have gotten you and your family out."

"Out?" he repeats, incredulous. "All we've built would be lost. We'd be destitute. That's not *protection*."

"What of Hamidi's family?" I demand. "What of all the others who disappear? What of the changes in the law that are hurting us? And—"

"*Us?* You are nothing but a street rat, and a mgeni at that. You have no place here."

"I may be a foreigner, but at least I honor this land and people. Unlike another mgeni you seem to be good friends with."

"Shut *up*," he growls.

I consider him, the fury burning in his eyes, and decide I have other, greater concerns than this argument. I give a little upward jerk of my chin at him and turn my gaze to the curtained window. It's time to escape.

Closing my eyes, I gather what magic I can, drawing on the creaking wood of the carriage with its memory of growth and sunlight; the slumbering power of the cobblestones beneath us, burrowed out of the earth and filled still with the heat of the day; the sea-salt-heavy breeze, breathing and alive. Then I send a tendril of magic down through the carriage, wrap it around a wheel, and tug.

With a great *crack*, the wheel snaps. The corner of the carriage teeters, dipping down and then slamming against the ground, sending me tumbling from my seat. Abasi yells as he hits the wall, and then again as I thump into him. One of the horses squeals, and the carriage swings wildly before slowing.

I shove myself off Abasi, scooting away on my backside, and lift my foot to kick at the door latch. All I manage to do is stub my toe. Biting back a curse, I push myself a half step back, my mind racing. I still have a twist of magic left. I use it to cut through the ropes binding my wrists. The acrid scent of something burning registers only a moment before I manage to yank my wrists free, the rope falling to the floorboards behind me, its

227

ends smoking. My skin smarts, but burns are the least of my worries right now.

"You!" Abasi yells, struggling upright to block the door as the carriage judders to a halt. "Don't think you're getting away. Jelani! *Jelani!* What's happening out there?"

"I think you lost a wheel," I say, keeping my hands out of sight behind my back.

"Stay where you are," he snaps, and turns to open the carriage door, yelling up to the driver once more.

I launch myself at Abasi, slamming into his back and sending us both flying out the door. He cries out again, a short, grunting gasp of a yell, and then his head cracks against the cobblestones. I clutch the fabric of his cloak, still half on top of him, terrifyingly aware of how still he lies. Panic nearly chokes me. He can't be dead. He can't—

"Get up!" Someone grabs my elbow, yanking me off Abasi. Even now, he doesn't move.

"What have you done?" a man cries from atop the carriage. I look up to see Jelani. Somehow, he's managed to keep his seat on the driver's bench, his arms straining to keep the horses from bolting. He glances from Abasi to the horses, to me. No, to *us*.

"Run," Kenta says, dragging me back another step.

"Wait." I pull my elbow free and drop down beside Abasi. Rolling him over, I press my fingertips to his throat—and find a steady pulse. "He's alive," I call up to Jelani, relief making me dizzy. Or perhaps that's the aftereffects of my magic-working.

Jelani manages to tie off the reins and jumps down, starting toward us. Beside me, Abasi gives a low moan.

"You're going to leave the girl alone," Kenta says, halting Jelani in his tracks. A glance at Kenta shows me why: he's dropped into a fighter's pose, a knife gleaming in his hand. He's also bare chested and barefoot, which somehow makes him look doubly dangerous. "We'll leave, and you can see to your master. Understand?"

"You're thieves, both of you," Jelani says, his voice laced with contempt.

"No," Kenta says. "We're members of the Shadow League, and Abasi betrayed us."

Jelani's eyes widen with fright, gleaming white in the moonlight. This isn't a fight he wants to have.

Kenta shifts slightly, his voice dropping to address me. "Get up. We need to go."

I look down at Abasi, wrapped in the cloak that symbolizes all that has gone wrong in Karolene, and fury courses through me. He didn't mourn Tendaji, didn't care what happened to Hamidi. That cloak is the evidence I need, and I'm not leaving without it. "All right," I say to Kenta. "But we're taking this with us."

Reaching down, I pull open the brooch that secures the cloak, grab the edge of the fabric, and pull *hard*. Abasi grunts, his eyes fluttering open. He looks up at me in a daze.

"What are you doing?" Jelani demands, taking another step toward us.

It is not exactly an easy thing to roll a full-grown man out of his cloak.

"Stop there," Kenta warns.

I grab the cloak again from farther down and pull it upward, and Abasi rolls over with a garbled cry. The cloak comes free, sending me sprawling. "Got it," I pant, staggering to my feet. The world sways once, in a way it is certainly not meant to, before righting itself. That's definitely the magic-working taking its toll.

Kenta nods once. "Run. I'll follow you."

Jelani watches us both, but there's no question that he's more concerned with Abasi than with stopping us. I make for the nearest alley, pushing myself into as fast a jog as I can manage. My head aches, but the worst should pass soon. I just hope Kenta can get away before Abasi manages to figure out what's happening.

I turn the corner and lean against the wall, clutching the cloak to my chest. I'm shaking now, the taste of iron on my lips, blood dribbling from my nose. As a rule, I don't use magic except in emergencies. But tonight has given me proof that whether I need it or not, I had better teach myself how to use my Promise. No one else is going to, and I can't afford to expend so much energy on a working that I end up unable to run afterward.

"All right?" Kenta asks as he rounds the corner.

I nod, relief rushing through me. I fall into step with him. He raises one hand uncertainly, as if to grasp my elbow and steady me, before letting it drop back down again.

"You're bleeding," he says as I wipe at my nose again.

"It's nothing," I assure him. "I fell when the carriage wheel broke." Both statements are true, though I'm not sure the second is fully relevant. I might be bleeding from getting knocked about, but I've also bled once or twice before as a result of pushing myself a little too far with my magic. Thankfully, Kenta just nods.

"That was a piece of luck," he says. "I wasn't sure how I was going to stop the carriage until that wheel gave out."

"Yeah," I say. And then I realize what his presence means. Warmth rushes through me. It's been so long since someone has been there for me. "Thanks for following me."

"What else was I supposed to do?" he asks gruffly.

I shake my head and stumble to a stop as the world dips precariously. "I don't know," I say, as if everything were perfectly normal with me. "But we need to find your clothes. You can't go walking through the city like that."

It takes me a moment to realize he's laughing.

"Oh hush," I say grumpily. My head aches. I very nearly killed a man. The last thing I need is Kenta laughing at me. "It's all very well and good being able to turn into a tanuki, but you need better pants."

"It's considered quite a feat to be able to shift with clothing at all," Kenta says. I swear he can see my mortified flush in the moonlight.

"I'll keep that in mind if I meet any other tanukis," I say in a strangled voice.

"Not too many around here. Are you steady on your feet now?"

"I'm fine," I assure him, glad for the change of subject.

"Good. Follow me." He takes a step forward, shrinking as he does. I blink, my eyesight blurring, and find I'm looking at a black-masked dog. Kenta gives me a sharp smile, picks up his knife with his teeth, and sets off down the alley once more, paws pattering over the stones.

8. GHOST

I'm not sure where I thought we were going, but it certainly wasn't the Golden Cup. Apparently, the Shadow League has friends in unexpected places.

This late at night—still a few hours till dawn—the Cup stands dark, the windows shuttered. Kenta leads me to the back of the building, stands up on his hind legs, and scratches at the window, whining softly. Unlike the rest of the buildings, a faint glow shows around the edge of these shutters. At Kenta's insistent scratching, they swing open.

"Kenta," Hamidi says with evident relief. "You're hours late. I've been to Kibwe's and back looking for you."

Kenta huffs once and turns in a circle, as if to tell Hamidi to look around a bit. He does, finally spotting me in the shadows.

"*Hitomi?*"

I nod, well aware that I'm going to have to explain everything.

Kenta backs up and takes a flying leap at the window. Hamidi presses himself to the side as Kenta sails past into the lamplit room. I shift from one foot to the other. My head throbs fiercely, and while I've managed to walk this far, I'm not sure how easily I'll be able to clamber over the high sill.

"She might need a bit of help," Kenta's voice says from within.

Oh no, I won't. "I'm fine! Just take this." I toss the cloak up to Hamidi, along with Kenta's spare clothes. He catches them as they come unfolded, then turns to set them down.

I reach up to grasp the windowsill, intent on getting up without admitting I need Hamidi's help. Unfortunately, my body is not as convinced of my ability, and it's a hard, ungainly scramble up the side of the building.

"Hitomi, let me," Hamidi begins as I pull one knee up.

"I'm fi—" I pitch forward, my other knee banging against the windowsill. Hamidi's arm swings in front of me, attempting to break my fall, but he's not fast enough and ends up staggering after me as I crash through his arms to the floor.

Kenta barks a laugh. "You've got to let people catch you once in a while, Hitomi."

I heave myself to my feet, cheeks burning. "Right. Whatever." I keep my eyes off Kenta, who is probably not dressed yet, and gesture toward the cloak, addressing Hamidi. "Did you look at that?"

Hamidi glances from the mound of fabric to Kenta. "Not yet," he says and turns to close the shutters.

I cross the room and sink onto a cushion beside the tea table. Kenta has, thankfully, dressed himself in a dark green tunic and pants. He must have known there were clean clothes here waiting for him. He and I went back to Abasi's house to retrieve our things first: my own package from the mango tree, as well as my sandals, and of course we needed Kenta's discarded clothes, thrown in a heap in the backyard, waiting for someone to notice them. Unfortunately for him, they'd fallen in the mud beside the empty washing tub. He gave them one uninterested sniff and led me on to the Golden Cup.

Now, he kneels at the tea table, reaching to lift the teapot from its charmed warming tile. Hamidi shakes out the cloak and holds it up to inspect it. He makes no comment, though, just rolls it into a bundle and sets it beside the table before seating himself.

"Tell me," he says quietly. His gaze, for some reason, keeps shifting from my face to my hands.

I wrap my fingers around the warmth of the little teacup, take a slow sip, and start talking. I'm slow about it, my head slightly fuzzy, but Hamidi waits patiently, and Kenta doesn't say a word. I'm grateful he lets me tell this my way.

"It was Abasi, then," Hamidi says when I am finished.

"Yes." I glance at him askance. "He also thinks you're dead right now, though he'll realize soon enough that I lied."

"He may not. How long ago did you tell him I was dead?"

I frown. "An hour, maybe two."

"Good." He picks up his teacup. "That will work."

I glance at Kenta, but he looks as baffled as I feel. "What do you mean?" he asks.

Hamidi smiles, but the expression doesn't reach his eyes. "If my family is to survive, and the Shadow League as well, then I better be dead, don't you think?"

"You're planning to change your name, take on a new identity," I say with sudden understanding. If only Abasi had been so committed. "But Hamidi isn't your real name anyway, is it?"

"No. My father made sure we both used nicknames." He pauses. "But Abasi knows my birth name. I won't give my birth name to a mage to be used against me, so he needs to think me dead. More than that, if I am to lead the Shadow League, I cannot have a history or a family for people to use against me."

"Which is why you have to die."

This time, his smile crinkles his eyes. "There's no need to sound so somber. I'm not *actually* going to die."

He is. If he gives up his family and his name and becomes only the leader of the Shadow League, who he is now will become a relic of the past.

"You don't intend to tell your family you're alive, do you?" I demand.

He drops his gaze to the table. "It seems better not to—except perhaps for my mother."

"There's a risk in that," Kenta says.

"And it's well worth it," I say firmly. "Your mother needs to know she didn't lose you both."

Hamidi looks at me, his head tilted and his eyes dark with sorrow. Does he truly understand what he's giving up? "Just my mother," he agrees, "and only after the period of mourning has passed."

"No, sooner," I argue. "Three days at most. She can pretend to grieve for you—she must know how to hide her true feelings to have kept your father's work safe. Whatever you feel now about losing your father, it's worse for her to have lost him, and you."

Hamidi raises a hand. "All right, Hitomi. Three days."

There, that will at least force him to face some of his grief when he meets his mother. Because all he's doing now is putting it off, packing it away. It's my own fault, pushing him to focus on the Shadow League, but he has to make space to grieve as well. I would know.

Only... I haven't done a good job at this either. I drop my gaze, aware of how my own grief—buried beneath the busyness of survival—has soured and turned to shame. A shame that has tainted so much of my life, that Tendaji saw it in me that day in the prison. *There is no shame in being afraid.* I've been afraid for so long of being abandoned, of having the next person I trust walk away from me, not need me. And that shame has made me weak—it has meant that when I fall, I've already pushed away the people who would be there to catch me otherwise.

The League wants strong people, and I've been afraid to show my weakness. That fear, that shame that I have no one, that I'm grieving and alone, is what has made me weak. I don't know how to fix that yet, don't know how to wrestle with a grief that has settled into my bones. But at least now I can see it. I can start learning to trust again, to not push people away. To not assume I'm a burden. That I can do.

Kenta shifts, glancing at Hamidi. "How will you ensure Abasi doesn't realize you're still our leader?"

I take a slow breath, turning my focus back to my friends.

"I'll have to change. Turn myself into something else." Hamidi considers the bundle of fabric beside him and a slow smile spreads across his face. "Perhaps I'll be a cloak. Though I might need to dye it."

"A cloak?" Kenta demands. "That's not even—that's a *north-lander* cloak."

"One Blackflame gave to Abasi. I'll use it to mock him. He can't even keep his presents from being used against him." Hamidi's smile is sharp enough to cut. "We'll undermine every step he takes."

"That cloak isn't going to hide your face from anyone who sees you," Kenta says. "People will recognize you on sight. It's not that easy to 'die.'"

Hamidi shrugs. "It won't be easy at all, but I'm sure we can figure it out."

Despite my misgivings, I find myself saying, "You can have the hood charmed to cast your face in complete shadow. That way, even your closest League members may not recognize you, at least not until you speak. And for that, there might be other charms."

"Shadow charms for the Shadow League," Hamidi murmurs. "You have to agree there's a certain poetry to it, Kenta."

"That may be how we started, but I don't think such *poetry* was meant to take your life from you."

Hamidi shakes his head. "I'll still have my life. I'll just hide my face and use a different name—a code name of some sort that can't be mistaken for a real name."

Kenta sighs. He is considering Hamidi's life with his family, his life separate from the Shadow League. Hamidi is thinking only of staying alive and keeping his family safe. And I'm wondering if there's a way to keep Hamidi from losing himself as I did.

"What kind of name?" I ask.

Hamidi shrugs again. "I don't know. I'll think on it." He looks toward the shutters, but the night is still dark. It's an hour or two yet till dawn. "We should sleep while we can. There'll be work to do come morning."

I hesitate. I want to discuss this further but I'm too tired to think. There'll be another chance when we wake. I pause, say carefully, "I'd like to be able to help then. In the morning."

"There's no need. Kenta and I will be fine."

At least this time, I was expecting his words. "I know," I say, as if they didn't still hurt. "But tell me this: at what point will you trust me enough to make me an active member of the Shadow League?"

The silence, this time, is suffocating. Kenta watches Hamidi, and I'm grateful for that—for the care he takes in keeping me from seeing his pity.

"You're young," Hamidi says. "I trust you, but it's better for you not to be involved."

Better how? I'll still be scrabbling to survive, regardless. At least with the Shadow League, I'll have something else to fight for. And people to work with who don't see me as a burden. But

I've shown my weakness to him, and I don't have a way to show I've changed, or that I'm trying to.

"You're wrong," I say baldly, and find I'm too tired to argue more, not when he isn't even listening. I push my cushion to the corner, lie down with my back to the room, and blink away my tears until I finally fall asleep.

I WAKE to the sound of a low conversation.

"Why are her wrists burned?" Hamidi asks.

Burned? Oh. That's right. My skin is tender where it touched the rope as my magic-fueled fire burned through it.

"No idea," Kenta says. "I didn't see it happen, and she didn't say."

"The bruises? And blood on her face?"

"From the carriage accident, I presume. I don't think Abasi caused them—she was too concerned that she'd killed him."

"She didn't want him to die?"

"I think," Kenta says, "that she didn't want to be the one to kill him. I'm fairly certain she hates him."

There's a brief silence. I'm about to open my eyes when Kenta says, "Why are you keeping her out of the Shadow League? Do you really not trust her after all she's done?"

I hold my breath, listening.

Hamidi sighs. "When we found her, my father made me promise to keep her safe. She'd already lost almost everything. He said we couldn't take her life as well."

"There's always more to lose," Kenta says dryly.

"What more could she lose? She has no family that she knows of. She needs all her energy just to keep a roof over her head."

Shows how much he knows. Nowadays, it takes everything I've got to keep a roof *under* my head. Although, to give him credit, I didn't realize he knew that much about my struggles. I wonder if he would have helped me if I'd reached out, and know at once he would have. He and Tendaji always did, no matter what. I just didn't want to seem weak to them, helpless. It was my shame again, closing all the doors that were open to me.

"If this is what she wants, I doubt you can really keep her from it," Kenta says. "She won't walk away from a need, and from how she's looking out for you right now, she's not done making sure you're all right. It will be much better for her and the League if you stop shutting her out."

"You mean," Hamidi says with a trace of amusement, "she'll do things alone if I don't give her the opportunity to work with us."

"Judging from the past day, we'd be deluding ourselves to think otherwise," Kenta says. "And while she could have escaped Abasi without me, there's no question that my presence helped."

"I see," Hamidi says.

"Do you? She needs a place to belong, Hamidi. If the Shadow League is going to be your new family, maybe it can be hers as well."

"It's hardly a family," Hamidi says, though his tone is thoughtful. "We operate in secret."

Kenta doesn't respond, at least not that I can hear, and Hamidi doesn't speak again.

After a few breaths, I shift and open my eyes. Hamidi sits against the wall beneath the window, Kenta a few feet away, his back against the side wall. They both look at me, then away.

"I'm going to go wash up," Kenta says, and lets himself out of the room.

Hamidi stares unseeingly at the deep-red cloak still sitting on the table. I want to ask him about the Shadow League again, to see if Kenta has swayed him, but Hamidi may realize I was listening if I do. I frown, studying him. "Did you sleep?"

His smile is more grimace than anything. "I think I dozed a little. My mind's too busy."

I know that kind of nervous energy when you can't stop thinking, or don't dare to, because then all that's left is feeling and you can't afford to do that. Except that, if you don't, you'll eventually break apart from what you're holding in, and that never ends well. "You need to grieve," I tell him bluntly. "Let it out."

"I'm not sad," he says. "I'm angry. I want to break every last thing Abasi loved into pieces. I want to set his house on fire while he's inside and listen to him burn. I want to—" He breaks off, takes a shaky breath, and says quietly, "But I'm not going to."

I watch him, wishing I could reach out and wrap him in a hug. But we've never been that kind of friend, and girls don't just hug boys they aren't related to here. So instead I ask, "Why not?"

"Because my father taught me better. He taught me to ... care. To fight smart. To keep my honor. To protect lives. He was—he was so damn *good*, Hitomi," Hamidi cries, tears streaking down his cheeks. "He deserved to live. *He* should have been the one to survive. Not me, and not that two-faced snake, Abasi."

"Don't you dare," I snap. He looks up, shocked. "Your father would have fought tooth and nail to keep you safe—he probably did. And you did everything you could for him. Don't you mention yourself in the same sentence as Abasi. You didn't betray your father."

"I'm alive," Hamidi says raggedly. "I'm alive and he isn't."

Just as I am, while I don't even have a grave to visit for my mother. All I have is the knowledge that I stayed behind to wait for her when I should have gone with her.

"I know," I say, choking on the words. "I know, and it is never not going to hurt, but your father would have given his life for you. He loved you, Hamidi. I saw it every single time you were together. He wouldn't want his death to break you. He wouldn't

240

want it to rob you of everyone you love in your life—not just him but the rest of your family. He wouldn't want you to turn hard, or cold, or ugly."

"So, what am I supposed to do?" Hamidi demands. "I don't know how to feel right now."

"I don't know," I admit. Perhaps I recognize some part of my own grief in him, but that doesn't mean his experience will be the same as mine. "Just—let yourself feel. Whatever it is that you're feeling, don't lock it away."

He swipes his arm across his face, then drops his gaze to his hands. His voice is oddly hollow as he asks, "Do you still grieve your mother?"

"Yes," I admit. "But it gets easier with time. It..." I gesture helplessly. "It's a weight you get used to carrying. It only feels like it's going to crush you sometimes."

He squeezes his eyes shut. "I'm sorry," he says, which makes no sense at all. Unless he means he's sorry he never understood what it means to lose a parent before, but how would he have? I'm glad he didn't, glad he had his family for as long as he did.

Kenta pushes the door open, breakfast tray in hand. He pauses as he takes in Hamidi's features, the faint wetness on his cheeks.

"Oh good," I say. "Food!"

Hamidi lets out a raspy chuckle. "Kenta is always good for food. Come, let's eat and plan."

"You're letting me help?" I ask before it occurs to me not to.

Hamidi offers me a faint smile. "If you truly want this, Hitomi, I won't keep you from such work."

"*If*," I scoff, but I'm beaming. "Just wait till Rafiki finds out I'm a proper part of the League now!"

Kenta coughs on a laugh while Hamidi shakes his head, smiling properly now. "You've earned it, Hitomi. I just don't want this to cost you."

"I know," I allow. "Some risks are worth the danger."

Kenta sets the tray down on the table beside the cloak. "Did you decide on a name, then, Hamidi? Or a title?"

Hamidi moves to the table, reaching out to lift the cloak. He holds it a moment before setting it on the mat beside him. "The only way I can survive is to keep my identity secret. If I cannot have a name or a face, then I cannot be found or killed." He meets our gazes, and the resolve I see in him has all the strength of tempered steel. "I will be the Ghost of my father, and I will not rest until justice is returned to our land."

I'm glad for this—I am. It's what the Shadow League and Karolene needs. But I don't want my friend to lose himself. "Hamidi," I say unhappily.

His aspect softens. "It's all right, Hitomi. I'll make another life for myself. I'll keep a few ties, but I'll have a new name there too. I can't erase myself completely—I don't want to. And I'll have you and Kenta to remind me of who I am."

"You certainly will," Kenta says and pours him a cup of tea. "Are we ready to plan, then?"

"Ready," I say and reach for a biscuit, my mind already focused on the future.

EPILOGUE

An hour later, Kenta and I leave the inn via the window, dropping to the dirt-packed yard one after the other. It's our job to call together the key members of the League for a meeting this afternoon, one where Abasi's betrayal, and Tendaji's and Hamidi's deaths, will be revealed, and Kenta will introduce the Ghost as their only successor, an heir kept in secret, so to speak. Together, we'll come up with a plan to ensure Abasi's silence regarding the members he knows—Rafiki chief among them. I don't yet know how we'll do it. Violence has never been the way of the Shadow League; at least I can rest assured in that.

"You all right?" Kenta asks as I pause to get my bearings.

"Of course."

He snorts. "There's really no 'of course' about it. You've been through a lot in the last day. Being part of the League doesn't undo the rest."

He's right, but he also doesn't realize just how much I've already been through. Tendaji's death will haunt me, that is true, but I'll make it through. "I'm well enough," I assure him. "Plus," I pat the package in my pocket again, "I have my things."

He shakes his head, his shaggy mane brushing his shoulders. "You'd better be careful with that bundle of yours, or you're going to lose it one of these days."

"I've managed to keep it safe these three years," I say testily. I start walking, following the wall of the teahouse toward the main road out front.

"Three years?" Kenta echoes as he paces me, brows raised. "What's in it?"

I hesitate. He watches me curiously, and I remember suddenly that he has a room. A place of his own. And that he's been there for me every time I've turned around since he allowed me to join him yesterday. "I'll show you," I say and sit cross-legged in the dirt.

Carefully, so carefully, I unwrap the package, unwinding the old strip of fabric that holds it all so tightly together. I lift out a hair comb first, slipping it free of its additional wrapping to reveal the carved end with its six pearls.

"That's..." Kenta shakes his head.

I know what he won't say. It's enough wealth to feed me for a season, maybe longer. But that's not what's important.

"It was my mother's," I say, setting it on my knee. Then I lift out the palm-sized leather-bound book, carefully open it to the first page. I touch the paper, my fingers just brushing the faded ink, the name written there.

"And the book?" Kenta asks.

I close it. "My father's."

I pack up the journal and hair comb in silence, making sure each is snugly wrapped and protected, and that the fabric won't open up in my pocket. "I don't have a room right now," I explain without looking up. "The safest place I can keep them is with me."

I stand once more, slipping the package into my pocket. Kenta looks toward the bustling street. "I could keep it for you," he says. "At least for a little while, till you arrange a new place to stay."

I hunch in on myself. This is what I hoped he'd say, but now that the words hang in the air between us, I don't want to hear them. I'd prefer these last things my parents left me stay in my pocket, with me always, a reminder that I was loved and had a home. I don't want to give them up, not even if it's more sensible. Not even if I wholeheartedly trust Kenta to keep them safe for me.

Kenta rubs the back of his neck, glances toward me. "Why don't you see my room and judge for yourself how safe it is? I can keep your package for you if you like, and if you'd rather not" — he shrugs— "that's fine too."

I hesitate. A girl shouldn't visit a young man's room alone, but I'm not dressed like a girl. And who is there to care about my following proper etiquette, anyway? It's only to ensure my things will be safe. And, most importantly, I trust Kenta.

Still.... "We need to get our work done first."

"We'll be passing by there to reach one of our members' homes who lives nearby. It won't be much of a detour," Kenta says. "Plus, we'll probably need to eat by then. There's a woman who sells fish cakes below my building."

"I don't have any coin," I admit, wondering if he heard my stomach grumbling earlier this morning. The tea tray was lovely, but it only had one plate of biscuits on it, and I wasn't going to embarrass myself by taking all of them. Though I did finish off the leftovers.

"My treat," he says, starting forward.

That pretty well decides it. "All right," I say, hurrying to catch up with him.

He smirks. "I think I know your weakness now."

I stiffen, my hand going to my pocket. "Weakness?"

"Food," Kenta says, his eyes twinkling. "Am I right?"

"I thought that was yours," I say, grinning in relief. "Our *friend* said you were always good for food."

"Guess that makes two of us," Kenta says. "Though I admit I like a good bottle of rice wine even more."

I grimace. "No getting drunk around me. I don't like drunks."

He laughs. "Finally, something you won't accept."

"There are many things I don't accept," I grumble. "Anyhow, if you really want to know my weakness, it's pineapple."

Kenta chuckles, a friendly rumble in his chest. "I'll be sure to tell our friend. I think he'll need all the help he can get with you."

"Oh, he'll be fine," I say firmly. "I'll make sure of it."

Kenta's laugh breaks from his lips this time. It's the warm laughter of a true friend. "I don't doubt you will."

ACKNOWLEDGMENTS

It's a rare thing that a book comes into the world without the help of at least a handful of people. In this case, *Sunbolt* had the support and encouragement of a wagonload of folks.

As always, a huge thank you to my husband and children, for being my cheer team and closest supports. Thanks as well to my parents, for stapling my first books together when I was three and supporting my writing ever after, and to my brother and sister-in-law, who are always willing to read a draft and voice encouragement.

I am also deeply indebted to the very many lovely people—writers, readers, and fans—who have befriended me since the first indie edition of Sunbolt came out in 2013, offering their encouragement through the highs and lows of my writing journey—from celebrations to the absolute exhaustion of burnout. I couldn't continue this path without you; I am so grateful to each and every one of you for your support.

Sunbolt has had the help of many, many beta readers, to whom I am very, very grateful. Thanks to my initial readers, writing circle cronies Janelle White and Nat Kutcher, for those first suggested revisions. Many thanks for the thoughtful constructive feedback of my Round One Beta Readers, in order of reading: Emory Colvin, Shy Eager, Ahmed Khanani, Tia Michaud, Alina Shosky, Bekah Trollinger, Kat Wise, Elisabeth Wheatley, and Janelle White.

Extra special thanks to my Round One teen beta readers:

Hohokam Middle School students Hailey McCann, Vauxn McQuillen, and Sophia Lewis; as well as British International School of Jeddah student Mus'ifah Amran. You guys rock!

Where there's a Round One, there's bound to be a Round Two. Huge thanks are due to Ann Forstie, Claire Hermann, Anne Hillman and Theresa Shreffler for everything from suggested scene changes to brilliant line edits to making sure my selection of fruits and fish in Karolene made sense. I can't thank you all enough! Additional thanks to Diana Cox and Batool Al-Khawaja for your proofreading prowess!

As Sunbolt relaunches with Snowy Wings Publishing, my sincere gratitude goes to Lyssa Chiavari and the rest of the team at SWP for all you do, from brilliant business advice to ongoing support to keeping me on track with all the deadlines publishing entails. You're the best!

Gratitude also to the good folks at the (now defunct) Feminist Book of the Month for selecting *Sunbolt* as their 2017 fall quarterly read, and asking for a short story to include. Over the course of a very intense sixteen days, *Shadow Thief* came to life with the help of beta readers Anne Hillman, Shy Eager, Anas Malik, Suzannah Rowntree, and M. K. Wiseman, and the copy-editing wizardry of Laurel Garver.

While the experience was amazing, I ended up unhappy with the story itself... I hadn't quite found its emotional heart. It wasn't until this summer, with the support of my Patreon and Kickstarter backers, that I was able to return to *Shadow Thief*. I took it through a new round of edits with the inimitable Sarah Chorn, plus an additional beta read with A.C. Spahn and Anela Deen, and then a final proofread with Diana Cox and Batool Al-Khawaja. (It *really* takes a village to make a story.) Thank you all so, so much!

A great big (additional!) shout out to all my supporters on Patreon and Kickstarter who not only helped make this new edition of *Sunbolt* as gorgeous as it is, but made it possible to include *Shadow Thief* at the end. Thank you all so much for believing in Hitomi!

As always, deep thanks to the bloggers and readers who have encouraged me by reading and reviewing my work. Thank you for your support, and for sharing your love of books with the world.

As a person of faith, I am ultimately grateful to God — for granting me the love of writing, a way to share my stories, and the support I need to keep going.

ABOUT THE AUTHOR

Intisar Khanani grew up a nomad and world traveler. Born in Wisconsin, she has lived in five different states as well as in Jeddah on the coast of the Red Sea. She first remembers seeing snow on a wintry street in Zurich, Switzerland, and vaguely recollects having breakfast with the orangutans at the Singapore Zoo when she was five.

Intisar currently resides in Cincinnati, Ohio, with her husband and two young daughters. Until recently, she wrote grants and developed projects to address community health and infant mortality with the Cincinnati Health Department — which was as close as she could get to saving the world. Now she focuses her time on her two passions: raising her family and writing fantasy.

To keep up with what Intisar is working on next, join her monthly newsletter at booksbyintisar.com/newsletter and follow her on Instagram at @booksbyintisar.

Printed in the USA
CPSIA information can be obtained
at www.ICGtesting.com
LVHW091121021023
759804LV00002B/225